Blast

David Hodges

© David Hodges 2017

David Hodges has asserted his rights under the Copyright, Design and Patents Act, 1988, to be identified as the author of this work.

First published by Endeavour Press Ltd in 2017.

This book is dedicated to my wife, Elizabeth, for all her love, patience and support over so many wonderful years and to my late mother and father, whose faith in me to one day achieve my ambition as a writer remained steadfast throughout their lifetime and whose tragic passing has left a hole in my life which will never be filled.

TABLE OF CONTENTS

AUTHOR'S NOTE	7
BEFORE THE FACT	9
CHAPTER 1	13
CHAPTER 2	21
CHAPTER 3	31
CHAPTER 4	44
CHAPTER 5	51
CHAPTER 6	58
CHAPTER 7	67
CHAPTER 8	75
CHAPTER 9	82
CHAPTER 10	92
CHAPTER 11	100
CHAPTER 12	110
CHAPTER 13	118
CHAPTER 14	135
CHAPTER 15	145
CHAPTER 16	157

CHAPTER 17	167
CHAPTER 18	178
CHAPTER 19	188
CHAPTER 20	199
AFTER THE FACT	204

AUTHOR'S NOTE

Although the action of the novel involves investigations by the Metropolitan Police and the Devon & Cornwall Police, these investigations, together with the story itself and all the characters in it, are entirely fictitious and drawn entirely from my own imagination. Similarly, while the story takes place in actual areas of the UK, The New Light Modelling Agency and specific premises, like The Philanderer's Night Club, The Blue Ketch Inn, The Beach House and The Old Customs House, are also products of my imagination and any connection between them and existing businesses or properties is entirely coincidental. I would also point out that this novel is not a 'police procedural', but a crime thriller. Consequently, to meet the requirements of the plot, I have adopted a degree of poetic licence in relation to the police structure and some of the operational procedures followed by both forces and I hope that these departures from fact will not spoil the reading enjoyment of serving or retired police officers, for whom I have the utmost respect.

David Hodges

BEFORE THE FACT

Shadows in the empty moonlit street. Curling around the vandalised lamp-standards. Masking the graffiti daubing the walls of the tenements and boarded-up derelicts. Discarded sweet wrappers and cigarette packets whirling in the low wind caressing the broken paving stones. Tin cans clattering along gutters, which had not felt the bristles of a council cleaning lorry's brushes since marauding foxes, raiding the over-full dustbins, had abandoned them after savouring their putrid contents. Decay and despair inhabited this North London street, infecting the very senses and settling on the shoulders of the wayfarer like a clammy dead hand.

At first sight, the hooded figure furtively hugging the shadows might have appeared to personify that decay – to be a product of the lost, no-hope community, which had long since turned in on itself and self-destructed. Yet appearances can be deceptive and there was something very different about this particular hoodie.

Missing was the cocky, bouncing slouch of the arrogant street thug, with his over-sized jeans and head and shoulders thrust forward like the aggressive Neanderthal he sought to emulate. In its place was a noticeable hesitancy – a nervousness, which would have been totally alien to the sort of vicious waste-of-a-skin that prowled many of the Met's so-called sink estates. Nevertheless, the body language of the lone walker communicated a degree of tension that would have aroused just as much suspicion in the mind of a passing police patrol. The figure constantly cast uneasy penetrating glances at the run-down buildings opposite and over one shoulder into the moon-splashed gloom behind, as if nursing a fear of being followed or the subject of surveillance, one hand snatching at the hood of the coat and tugging it forward as the wind did its level best to peel it back. It was clear that this was not some mindless tearaway who had taken to the streets, looking for any windows to smash or bus shelters to wreck. It was someone with a definite sense of purpose. Someone who had intended to be in this particular street at this particular time.

It became evident that they also had a specific address in mind when the figure finally stopped outside a derelict terraced house, flanked by other abandoned properties with boarded-up doors and windows. A dim light filtered into the street from a curtained upstairs room and the front door stood ajar – as it had on the visitor's previous visit a few weeks before.

The door opened easily to the touch and the next instant the beam of the torch held in one gloved hand was probing the dark hallway beyond. Nothing stirred. The house seemed to be dead. Glancing quickly up and down the street, the hoodie stepped over the threshold and after further hesitation, turned immediately left to climb the staircase to the upper floor, thick crepe-soled shoes making hardly any sound despite the bareness of the wooden treads.

A bar of light showed beneath a closed door on the landing and a chair creaked several times behind it, as if the occupant of the room was trying to ease into a more comfortable position. The need to knock turned out to be unnecessary. A heavily-accented male voice called out suddenly from inside, indicating that the visitor's arrival had already been detected: 'Entrez, my friend.'

Pushing the door wide, the hoodie stood for a moment in the opening, surveying the room through narrowed eyes.

A thin, bearded man, dressed in jeans and a sweater, sat at a rickety table illuminated by a portable battery-operated lamp, a haversack on the floor beside him. Save for the table and the chair, the room was unfurnished. The man treated his visitor to a brief smile that failed to reach his eyes. 'Nice to see you again,' he said. 'I thought you might not come back after our first meeting.'

The hoodie considered the statement, but ignored it and said softly, 'You have the package?'

The other nodded and bending down, unzipped the haversack before carefully lifting out a cardboard box and placing it on the table in the pool of light cast by the lamp. 'I always deliver,' he replied, his guttural East European accent even more pronounced. 'You have the rest of my money?'

'Of course.'

The hoodie undid the coat and unclipped a wide body-belt before stepping forward a few paces to drop it on to the table. He stared at the wrapping on the box and commented cynically, 'Chocolates?'

The bearded man chuckled, stacking the wads of notes from the pockets of the belt on the table in front of him. 'Open it and see,' he invited. 'What I have for you is sweeter than a woman's smile.'

The hoodie carefully lifted the lid off and stared at the tray of dark chocolates. He nodded slowly. 'And exactly how sweet would that be?'

Another chuckle and the other reached across to lift the tray out.

'Just so,' he said. 'Complete with all the instructions.'

The hoodie stared at the contents and emitted a hard laugh. 'Very nice too. You have done well.'

An indifferent shrug as tobacco-stained fingers began counting the money 'It's what I do, what I've always done – since the old days.'

'Pity you won't be doing it anymore then,' his visitor said.

Pulling a pistol from a side pocket, the hoodie shot him once between the eyes. Then, carefully slipping the chocolate box into a canvas bag produced from another pocket, the cold-blooded assassin scooped up the money and the body-belt and disappeared into the night without a backward glance.

CHAPTER 1

It had come at seven in the evening. Unheralded. Unexpected. A thunderous, rendering blast of destructive energy, which knew no ally or foe, but mercifully anaesthetised the young woman's brain in an instant, blotting out the screams, the mutilation and the pain.

The police said afterwards that some new terrorist group had claimed responsibility for the bomb, which had been planted at the select Philanderer's Night Club in London's Mayfair. 'Christians Against Sexual Exploitation' or something, they'd said. But she didn't really care. All she knew was that the blast had scarred her body beyond repair.

The surgeons had done their best, of course, but the wounds had not been suitable for plastic surgery. As a result, the tracer-like scars were still visible and lying naked on the hot sand of the secluded little Cornish cove, making the most of the Indian summer and roasting in the unexpected early autumn sun, she knew that even a good tan could never conceal the hideous marks, no matter how much she tried to delude herself. Maybe it would have been better if she had actually died.

To think that, until the moment of the blast at the celebrity fashion show, she had been a successful glamour model. A 24-year-old raven-haired beauty, with large almond-shaped eyes the colour of a stunning hypnotic green and a flawless skin, which had once tanned a rich nut-brown at the merest hint of sun. She had been tipped as one of the prime contenders for a contract with a major fashion house and their scouts had been given VIP seats at the show so they could make their final selection. The club's spot-lit catwalk could have taken her to the top of her profession, with the prospect of a fortune in earnings from film and glossy magazine advertising at the end of it.

She would have been the envy of every woman, the desire of every man. Mixing in the most exclusive social circles and enjoying the company of a succession of wealthy admirers, with their Porsches and ocean-going yachts. Now? Now she was just another ex-model, with nothing to show for five years of spitting, clawing graft, except an album of photographs and a future already heading deep into oblivion. As for the men in her life, like her most recent ex, Greg Norman, they had melted away faster than ice-cream when it hits the hot sand.

She turned over on to her back and applied more sun-tan lotion to the front of her body, the burning orb in the fierce blue sky just a fuzzy white spot through the lenses of her sunglasses. Staring down at herself, she grimaced. The shape hadn't changed. The long legs, flat stomach and pert breasts were just the same. But the disfiguring scars from the flying glass and other debris were clearly visible. In fact, her tan actually seemed to have accentuated them and she knew one side of her face and under her chin were just as badly marked.

She remembered the day the boss of the New Light Modelling Agency, fat Freddie Baxter, had paid her off, patting her arm with one podgy bejewelled hand, which was better manicured than her own. 'Don't worry, sweetness,' he had consoled with an oily, insincere smile. 'You'll be back just as soon as those scars have healed. Don't forget, Lynn Giles is already a household name. There'll always be a job for you in this business.'

''Course there will,' Felicity Dubois, her arch-rival, had purred from the usual position she occupied draped across the sofa in Freddie's plush office. 'You can always model for the winter catalogues, *dahling*. You know, hats, overcoats, that sort of thing. Maybe wear one of those little black veils too. Very chic.'

'Bitch!' Lynn muttered, her resentment burning like acid through her veins at the thought of how her disfiguring scars had ruined everything. Feeling for her shoe, she used the heel to savagely crush an over-inquisitive wasp as it settled innocently on the rock beside her, pulverising it with blow after blow. Damn Felicity! Damn the agency! Damn the whole rotten world!

Then abruptly the all-consuming fit of rage subsided, her eyes misting over behind the designer sunglasses as she fell back on to the sand. Brave words, she mused bitterly, but what the hell was she going to do with her life now? She was single and had known nothing but modelling since fat Freddie had spotted her working as a pole-dancer in a London bar. So she had no other job experience and very few skills that could be transferred to any of the more up-market mainstream – and therefore highly paid – careers, which might have proved attractive to her. Okay, so the financial settlement Freddie had been forced to agree to when he had terminated her contract, coupled with the big insurance pay-out she had received, guaranteed her financial security for the foreseeable future. But even that wouldn't last forever and as an ambitious Type A achiever, she couldn't see herself remaining in her beach-side bungalow, hiding behind the name Mary Tresco for longer than a few more weeks anyway.

That said, the place itself had certainly been a boon. Renting out her luxury flat in London's Mayfair and burying herself in this isolated spot by the sea had enabled her to escape the media feeding frenzy, which had inevitably followed the bomb outrage. The tabloid press had tried every trick in the book to get some revealing pictures of her scarred body. At least here, living under her assumed name, she was safe from their long lenses and with her hair now cut short and treated to a blonde dye, it was unlikely anyone in this back of beyond place would recognise her from the glossy photo-shoots. Unless they were into fashion modelling, which she doubted.

Losing her identity for a while was vital for another reason too. Although she'd told the police that she was unable to remember anything about the bomb blast itself or even her own routine on that fateful day – what her psychiatrist had called selective amnesia due to shock – she had revealed a vague recollection of seeing something out of the ordinary prior to the explosion. But her traumatised brain had so far stubbornly refused to give up the information despite specialist therapy. Because of this and the fact that the experts expected her memory to return one day – possibly producing vital evidence, which could make her a crucial witness – the senior police officer leading the case, Detective Chief Inspector Mick Benchley, had expressed concern that the terrorists might come after her and had strongly recommended she disappear for a while. He had also recommended that, apart from himself, no one should be told where she had gone to ground.

She had reluctantly agreed to it all, but contrary to his advice had given her new address to Freddie Baxter, just in case he was able to find her another lower-profile modelling job – Felicity's winter catalogues suggestion, for example, she thought bitterly. But she wished now she hadn't said anything to the police in the first place. She should have kept her big mouth shut. Having set the hare running, however, it was too late for her to do anything about it now.

The irony of it all was that, despite the potential evidence still locked in her subconscious, it seemed she was not actually considered important enough to be offered the usual protection afforded vulnerable witnesses anyway. To be fair, the last thing she wanted was some armed chaperone invading her life and following her about everywhere for months on end, but it would have been nice to have been given the option of refusing such an offer. Benchley had denied her that opportunity. 'Sorry,' he'd said, 'but we don't know for certain that the information you hold would be of any significance to our inquiry. Without an arrest and an imminent court case, I'm afraid you don't qualify under the witness protection programme, and the economic situation being what it is ...'

His voice had trailed off and he'd shrugged, like the good detective he was, washing his hands of any responsibility for the decision. But he *had* assured her that he would pull out all the stops with the local police force if she rang him with a problem. No offer of boots on the ground, though, just a grimace and the almost prophetic words, 'We'll be in touch if there are any new developments.'

'I bet you will,' she said drily, 'but I won't hold my breath.'

'Hello there, talking to yourself then?'

The dark figure blotted out the sun completely and jumping to her feet, she snatched up her towel and held it over the front of her body – for the first time in her life conscious of her nudity.

The speaker was a tall, athletic-looking man in his 30s, with a mop of jet black hair, wearing very dark sunglasses and a pair of blue boxer shorts, and he was accompanied by a black Labrador dog, which he held on a short lead.

'Where the hell did you spring from?' she demanded. 'Don't you know this is a private beach?'

There was a soft laugh. 'My apologies,' he replied, without taking his eyes off her, 'but Archie here cannot read notices and where he goes I follow, I'm afraid.'

She snorted. 'Well, now you know it is private, perhaps you and Archie here will push off again.'

The lean handsome face flashed her an engaging smile. 'Now, that's not a very nice welcome for your neighbour, is it? I assume you are the lady living in The Beach House?'

'Neighbour?' she echoed, without answering either question.

He extended his free hand. 'That's right. Alan Murray. I'm renting The Old Customs House on the headland above Diamond Cove. Arrived shortly after you.'

She scowled, doubting his explanation and suspecting a chat-up line. 'I thought that place was empty – I was told it's been shut up for years.'

He nodded. 'So it has been, but I've opened it up again. Rented it for a song too.'

He changed the subject. 'You must be Mary Tresco, eh?'

She ignored the proffered hand and shook her head in disbelief. 'You're incredible. I mean, do you normally barge on to private property and try to introduce yourself to naked women you have never met before?'

His jaw dropped and he snatched his hand away as if she had bitten it, while the Labrador crouched down in the sand with a nervous whine. 'Good Lord,' he gasped, 'are you saying you've got no clothes on?'

She tossed her head contemptuously. 'Are you blind or something?'

He smiled again, but this time it was ironic and lacking in warmth. 'Yes, I'm afraid I am,' he said. 'Why else would I walk across a beach with a dog on a lead?'

Lynn stared at him and unwittingly allowed the towel to slip through her fingers and drop to the sand. 'You're blind?' she whispered, feeling embarrassed now for an altogether different reason. 'Look, I … I'm so sorry. I just didn't realise …'

He silenced her with a wave of his hand. 'No need,' he said curtly. 'I should be the one to apologise. After all, you're quite right: I am a trespasser. Come on, Archie, time to go.'

Before she could think of anything else to say, he had turned on his heel and was allowing the dog to guide him back across the beach towards the footpath, which led up on to the headland. 'Damn!' she breathed as she watched the muscular figure disappear from view. 'Damn! Damn! Damn!'

****

Over nine hours later, in an entirely different kind of environment some 300 miles away in London, the young police patrolman, ensconced in his patrol car at the back of Wong's Chinese Restaurant, swore and dumped his take-away on the front passenger seat to take the message which had just come in over his personal radio.

Switching on the car's interior light, he scribbled down the address he had been given on the lid of the box containing his extra-large chow mein. Just his luck. It wasn't often anyone could cadge a freebie out of Fu Wong and now that he had succeeded, the bloody thing was going to be cold before he could even stick his plastic fork into it.

With five years at the sharp end of the Met, Dennis Jordan was well used to attending the bogus shouts as he and his colleagues liked to call the multitude of spurious alerts, which came in during the late evening when the pubs and restaurants turned out, and it was easy to get complacent about them. But the young bobby knew there was always a chance that one of them could be genuine and ignoring them was not an option, even if it did mean sacrificing one of Fu Wong's best.

Starting the engine, he turned out of the small car park at the back of the restaurant and joined the late-night traffic pouring back into the suburbs from the West End.

He managed a few mouthfuls of his Chinese take-away on route, but then had to dump it on the seat again when he swung off the main road and shortly afterwards entered a familiar labyrinth of mean, unlit streets populated solely by shadows. His headlights caught a couple of those shadows peeling away from the front of a terraced house as he approached and with a wry smile he watched them disappear down an adjacent alleyway. He recognised them both as a couple of his resident dossers. Tenants of a twilight world of booze and drugs, who spent their days begging and shoplifting and their nights crashed out in any available derelict, sleeping off a skinful or an illicit fix. If they'd had anything to do with this call, he mused, giving his cold Chinese a rueful glance as he climbed out of his patrol car, then it looked like being yet another of the night's hoaxes. But as it transpired, he could not have been more wrong.

No lights showed in the windows of the rundown terraced house and the front door was wide open. Frowning, he directed his torch into the blacked-out hallway, then focused it on the staircase.

'Police,' he called, his voice echoing in the hallway. He knocked on the door with the base of his torch. 'Anyone here?' There was no reply. Although that was not surprising, as the place was obviously derelict, for some reason he felt a stab of apprehension and his heart began to race.

He frowned. What was the matter with him? Okay, so checking derelict houses at night usually produced an adrenalin rush – you could never be sure what was waiting for you on the other side of the door – but he must have checked scores of them in his service and none had affected him quite like this. What was it the control room had said? A report of a break-in? But why would anyone want to break into a derelict? He checked the door. The lock was smashed and rusted. By the look of it, it was something that had been done a long time ago. Nothing to do with a recent break-in.

Taking a deep breath, he moved towards the stairs, feeling the oppressive silence of this dark, creepy house pressing down on him with an almost tangible force.

The bare risers creaked twice on his ascent, and reaching the top he quickly flashed his torch around the landing, half expecting a nightmare figure – like the murderous transvestite in Alfred Hitchcock's *Psycho* – to rush at him out of the darkness, wielding a long-bladed knife. But apart from the distant sound of a train, nothing stirred.

A number of rooms led off the landing, their open doors leering slashes blacker than the gloom around him, but immediately on his left one door was tightly closed for some reason. He knocked on it twice, calling again, 'Anyone here?'

From the street below, he heard the sound of a car drawing up and the metallic chatter of a radio. Another unit, thank goodness. As was usual in these cases, the control room had detailed some back-up.

Feeling a lot more confident, he turned the handle of the door and pushed it open.

The flies rushed out at him like angry hornets, forcing him back with a sharp cry as he swept them away from his face with both hands. His torch beam grazed a tattered blanket covering the window before splashing light wildly across the ceiling.

'You okay, Dennis?' his colleague shouted from the foot of the stairs. But Dennis Jordan was unable to reply. His horrified gaze was fixed on the figure slumped in the chair behind the table. That the man had been dead for quite some time was evident from the condition of the body and the stench which filled the small room. But the energies of the remaining flies, still feasting on the remains abandoned by the rats, lent a kind of grotesque quivering life to the partially decomposed facial muscles, which were locked into an obscene rictus grin.

CHAPTER 2

The Old Customs House was a white, two-storey building, which stood on the clifftop with its back to the sea and was bordered on the land side by tall shrubs. A notice on the slatted wooden gate warned, "Private. Beware Land Mines", and Lynn smiled as she pushed it open. Mr Alan Murray obviously had a sense of humour, in spite of his disability.

Just inside the gate, a turfed path ran down the side of the property for its entire length, between the line of shrubs and the house wall. Turning right, she followed it to the front of the place and a broad hard-standing where a lane trailed away through crowded woods, no doubt eventually connecting with the main road. A porch partially enclosed the front door, but there was no bell or knocker in evidence. She didn't bother to rap on the weather-ravaged wood. Instead, she backtracked past the gate she had just used, down the side of the house, then at its end followed a high perimeter wall towards the sea.

In just a few yards the path seemed to finish before a broken-down fence, close to the cliff edge, but that turned out to be an illusion. Closer inspection revealed that it actually struck off at a sharp right angle along a continuation of the perimeter wall behind the property, just a few feet from the sheer drop to the sea. It then disappeared into a tangle of gorse and bracken, only to re-emerge some 20ft further along, where steps crept down the cliff face between twin stone pillars. On the seaward side of the path, broken walls thrust their way up through the scrub masking the edge like jagged teeth and though the battered wooden sign just in front of her said nothing about land mines, it warned, "Danger. Concealed Mine Shafts".

She gripped the end post of the broken fence for support to peer over the cliff edge and shivered when she glimpsed a spit of sand scattered with rocks at the foot of the stone steps far below. It was one hell of a long way down and she had no intention of going any closer.

Backtracking again, she discovered a stone archway set deep in the wall to her left, almost hidden by a tangle of climbing roses. A flight of steps climbed up through the archway and investigating further, she found herself on a small patio enclosed on the other three sides by another wall, this time only about 3ft high. She also found Alan Murray.

He was dressed in a pair of khaki shorts, a green T-shirt and the ubiquitous sunglasses, and sitting at a round wooden table, talking into a Dictaphone. Archie, the Labrador, was stretched out beside him.

The animal looked up quickly as she climbed the four steps on to the patio, and began to wag its tail in recognition. No doubt hearing her footfall, its master glanced towards her and switching off the Dictaphone, pushed his plastic chair back and stood up with a smile.

'Ah, good morning, Miss Tresco. I wondered if you would call and see me after yesterday.'

She stopped short. 'I thought you were … were …'

'Blind?'

'Yes.'

'So I am.'

'Then how could you possibly have known it was me?'

He laughed outright. 'I may be blind, but there is nothing wrong with my sense of smell – the suntan oil you wear is quite distinctive, if I may say so.'

'Elementary, my dear Watson, eh?'

His smile broadened. 'Something like that. Also being blind, my other faculties tend to be sharper. Your lightness of step gave you away as a young lady and since I see precious few young ladies – particularly those who would walk round to the back of my house – I made a calculated guess.'

She inclined her head in rather pointless acknowledgment. 'Maybe your "Beware of Land Mines" sign put off all the young ladies there might have been?' she suggested mischievously.

He laughed. 'That was just a bit of fun actually. Got a local chap to do it for me, but obviously I haven't seen the thing myself. Good, is it?'

'Well, effective anyway.'

He laughed again, then looked serious for a moment. 'Having said that, there *are* mines all along the cliffs here – old tin mines. Hidden shafts everywhere, and the cliffs are crumbling in places with deep fissures opening up which are concealed by the gorse. Even the public footpath on the other side of my patio wall has disappeared at one point. So it doesn't do to wander too near the cliff edge.'

'Yes, I saw the other warning sign just now.'

He raised his eyebrows. 'I didn't know there was one. So you must have had a good look around, then?'

She chuckled. 'Just nosing. It's a woman thing. Your own warning hint to stay away is pretty clear on its own, though?'

He winced and pushed a second plastic chair towards her. 'Yes, I must admit I do not normally encourage visitors. Bit of a recluse actually. But that certainly doesn't apply to you, so please have a seat. I'm really delighted you chose to come.'

She manoeuvred the chair and sat down a little uncertainly. 'I don't know why I did actually, except to apologise for my rudeness yesterday.'

Another laugh and she noted how white and even his teeth were. 'There was really no need, but I trust you are fully clothed now?'

Lynn glanced down at her neat white shorts and matching blouse. 'Oh yes, very respectable.'

'Glad to hear it. But you must be thirsty. What would you like to drink?'

'No, really—'

'I insist.'

'Then I must help you.'

'No, damn it!'

The rejection was sharp, almost violent, and his face had darkened appreciably. Half out of her chair, she sat down heavily again. Almost at the same moment his smile was back, as if he realised he had over-reacted.

'I … I can manage, honestly. I'm well used to where everything is now.'

She watched curiously and with growing admiration as he felt his way across to the open patio door and disappeared inside.

If she expected the sound of breaking glass and a muffled curse as he knocked something over, she was pleasantly surprised. He was back with a selection of bottles and some glasses on a tray within minutes, setting them carefully on the little table beside her.

'What would you like? Whisky, vodka, gin or just orange?'

She smiled unnecessarily. 'The orange will do just fine.'

He picked the right bottle first time and poured without spilling a drop before half-filling another glass for himself from the whisky bottle.

'You're absolutely marvellous,' she said, without thinking, as she took a sip.

'And you are patronising,' he retorted sternly.

She bit her lip. 'I was trying to be complimentary. There's no need to take offence at everything I say.'

He sighed and sat down opposite, ruffling Archie's ears as the animal nuzzled his leg. 'Look, I'm sorry, Mary. Can I call you that? I'm afraid I'm a bit touchy about my … ah … disability. It's very hard for sighted people to understand how important it is for a blind person to be treated normally and not to be regarded as some kind of a freak.'

Lynn nodded grimly, remembering the intense press interest in her own condition, following the bomb outrage – the lengths to which the journalists had gone to obtain photographs of the scarred body, which had once adorned the glossy magazines. Sick, sick, sick.

'Not only blind people either,' she muttered bitterly, then added, 'How did it happen?'

Her sudden directness even shocked herself, but he seemed unperturbed by it.

'Car accident couple of years ago,' he replied. 'Wrecked the optical nerves as well as my life. My wife was killed instantly.'

Lynn shuddered. 'How on earth can you keep going?' she whispered.

'What do you suggest I do instead?' He drained his glass and sat back in the chair, playing with the rim. 'Fate doesn't give you a choice. Oh, I thought about the usual things – suicide, revenge against the drunken arsehole in the other car who had caused the accident – but in the end I recognised the futility of it all and just made the best of it.'

'Aren't you lonely out here all on your own, though?'

'Not really. I have Archie and although he's not much of a guard dog – bit of a coward actually and rarely barks or anything – he's good company for me and he's my eyes, of course.'

'So, what do you do with yourself all day – apart from walking in on naked ladies on the beach?'

He chuckled at the dig. 'Creative writing has been my salvation. I'm not famous – only mid-list – but I don't feel I'm doing that bad and it pays the rent for this place.'

Lynn raised her eyebrows and leaned forward in her chair. 'Writing? What, books, you mean? But how on earth—?'

He tapped the Dictaphone on the table. 'I use this. It goes everywhere with me – even to the bathroom.'

'But don't you find it difficult coming up with ideas when—?'

'I'm blind? Don't be frightened of the word, Mary – it is in the dictionary, you know. But to answer your question, no, I don't find it difficult. In fact, I find it easier than when I had my sight. You see, as I indicated when you first came here today, the other senses like touch, taste and smell become more acute when you are in this predicament, and loss of sight also makes your imagination that much stronger.'

'But what sort of books do you write?'

'Oh, gory thrillers, I'm afraid. People being strangled, stabbed – even thrown off cliffs – anything goes really.'

'I shall have to pop into my favourite bookshop in Helston and get hold of one of your novels unless, of course, you have a spare copy here I could buy?'

He shook his head. 'Not available in hard copy, I'm afraid. All my books are digitised. It's the way of the world now.'

She shrugged. 'Well, I do have an I-pad, so I can easily order one. Have you a title for me?'

He frowned and waved a hand dismissively. 'Oh, I wouldn't bother. You wouldn't like them.'

'You might be surprised. Do you write under your own name?'

'Er ... no, I use a non-de-plume.'

'Which is?'

'I'd rather keep that to myself for now.'

'Whatever for? Being a professional writer is a real achievement. I'm impressed.'

'Maybe if you read my stuff, you wouldn't be so impressed. The books are rather ... er ... risqué.'

She grinned. 'Risqué? What, you mean with naughty bits? That might be right up my street.'

He fidgeted in his chair, obviously embarrassed. 'Look, let's just drop it, shall we?' he snapped.

Her mouth tightened, but sensing he was getting irritable and that she was not going to get anywhere anyway, she abruptly changed tack. 'So are you working on something at the moment?'

He nodded, relaxing a little now. 'Since yesterday actually. Stumbling upon you on the beach gave me a marvellous idea for a new book.'

'Me?'

His smile was back and he chuckled again. 'But of course. Mystery girl lying naked on the sand in a hidden cove. Who is she? What is she doing there? Excellent ingredients for a thriller.'

It was her turn to laugh now. 'Touché. But I'm hardly a mystery girl. After all, you know my name.'

He shrugged. 'Do I? So what's in a name? I was able to get that from the local pub. But maybe it isn't the right one, eh?'

Lynn tensed. His face was turned towards her, but with his eyes hidden behind his sunglasses, it was difficult trying to read his expression. 'What makes you say that?'

'Oh, just a feeling I get. Maybe you're running away from something. Trying to hide from the world perhaps?'

'That's silly. I … I'm just having a break, that's all.'

'A break? So what do you do when you're not having a break?'

She hedged. 'Nothing especially. I … I'm between jobs at the moment.'

'Doing what exactly?'

She thought quickly. 'I … er … I'm in teaching.'

'Well, that's interesting.'

'Not really. Actually it's quite boring.' Lynn stood up sharply. He was getting far too close. 'Now, if you're through analysing, I must be off. I only came to apologise.'

He must have sensed she was no longer sitting down, even though she had got up without moving her chair, and he stood up also, hand extended. This time she took it and felt a strange thrill run through her at the firm, dry grip.

'When can I see you again?'

The question was quite unexpected and it caught her off balance. Before she could stop herself, she blurted a reply. 'Well, you know where I live.'

He smiled broadly. 'And you know where *I* live, so why don't you come over for dinner – say, Friday evening, eh? I'm quite a passable cook, though do I say so myself. Let's say eight o'clock?'

It was a skilful tactic on his part and Lynn felt she had been manoeuvred into a position where she could not refuse.

'Thank you,' she heard herself saying. 'That's very nice of you.'

'Then it's settled,' he replied firmly. 'Red or white wine?'

****

Detective Inspector Maurice Morgan usually prided himself on having a strong stomach. Fifteen years in the Metropolitan Police, including service on the Drug and National Crime Squads and now a DI at Islington, should have equipped him for anything, but for some reason the stench from the partially decomposed corpse slumped in the chair in the morning sunlight now streaming through the window of the small bare room brought the bile racing up into his throat. Maybe he was getting old and past it. It was at times like this that he wished he'd stayed in his native Jamaica.

'Looks like a single bullet in the head did the trick,' the pathologist commented cheerfully from behind his face mask and straightened up from the body. 'But I won't be able to carry out a proper job until we get him out of the chair and down the morgue.' He nodded towards the window. 'At least I've had some light to work in since your people took down the damned blanket, but I still have only been able to do a preliminary examination.'

'The morgue will have to wait until the evidence recovery unit has done its stuff, Doc,' Morgan said heavily, adjusting his own mask and stepping away from the door to allow two figures in protective white overalls to enter the room. 'My CSIs will need to complete a full crime scene examination, with the body in situ, and also take some detailed photographs before we move him out.' He hesitated, running a hand through his thick, black curly hair. 'No idea what sort of firearm was used, I suppose?'

Doctor Julian Hake shook his head, using one gloved hand to swat a fly which had landed on his face. 'Something for ballistics to determine, Maurice,' he said, adding, 'It is completely outside my field of expertise, as well you know.'

The policeman cleared his throat noisily. 'So what else can you tell me?'

Hake turned to study the corpse again. 'Well, he's male—'

'Yeah, I'd rather gathered that, thank you.'

'Late 40s, I would say – some bad dental work to his upper teeth and it looks like a congenital deformity to his left hand.'

'How long do you reckon he's been dead?'

'Difficult to say. Weeks certainly, couple of months or so probably, but the cadaver is remarkably well preserved under the circumstances. Possibly something to do with the ambient temperature of this room.'

Morgan studied the ceiling. 'Well, if this is a well-preserved stiff, I'd hate to see a badly preserved one, that's all I've got to say.'

The pathologist chuckled. 'Who found him?'

Morgan shrugged. 'No idea. A dosser looking for somewhere to kip, we reckon. We got an anonymous three-nines.'

Hake grunted. 'Strange no one found him before?'

The DI nodded. 'Probably someone did, but dossers tend not to contact the police and I understand these places are due for demolition soon anyway, so no one would have had any other reason to pop in, would they?'

Hake peeled off his surgical gloves and began unzipping his protective overalls as he turned for the stairs with Morgan in tow.

The uniformed policewoman guarding the front door stepped aside when she heard them approach. The DI nodded to her perfunctorily as he followed Hake to his car, ignoring the army of press photographers snapping them both from the other side of the road.

'I'll let you know when we've scheduled the PM,' Hake said and grinned. 'Wouldn't want you to miss your afternoon out at the morgue.'

Morgan scowled. 'I'll look forward to it, Doc,' he retorted drily and turned back towards the house as the pathologist drove away.

The crime scene investigators were well into their work when he got to the top of the stairs again and he chose not to disturb them, taking a good look around the upper floor instead. He found nothing of interest, just a wrecked bathroom and toilet, and a couple more of what had probably once been bedrooms – bare except for piles of rugs, old clothes and in one case a stained mattress. His foot struck an empty wine bottle as he turned to leave the second room, sending it skating across the floor into a discarded carton of what had once been some sort of take-away meal. He grimaced. 'Bloody dossers,' he muttered. 'Ought to be exterminated.'

There was a soft chuckle behind him. 'That was a bit harsh, Maurice?' the young woman in protective overalls exclaimed from the doorway. 'Commissioner wouldn't be too happy to hear you talk like that.'

Morgan snorted derisively but ignored the censure, eyeing the Scenes of Crime manager narrowly instead. 'Okay, Sheila, so what have you got for me?'

Sheila Lambert shrugged. 'Come and see.'

Following her across the landing into the room with the corpse, Morgan stopped and stared at the large unzipped haversack on the floor beside the table.

'Started going through it, then thought we'd leave it alone' Lambert said, her eyes studying him fixedly over the top of her face mask. 'At first we thought it contained just old clothes, but then we found something a lot more interesting further down. Obviously the clothes were put in there to conceal it.'

Bending over the haversack, she carefully pulled back the flaps a little wider, inviting him to take a look. He moved closer and immediately glimpsed the transparent plastic wrapping tangled up inside a sweater.

'Have a sniff,' she said.

He bent even closer, but at first all he could smell was the stench of the corpse.

'You'll have to get lower than that,' Lambert commented.

Casting her a sour look, he got down on to one knee and tried again, his face almost into the bag. At once he detected another much sweeter smell, faint but still discernible. 'Marzipan,' he declared, straightening up.

She nodded. 'Going by the condition of the corpse, he must have been here quite some time, yet you can still smell it off the plastic – probably because the bag was zipped up, holding the odour in.'

'You're suggesting gelignite?' he queried incredulously, remembering his early forensic training on CID and picking up on her insinuation. 'You're saying the bag contained gelly?'

She shrugged. 'Either that or he had one hell of a sweet tooth. The smell is quite distinctive. None of the stuff there now, as far as we can see without taking the lot out, just the wrappings. But in one of the compartments we found packets of batteries and several apparently new strapless wristwatches, suggesting that our man had been on a shopping spree. More importantly there were also a couple of what look like pencil detonators.' She now straightened. 'I've sent someone to call up for explosive support, just in case there's anything else in this place likely to be a bit nasty.'

'You're saying the stiff was a bomb-maker?' he said grimly.

'Certainly looks like it.'

'Bit behind the times, though, wasn't he? I didn't think people in his profession used gelly anymore.'

'No idea, maybe he was an old safe-cracker – a Peterman I believe they called them. But in any event, one thing is clear, he liked to change his ID a fair bit.' Picking up an as yet unsealed evidence bag off the table, she held the flap open in front of him so he could see the passports. 'Found in another pocket,' she said. 'Three of the little buggers in a variety of names – all in pristine condition and undoubtedly recently produced. Another shopping trip, I would think. Seems he was gearing himself up for more contracts and a bit of travel thrown in.'

Morgan's heart was racing. What at first had seemed like the random shooting of a nondescript vagrant had taken on a whole new meaning. 'Problem is,' he said, 'if there's no explosive in the haversack now, where the hell is it?'

Lambert emitted a hard laugh. 'That, Maurice, is the million dollar question – which is why I'm so happy to be just a humble crime scene manager.'

It was then that Morgan felt something begin to crawl around his insides.

CHAPTER 3

The revelation by Alan Murray that, despite his blindness, he had managed to pursue a professional crime-writing career had enthralled Lynn and she couldn't wait to check the internet for one of his novels the moment she got back home, even though she had no title to work with and didn't know the name he was writing under. But to her annoyance, her laptop packed up within seconds of being switched on. There was no loud bang – not even a hiss – just a silent expiration as the screen went blank and the thing refused to function. She tried recharging the battery, plugging the computer into different mains sockets. When after an hour that didn't produce a result, in her ignorance of such sophisticated technology, she even shook it several times in the hope that she could dislodge something and somehow shock it back into life. All to no avail. The six-year-old machine had finally bitten the dust.

Resigned to the situation, rather than angry about it – after all, she had been warned by her ex months before that the laptop was on the blink – she exchanged her white shorts for a pair of faded blue jeans and boaters and drove to Helston instead, parking in a car park close to the centre of town. Helston was only half an hour's journey from The Lizard and she liked the town, which had a nice library with good internet facilities, so she felt sure the trip would be worth the effort.

There was hardly anyone in the library when she arrived and she was immediately able to settle in front of one of the computers provided for public use. But she was not really surprised to find that there was no record on the net of any crime-writer by the name of Alan Murray. Well, there was unlikely to be if he was using a pseudonym, was there? It had been just a long-shot on her part. She had thought, though, that as many other writers who used pseudonyms were still known to the public by their real names – Ruth Rendell, for example, who also wrote under the name Barbara Vine and Jack Higgins whose real name was Harry Patterson – there was a chance that Alan Murray's name might throw up his own pseudonym. But no such luck. Maybe his novels were a lot more risqué than she had imagined, which might explain his reluctance to lay them open to scrutiny.

Feeling disappointed, frustrated and not a little mystified by it all, she finally gave up looking altogether and headed for the car park – only to be stopped in her tracks a few yards from the library by a loud shout: 'Lynn? Lynn Giles?'

Spinning round, she saw a red-haired woman in her 30s, dressed in jeans and a floppy white sweater, crossing the street towards her at a half-run. Her heart sank. She recognised the woman immediately – Cate Meadows, New Light's publicity and advertising manager. Known in the agency as the "Sidewinder" – after the poisonous pit viper – because of her vicious tongue and back-stabbing reputation, she had been one of Freddie Baxter's earlier "bits on the side" before he had snared Felicity Dubois, and she was the very last person Lynn wanted to meet.

'Sweetie,' Cate exclaimed, grasping Lynn by both arms and planting an indelible kiss on each cheek, 'fancy meeting you down here.'

Still holding on to her arms, she stepped back a little and studied Lynn's face with a disapproving frown. 'What have you done to your hair? Dreadful, my dear, absolutely dreadful.' She peered at her more closely again. 'Scars have healed, I see, after that awful business at The Philanderer's Club, but really, dear, you should use more foundation. Girl's best friend, you know.'

Her high-pitched OTT delivery seemed to be attracting looks from passers-by and Lynn gently extricated herself. 'Nice to see you again, Cate,' she said, forcing a smile and edging back towards a shop front. 'But why are you in Cornwall?'

'Hols, sweetie,' the other replied. 'Two weeks away from that horrible agency and that equally horrible fat man. Bliss, absolute bliss. But what are you doing here?' She glanced quickly around her and lowered her voice a fraction. 'This where you've gone to ground, is it? Mum's the word, dear. You know you can trust me.' Another frown. 'Er … so, where are you living now? Near here, is it?'

The question was put in a casual, off-hand way but there was no disguising the sharpness of the blue eyes and the business-like set of the thin, slightly crooked mouth and Lynn had no intention of enlightening her anyway.

'You've picked up a tan already, Cate, I see,' she said, quickly changing the subject. 'Obviously you chose the right weather for it.'

Meadows blinked, seemingly taken aback by the abrupt put-off. 'Er … yes, thank you, but look …' and her voice suddenly dripped enthusiasm '… we must find somewhere to have a coffee and a chat about old times.'

There was no way out of it and inwardly cursing her misfortune, Lynn guided her to a teashop she knew in one of the backstreets of the town. The place was busy, with every table occupied, but there was another smaller room at the rear and they were lucky enough to find a corner table on their own. The coffee and pastries were good, but the promised chat was more like an interrogation. Meadows virtually hogged the next half hour as she quizzed Lynn relentlessly about her situation and where she was now living.

Lynn was a match for her, however, giving nothing away and constantly batting off awkward probes with questions of her own about the agency and the people she had once worked with. That proved to be the perfect tactic and eventually Meadows warmed to the opportunity of providing some malicious gossip – she just couldn't help herself. In fact, she managed to dismember the characters of at least half a dozen senior staff, including Freddie Baxter, for whom she reserved the worst vitriol, before she finally seemed to accept that she was not going to get anything of value out of her former colleague. Glancing at her watch, she made the excuse that she had to get back somewhere and planted two more kisses on Lynn's cheeks before heading for the street, leaving her "long lost friend" to pay the bill.

Lynn thought a lot about her chance encounter with Cate Meadows as she headed for the car park. Of all the people to run into right out of the blue, it would have to be the Sidewinder herself, wouldn't it, she mused? What were the odds on something like that happening, she wondered? Probably 100-1 – a safe bet even for the most cautious bookie. Just her luck.

She was surprised that New Light's publicity and advertising manager had chosen Cornwall for a holiday destination too. Especially as she knew that as a single divorcee with more money than she knew what to do with, Cate Meadows tended to favour continental resorts, like Benidorm, Ibiza, and the Algarve, with plenty of male action. Maybe she had actually run out of money now or just wanted somewhere quiet for a change?

Whatever the reason, as someone who didn't believe in coincidences, Lynn couldn't help feeling strangely uneasy about the encounter. It was almost as if it had been contrived. But why would that be and how would Meadows have known she was living on The Lizard? Unless she had been keeping tabs on her movements, of course, which was most unlikely since she obviously had no idea where Lynn's home actually was. And anyway, what possible ulterior motive could the Sidewinder have had? No, the whole thing had to have been down to chance, but Lynn knew she would have to keep her wits about her in future to ensure she didn't run into the woman again or inadvertently lead her to her bungalow. The thought of sitting on her decking, sipping gin and tonics with a bitch like that was not something she would ever want to contemplate.

She was still turning things over in her mind when she got to the car park and flicking the button on her remote control, had the satisfaction of seeing the lights of her Mercedes flash in welcome from a bay in the far corner. But hand on the door, she froze for a second, sensing that she was being watched. It didn't take her long to spot the watcher either. The beige Volvo XC90 was parked about 30 yards away and she glimpsed the thin face and red hair a second before the figure behind the wheel ducked out of sight. Damn it! Cate Meadows again. What the hell was the woman up to and why was she so interested in her? Okay, so she could have just returned to her car as Lynn had or was adjusting her sat-nav to take her back to where she was staying, but it was all mighty suspicious.

Climbing into the driving seat, her mouth set in a thin hard line, Lynn started the engine and pulled away, cutting across the car park diagonally the wrong way and ignoring the blast of a horn as she narrowly missed another car dutifully following the directional arrows. Out in the street beyond, she glimpsed the XC90 lumbering after her, maybe 100 yards away, and put her foot down.

Fortunately the town was not that busy and she was able to get clear of the place remarkably quickly, but as she headed towards the big naval air station at Culdrose, she glanced in her mirror and saw that the XC90 was still on her tail, though holding back as if to avoid detection. 'Persistent cow!' she muttered, but increasing her speed, she found that the Volvo easily matched it.

She was left with no other option but to resort to diversionary tactics and after leaving the base behind, she turned left at the next roundabout, towards Truro instead of Lizard town. At the same moment providence came to her aid. A slow-moving articulated lorry pulled out just behind her at the roundabout directly in front of the Volvo, obstructing Cate Meadows' view and enabling Lynn to increase the distance between them as a stream of cars heading past in the opposite direction put paid to any chance of an overtake.

Then the sign for Gweek village was there and without a signal, Lynn swung across the carriageway into the turning, heedless of the flashing headlights and blaring horn of an oncoming van. Shortly afterwards she was threading her way through the lattice-work of narrow lanes, so typical of Cornwall, that opened up before her. The Volvo did not materialise again and she took comfort from the fact that she appeared to have shaken off her tail at last, which meant that Cate Meadows would likely end up following the artic all the way to Truro before she realised her mistake.

But despite her sense of satisfaction, she couldn't help feeling uneasy as to why the Sidewinder seemed so interested in her. The chance meeting in Helston had been surprising enough, but to find Baxter's publicity manager apparently going to the extent of following her afterwards really jangled the alarm bells in her head. Okay, so Meadows was a nosy, vindictive bitch who would have delighted in the opportunity of broadcasting Lynn's whereabouts to the rest of the staff at New Light, but to go to the extent of trying to tail her to her home was well over the top even for her. It was really unsettling.

Lynn continued to ponder the issue as she headed on her roundabout route back to The Lizard, but after pulling up in front of The Beach House, thoughts of Cate Meadows were soon expunged from her mind. The sharp breath-taking chill of the ocean had the instant effect of redirecting her focus as she slipped naked into its creamy surf. But as she struck off in an effortless crawl towards the mouth of the cove, she was completely unaware of the figure crouched on the clifftop above, studying her through a pair of powerful binoculars.

****

Detective Chief Inspector Mick Benchley was not a happy man. It was three months into the bombing investigation, which had scarred Lynn Giles for life, and it seemed he and the disenchanted members of the Major Investigation Team he led as a senior member of the Met's Homicide & Serious Crime Command were no further forward than at the start of the inquiry.

Slouched in the worn leather chair in the incident room commander's office, the heavy, balding ex-SAS man drummed on the top of the desk with the fingers of his right hand, scowling unseeing at the picture of Her Majesty the Queen on the opposite wall as, for the umpteenth time, he turned over in his weary brain what little information on the case had so far come to light and tried to make some sense of it.

The bomb had been planted at The Philanderer's Night Club in Mayfair prior to a celebrity fashion show and although several people in the vicinity had been slightly injured by the blast, Lynn Giles was the only one to have suffered so much physical damage. The crime scene investigation team had found the remains of some cardboard wrappings among the debris, which the forensics laboratory had painstakingly reassembled, to reveal that the device had probably been concealed in a box of chocolates. Laboratory examination had also found traces of gelignite on the wrappings and a partial thumbprint on a small fragment of glass, which was said to have come from a wristwatch – obviously used as the timer. No matches had been found for the thumbprint on the criminal record data base, suggesting the bomber was an unknown, and the only observation SO15's Counter Terrorism Command had felt disposed to make was that the device seemed to have been crude and the type of explosive used "unsophisticated" – whatever that meant. Crucially, they had never heard of the group, Christians Against Sexual Exploitation, which had claimed responsibility for the attack, and had concluded that the bomber was more than likely an amateur and therefore not an ongoing terrorist threat.

Benchley grunted to himself. Bloody SO15. They had been all over the incident at the beginning – only too keen to take on the lead role in the investigation. But all that had changed when the countdown to a major London-hosted international conference on terrorism – which had been leaked to the press – had got under way. In the absence of any positive intelligence suggesting terrorist involvement in The Philanderer's Club bombing, the incident had been downgraded from possible terrorist status to that of a crank crime. This had enabled the elite specialists to drop out and the police hierarchy to focus their attention on the more definite threats to national security they believed to be in the pipeline.

As a result, Detective Chief Inspector Mick Benchley had suddenly found himself flavour of the month again and handed back what he preferred to call "his poisoned chalice" as senior investigating officer, though with the caveat that SO15 reserved the right to maintain a watching brief should it be necessary for them to become further involved. In other words, he carried the can if the investigation went pear-shaped, but they could come back in if his inquiries turned up anything tasty and take the whole thing off him again. Bloody typical.

The point was, where did the team go from here? No suspects. Little forensic evidence, apart from the partial thumbprint. No surveillance footage from the CCTV system covering the venue, as it had been down for months. Not even a tenuous lead to follow up on. In short, not the faintest glimmer of light at the end of the tunnel. They had hit the buffers and that was certainly not good for his future career.

Leaning back in his chair, he lit a cigarette and blew smoke rings at the already yellowed ceiling, ignoring the "No Smoking" notice on the wall.

The crime was certainly a strange one. Okay, so whoever had planted the bomb obviously had a hang-up about scantily clad young women cavorting on a catwalk. But why now and how come the crank or cranks responsible had not struck again somewhere else or made any demands or threats? There had been other fashion shows, both in the city and outside it, since the event at The Philanderer's Club and all had gone off without incident. It just didn't make sense.

Benchley was uneasy about Lynn Giles too and the fact that she was no longer living on his manor didn't help his developing ulcer. What if the bomb had not been planted to kill and maim indiscriminately, but had actually been specifically meant for her? What if this crap about Christians Against Sexual Exploitation was just a blind to muddy the waters? So she had taken his advice and disappeared to the seaside for a while and as far as he was aware, he was the only person who knew her whereabouts. But that didn't mean she was safely out of the way. If someone was after her, they wouldn't give up now, would they? And it would be the height of naivety to think that she could remain hidden for ever. Yet there was nothing he could do to guarantee her safety. Unbeknown to the ex-model, he had desperately tried to get her on to the witness protection programme, but his commander had emphatically refused to sanction it.

'She doesn't qualify, Mick,' he'd explained. 'There's nothing to suggest she is a specific target, we have no suspects in the frame and what you're asking me for is an open-ended commitment at a time when our resources are already being stretched to the limit. It cannot possibly be justified.'

The trouble was that deep down Benchley had to agree with him. The model's vague recollections about seeing someone or something suspicious on the day of the blast didn't really amount to anything and as she was allegedly still suffering from amnesia and couldn't come up with anything definite, she was no threat to anyone, so why would she be in imminent danger? Pretty unlikely. That didn't stop him worrying, though.

He glanced at his watch and reached for his anorak on the back of the chair. Lunch-time anyway. Time for a sandwich and a pint at his local.

'Moira,' he shouted through the half-open door. 'Get your bloody coat on. Lunch, and it's your round this time.'

A thin, dark-suited woman in her 40s appeared at the door even quicker than he had expected. Detective Inspector Moira Angel was unsurprised at being summoned by a yell. The grey-haired, bespectacled detective had worked with Benchley for a very long time now and she was well used to his abrasive, intolerant personality, enduring it with the quiet fortitude of someone who actually nursed a secret affection for the lonely bachelor.

'Well, come on, woman,' he exclaimed, frowning as she just stood there, looking at him with a sober expression on her face. 'Stir yourself. Mine's a pint.'

She shook her head. 'I don't think so, Guv,' she said.

His frown deepened. 'And how's that?' he queried. 'I got them in last time.'

'We've just had a shout from Islington. They've got a stiff in a derelict over there.'

'So? Why would that be of interest to me? Probably some bloody dosser blown away on crystal meth.'

She raised an eyebrow. 'Actually it seems like their John Doe was shot in the head.'

'Shot?'

She nodded. 'And from the stuff they've found in a haversack he had with him, it looks like he was into explosives.'

Benchley stared at her. 'You what?' he exclaimed.

Angel nodded. 'I know it's a long-shot, but it could be there's a link here to The Philanderer's Club job.'

Benchley didn't make further comment. He was already on his feet, wrenching his coat off the back of the chair, and she smiled slightly. 'Lunch off now then, is it, Guv?' she asked mischievously.

****

A yellow-and-black-coloured police "Crime Scene. Do Not Cross" tape was in evidence across the door of the Islington derelict when Benchley and Angel pulled up outside. Maurice Morgan was actually there, waiting for them, and as soon as they had donned the necessary protective overall and booties, the uniformed police constable on guard duty lifted the tape to allow them to enter the evil-smelling premises.

The Met explosives team had already left the area after checking the dead man's haversack and giving it a clean bill of health, but SOCO were still carrying out their forensic examination and were likely to be there for some time.

The visit didn't last long – there wasn't a lot to see and corpses were corpses as far as Benchley was concerned, coupled with which Morgan had something else to show them anyway.

The old Ford van was parked on waste ground at the end of the street, a couple of hundred yards or so from the murder scene and overlooked by several grey concrete tower blocks.

'Local area plod pointed this out to us,' Morgan explained. 'Looks like it might have belonged to our stiff. He had a set of Ford ignition keys in his pocket and they fit the ignition slot and one of the door locks exactly. There are no other motors abandoned in the area, so it figures this one was his.'

Mick Benchley stared at the vehicle for a few moments with an expression of weary cynicism on his craggy face. It was apparent that the van was of no value to him whatsoever. Someone had torched the thing and much of the interior had been reduced to a scorched, blackened shell ironically bearing a nice "Police Aware" notice.

'Pity our bomber hadn't stashed some of his explosives inside,' he commented drily. 'At least then our little arsonist wouldn't have been around to do any more torching.'

'Local skipper tells me it happened a couple of months ago,' Morgan said. 'No witnesses, of course, not in an area like this. Fire Service managed to put out the blaze before it destroyed the van completely and the local authority should have arranged to have the motor shifted to the car pound by now, but obviously forgot about it. One of dozens on their manor, I expect.'

Benchley bent down to stare at the twisted bumper bar beneath which the registration plate should have been attached. 'Index number?' he queried.

Morgan nodded. 'All checked out by the plods, Guv. Did a thorough job, too. Plates belonged to a Jag stolen from Billericay in Essex two years ago and never recovered. Engine and chassis numbers check out with a van which was scrapped by the original owner and sold to a dodgy breaker's yard Chiswick way. Yard has since closed down after the owner got wasted in a gangland hit, so there's no trail to follow after that.'

Benchley grunted. 'Convenient,' he said sarcastically. 'So another brick wall for my team. Brilliant! Any other little gems of info you have for me?'

Morgan shook his head. 'Only that the pathologist reckoned the stiff was shot just once in the head and that that could have been as long ago as a couple of months.'

'Round about the time of the bomb blast at The Philanderer's Club then?'

The DI shrugged. 'I don't know much about that particular job, but if you say so.'

'Don't know a lot, do you?'

Morgan's mouth tightened. 'No, Guv,' he snapped back. 'I sort of left my crystal ball back at the nick.'

Benchley ignored the response, accepting that he had asked for it. Then leaning back against a broken-down wall, he pulled out a packet of cigarettes, selected one and proffered the packet to his two colleagues. Morgan took up the offer, but Angel refused.

'So what have we got?' he said, lighting up and passing his lighter to Morgan. 'A stiff in a derelict house with a bullet in the head, whom we believe to have been wasted several weeks – maybe months – ago and who may have been carrying an explosive device when he was shot?'

'No device there now, though,' Morgan cut in, puffing out smoke. 'We only found a trace of what we believe to be gelly on some wrappings.'

'But there were other items in his haversack. I think you said some cheap wristwatches and quite a few batteries and pencil detonators?'

Morgan nodded. 'Oh, I reckon he was a bomb-maker all right, but until DI Angel here called me, I had no idea what he might have done with the gelly or who his intended target could have been. Presumably he was constructing a device for someone and that particular someone collected it, then wasted him.'

'Which begs the question, why?' Angel put in.

'That's easy. To make sure he couldn't talk.'

Benchley straightened up, stabbing a finger at him, smoke curling from the cigarette in his other hand. 'Exactly, which suggests our bombing was to be a one-off job – the killer only needed the one bomb and he didn't intend using his man again.'

Angel frowned. 'I agree, he obviously didn't need his services anymore, but that doesn't mean our bombing was a one-off job. Maybe the killer walked away with more than one device.'

Benchley snorted. 'Oh come on, Moira, we're not talking about a cash-and-carry warehouse here. Can you honestly imagine someone calmly walking down a London street with a holdall full of ready-made poppers? Hardly likely, is it?'

'So what are you saying?'

'I'm saying that the actual bomber was unlikely to have been a terrorist, but someone who had planned a single hit.'

Morgan drew on his cigarette, then nodded again. 'That seems to fit – especially since, according to the SO15 guy who turned out to this job with the explosive team, no self-respecting terrorist would have used this particular bomb-maker anyway. He reckoned that the kit in his bag was about as sophisticated as the stuff a Seventies trainee anarchist would have used – and probably just as reliable.'

Benchley went into a fit of coughing over his cigarette, attracting a reproving stare from Angel. 'So a has-been or an amateur maybe,' he wheezed. 'But we have no ideas as to his identity.'

Morgan shook his head. 'He was in possession of three passports – one Serbian, one Croatian and one Albanian – in three different names, which suggests he got about a bit, but we've yet to print him and do a full check.'

'And no trace of the weapon or any clues as to what sort of firearm was used?'

'No sign of the weapon, no, and as to what it was,' Morgan shrugged, 'that's down to Ballistics when they have had time to examine the round.'

'And there were no witnesses at the murder scene?'

Morgan emitted a short laugh. 'If there were, no one is likely to admit to it. We're talking doss city here, Guv – junkies, alkies and roadsters, most of them wanted for something somewhere. And whoever belled us to report the stiff is probably long gone now.'

'So our bomb-maker was a foreign national, using a variety of identities, who most likely hailed from the old Yugoslavia or somewhere close by?'

'More than likely, yes.'

'But if that's the case, what was he doing in the UK? And if he was behind the bombing, what was his connection with the glamour industry?'

'Maybe he had no connection at all with it?' Angel suggested. 'Maybe he was just someone for hire?'

'And by the sound of it, not very proficient in his chosen profession. Doesn't say much for the person who hired him, does it?'

'Perhaps he was an amateur as well?'

Benchley pinched out his cigarette and tossed it over the wall. 'An amateur who was able to shoot a man in the head and to need only one round for the purpose,' he retorted bleakly. 'Unusual skill for the sort of nutcase we've been looking for, don't you think?'

Angel shrugged, but said nothing.

Morgan took another long pull on his cigarette. 'Don't ask me, Guv,' he replied after a brief pause. 'I haven't the faintest idea what sort of person you're looking for.'

Benchley smiled without humour and tapping Angel on the arm to indicate it was time to go, he headed back to his car. 'Well, maybe you should give that old crystal ball of yours a rub when you get back to the nick, eh, Maurice?' he said over his shoulder. 'It might save us all a lot of time.'

CHAPTER 4

The extension telephone in Lynn's bedroom shrilled at just on 10 in the morning. Thinking with a sharp stab of apprehension that it might be Murray and hoping he wasn't about to cancel his dinner invitation that evening, she rolled over in bed and propped herself up on to one elbow, squinting in the sunlight which streamed through the partially open blinds and acutely conscious of the screaming of gulls outside the window.

'Yes?' she snapped irritably.

'Hi, sweetness.'

'Freddie?' she exclaimed, recognising the wheezy voice of the boss of the New Light Modelling Agency. 'What do you want?'

There was a soft chuckle. 'Now, you be especially nice to Uncle Freddie,' he said. 'He might have something for you.'

Lynn tensed, then wriggled herself up into a sitting position. 'What? You mean a work-type something?'

'Could be.'

'But you paid me off?'

A confirmatory grunt. 'Said I'd keep looking around for you, though, didn't I, luvvie? Thing is, someone like you will always be in demand.'

Her eagerness spilled over. 'So what sort of work are we talking about?'

Another chuckle. 'The sort you know best.'

'But – but what about my scars, Freddie? Is this a joke?'

The voice on the other end of the line tutted. 'Joke? Of course it's not a joke. Look, can I bring someone down there to see you. Say at around 11 tomorrow?'

'But I still don't see—?'

'Let me worry about that, sweetness. Trust me. Tomorrow then.'

The line went dead.

Mystified, excited, but at the same time not a little apprehensive, Lynn got up and showered, thinking carefully about the phone call.

What on earth had Freddie arranged? She was suspicious of the devious little toad, but he had so many contacts that it was just possible he had managed to set something up for her. The idea thrilled her and she thought again of the money, the clothes and those golden-haired playboys with their Porsches and yachts. Could it be that she would be back to modelling again? So probably not lingerie or swimwear, but it was possible Freddie had fixed up a contract with some big clothing manufacturer for her to model dresses, coats or even shoes. Yeah, she thought with a bitter grimace as she remembered Felicity's sarcastic comment about wearing a veil, maybe it was shoes then.

Quitting the shower, she made herself a mug of coffee and took it out on to the little patio overlooking the cove, dressed in just a white towelling robe. She sat there for a long time, taking in the sun and watching the gulls wheeling noisily above her head. Then finally stirring herself to prepare a light lunch, she washed down a delicious crab salad with a glass of Chardonnay. She would have had a second glass too – after all, what else was there to do – but the pull of the azure blue sea was too much to resist.

Making her way down to the beach in her white bathrobe and checking around to make sure her privacy was not about to be invaded yet again, she slipped out of the robe and once more plunged naked into the white-crested breakers. The water was ice-cold and for a second it took her breath away, but it was also exhilarating and she swam with the long-accustomed strokes she had mastered years before at school as a sixth-form athlete.

Without realising it, she swam right out of the cove and around the headland so that her beach house was no longer visible. Instead, she saw the blaze of another small beach and above it, on the clifftop, a familiar white house. Well, well, well, so this was what Alan Murray's place looked like from the seaward side.

Motivated by a sort of inner compulsion, she swam slowly towards the shore for a closer look and only yards from the beach, she saw him. Swinging to her left behind some rocks, she crouched down in the water, feeling the sharpness of shingle on the soles of her feet.

He was going for a swim and, like her, he obviously had not expected to meet anyone, for he was wearing nothing but a pair of black goggles. Archie was already in the water, barking and biting at the hissing foam around his feet. At least here Alan had no obstructions to bump into and his faithful companion could take some time off. But she could not help but wonder how he had managed to negotiate the steep cliff steps to the beach and she was filled with admiration for his determination to overcome the most difficult of obstacles, despite his disability.

She was conscious of other more basic feelings too and studied the lean tanned body with a sense of excitement. The long straight legs. The muscular thighs. The wide, powerful shoulders. He was absolutely beautiful and she just couldn't take her eyes off him. Why, oh why did a man like that have to be blind?

Then he was gone. A bronze arrow cutting through the surf away from her, out to sea. For a moment or two more she remained where she was, anxiously watching his progress. How on earth would he know when to head back or in which direction land lay. But as she tensed herself for a rescue mission, she saw him execute a sweeping turn and head back towards the shore. There was one very good reason for the manoeuvre too. Archie was standing on one of the rocks behind which she sheltered, looking down at her with a crooked grin on his face and barking for all he was worth. What was it Alan Murray had said about his dog being the silent type?

'Spoilsport,' she mouthed and splashing the dog quickly with one hand, plunged back into deeper waters and struck out for home.

****

Detective Chief Inspector Mick Benchley decided to drop in on The Philanderer's Club the morning after his visit to Islington.

Why he had decided to go back to the scene of the bomb blast he wasn't really sure. Something was nagging at him about the incident, but he just couldn't put his finger on it. 'Wasting your time, Guv,' DI Angel had said. 'Be nothing for us there now. Scene is three months old.' Maybe, Benchley thought, but something was wrong, he could feel it in his water. There was something he had missed on his original evaluation of the incident. But what?

The club was shut up when he arrived. It was strictly a nocturnal venue as a rule, so he wasn't surprised. Come 8pm each evening the bars would be heaving, but right now it was just an empty shell, taking a breather from its frenetic after-dark activities. A security guard, built like a brick shed, answered Benchley's persistent knocking and treated him to a belligerent glare. 'On your bike, arsehole,' he growled.

Benchley flashed his warrant card. 'Open up, dickhead,' he retorted and smiled his satisfaction as the man's attitude abruptly changed.

'I'll tell the boss you're here,' the gorilla said helpfully.

'You do that,' Benchley replied.

The boss turned out to be the club's under-manager, Wilfred Kent, and he didn't seem too pleased about the impromptu visit, accompanying his visitor with undisguised reluctance to the ornate function hall where the fashion show had been staged on the fateful evening.

Money obviously talked because despite the damage the place had suffered in the blast, restoration now seemed almost complete.

'Nearly back to normal,' Kent said proudly. 'Just one or two tweaks needed.'

Benchley stared around the room, frowning at the garish red and gold decor. 'You were on duty the night the bomb was detonated, if I remember rightly?' he said. 'I believe my DI interviewed you when you came out of hospital.'

Kent nodded and pointed to the side of his face. The long narrow scar was very evident, running like a cord through his neatly trimmed black beard. 'Got my own souvenir of it,' he replied sourly. 'Several of my staff and a few of the guests took some minor injuries too. But the young model … what was her name?'

'Lynn Giles.'

'Ah yes. Well, she got the worst of it. When it went off she was actually about to walk into the changing room, which probably saved her life.'

Benchley grunted and pointed towards the curtained stage at the far end of the room. 'You extended the catwalk from there, didn't you?'

Kent followed him across the room as he threaded his way among the small round tables. 'Yes,' he confirmed. 'And we had tables set in rows on either side of it – the principal guests at the front.'

'But none of them was injured?'

'No, the bomb blew a nice hole in the studded wall over there, showering everyone with glass and plaster, but fortunately the VIPs were too far away to be at much risk—'

He broke off and glanced at his watch. 'Look, I told you and your guys all this at the time.'

Benchley gave him his best smile. 'Then you won't mind going through it all again with me, will you?' he said.

Kent forced a smile of his own. 'No, no, of course not, but I don't see what else I can add.'

'Well, let's take a look at the dressing rooms for a start.'

Benchley allowed him to lead the way, following him up a short flight of carpeted steps to the stage and then across it, through a curtained doorway to their right, into a small, even more thickly carpeted lounge area. Another curtain on the other side turned out to be masking a narrow corridor, with a row of doors on both sides and a door marked "Emergency Exit" at the far end. The policeman remembered most of it from the night he had attended the club, but following the restoration the layout was now much clearer.

'Could anyone have got in here via that exit door?' he queried.

Kent made a face. 'No way. It was padlocked on the night. Fire service and the HSE weren't very happy about that and we've just been told we are being done as a result.'

'Quite right too. Any other entrances?'

'Only the front doors and we had them covered by heavy security, with ticket-only entry.'

'What about this lounge? Could anyone have secreted themselves in here? Pretended to be staff or something?'

'No way. In any event, Mr Baxter, the owner of the agency who was running the show, was in here supervising the process for most of the night. Fortunately for him, he had apparently only just gone down to the end dressing room to speak to one of the models when the bomb went off. He was a very lucky man.'

Benchley thought about that for a moment, then said, 'And I gather your CCTV system covering the car park was down?'

'Yes, been out for months. We have just had it completely replaced, so it is in full operation now.'

'Bit late though, eh?'

Kent grimaced again but said nothing in reply. Changing his focus, Benchley flicked open a door on his right, staring into a small cubby-hole of a room fitted with full-length, wall-to-wall mirrors and equipped with a dressing table, sink and a wheeled clothing rail. The room smelled of paint and new carpet.

'This is where the blast occurred, I believe?' he said, turning towards Kent, who was standing behind him in the corridor, fingering his wristwatch impatiently.

'So your people told us, and at the time this whole area was a bit of a mess. Could have been a lot worse, however, and I gather the bomb was thought to have been a rather Heath Robinson thing and not powerful enough to cause major damage. One of your chaps said they thought the bomb-maker was probably an amateur or someone using inferior materials.'

Benchley gave a noncommittal grunt. 'Looks like you've managed to repair the place nicely since the blast, though?'

'We were lucky to be able to engage an excellent firm to do the job.' An irritable sigh. 'But listen, Chief Inspector, I really must get on. We have a variety show tonight and—'

Benchley ignored him. 'You were standing ... where?'

'Oh, out in the main function room, a bit too close to the wall, which blew out unfortunately.'

'And remind me, this was whose dressing room?'

Kent frowned. 'Well, it was originally assigned to a black girl. Felicity something – Oh yes, I remember, Felicity Dubois. But she said it was too small for her and made her manager move her to one of the slightly bigger rooms further down the corridor.'

Benchley raised an eyebrow. 'So the room was changed on the night, was it? I didn't know that.'

An irritable sigh. 'Yes, yes, Chief Inspector, that's why this Lynn Giles person was given it instead.'

'I don't recall you mentioning this to us at the time?'

'It probably didn't strike me as relevant.'

Benchley's heart had begun to beat a lot faster, but his thought processes were easily outstripping it. Rooms being switched at the last minute? The one containing the explosive device occupied by a different model? What if, as Counter Terrorism Command had already suggested, there was no terrorist group at all, but a single person with an axe to grind against a particular individual? And what if the crime had not been committed by an outsider, but was actually an inside job? Could the

Felicity Dubois he mentioned have been involved in some way with the bombing? Could she have changed rooms so as to be as far away as possible from the device, which had been smuggled into the club? Was this new information likely to lead to the break Benchley had been hoping for? Only time would tell.

'Not relevant, Mr Kent?' he echoed as he swung back towards the door. 'You might be wrong about that.'

CHAPTER 5

'Well, am I or am I not a superb cook?'

Lynn paused in the act of taking a sip from her brandy glass. She smiled at Alan across the table in the soft orange glow of the lights mounted on the corners of the low wall enclosing the seaward end and right-hand side of the patio. It was a secret knowing smile, which after her clandestine sighting of him that afternoon, said it all. Dressed in a blue open-necked shirt and fawn casual trousers, he looked very relaxed, although the ubiquitous dark glasses seemed to take away some of the warmth from his face and she couldn't help wondering what colour his eyes were.

Little now remained of the first-class meal he had set before her and she almost regretted having to wash away the taste of the mouth-watering profiteroles, which had completed it, even with the excellent cognac.

'I'll tell you one thing you're not,' she said, a mischievous gleam in her almond-shaped eyes, 'and that's modest.'

He laughed outright. 'Modesty is for children and old people,' he replied. 'But,' and he grimaced, 'I'm not only immodest, I am also a fraud.'

She raised her eyebrows. 'Oh?'

He nodded soberly. 'Yes, I'm afraid you owe tonight's culinary delights – the seafood platter starter, the rack of lamb *and* the excellent profiteroles – to Tremanny Enterprises, a local upmarket catering firm. They set it all up for me. Put everything where I wanted it in the kitchen, even provided the hot trays. All I had to do was show you to your seat.'

Lynn laughed with him. 'I don't care who did the cooking,' she replied. 'It's been a wonderful evening and it must have cost you a small fortune.' Her smile faded. 'Why did you do it?'

He sat back in his chair and warmed his brandy glass in his cupped hands. 'Why did I do what?'

'All this … invite me to dinner in the first place.'

'Why not … for a beautiful lady?'

Lynn's face hardened and the magic of the evening began to melt away in a surge of bitterness. 'How can you say that?' she snapped. 'For all you know, I might be as ugly as sin.'

He shook his head slowly. 'Beauty is not just about looks, Mary,' he replied. 'It comes from the inside and has to do with you as a person. Looks soon fade with time, but the nature and personality of a person usually stay the same.'

She hardly heard him, but stood up quickly and took her glass over to the patio wall. Staring across the two- to three-yard wide strip of shadowy low-level scrub which lay between the wall and the cliff edge, she studied the vast expanse of moonlit ocean stretching away to infinity. It was a velvet night, warm and clear. The heavens brimmed with stars and the ocean had a strange luminous quality as it chuckled and hissed over invisible rocks.

She heard the scrape of Alan's chair and the next moment he was beside her. She drew away from him as his hand ruffled her hair. 'Why did you do that?' he demanded.

'Do what?' she queried.

'Pull away from me? Are you afraid?'

'Of course not,' she said, suddenly on the defensive.

His hand was ruffling her hair again, then gently travelling down her face, strong sensitive fingers examining the high cheekbones, finely chiselled nose, partly open mouth. He was so close she could actually smell the aromatic perfume of his aftershave above the fresh salty tang of the air.

She swallowed hard, conscious of a dryness in her mouth and a trembling in her knees. She wanted to draw away again, but was unable to make the move. Instead, she closed her eyes and tilted her head to one side, trapping his hand between her cheek and her bare shoulder.

'No, please don't,' she whispered.

'Don't what?'

'Just don't,' she said more sharply than she had intended, then immediately regretted the way she had spoken as he quickly pulled away from her, freeing his hand quite roughly.

His voice was cold when he spoke to her from a few feet away. 'I assure you I was not trying to seduce you,' he said. 'I was simply trying to capture a picture of you in my mind – and he added almost brutally, 'It's what blind people do!'

She turned quickly, embarrassed by her own reaction. 'Oh Alan, I'm sorry,' she blurted, reddening in the darkness. 'I didn't mean—'

'Of course you did,' he retorted, 'and I'm sorry too. Now, I think I had better see you home before there are any other misunderstandings.'

She shook her head unnecessarily, blurting out her tactless reply without thinking. 'No, you won't. I am quite capable of making my own way back.'

Almost as the words left her lips she winced, realising too late how they must have come out. But she dug another hole for herself in trying to make amends. 'No, what I meant was, it's pitch black out there—'

'And in my condition I might not be able to see where I'm going?' he cut in, treating her to a smile which was as cold as his voice had just been. 'Oh, don't worry about the dark, Mary. I'm quite used to it by now.'

And before she could think of anything else to say, he had made his way slowly through the living room into the hall, fumbling for her coat on the peg beside the front door, then holding it out for her.

'Goodnight, Mary,' he said quietly. 'Thank you for coming.'

You certainly handled that well, she mused bitterly as she struck out across the moonlit headland. Just like some neurotic, virginal teenager, in fact. So what if Alan *had* intended to bed her? What was wrong with that? He was hellishly attractive and he turned her on like no man she had ever met. And at least, being blind, he would not have been put off by her scars – not like Greg.

She thought about her last ex with even greater bitterness. Poor old Greg. It must have been a real shock for him the night he had seen her naked in the shower while the scars were still healing. Couldn't get it up after that, could he? Some sort of mental block. Psychological thing probably. Six months they had been together and yet he had dumped her just two days after she had been released from hospital. Needed time to work things out, he'd said, and he was apparently still working them out while he shagged the arse off the ever-accommodating Felicity, no doubt in every conceivable position. A perfect end to a perfect relationship, she mused, just like the perfect end to this perfect evening, and she wondered what else the nasty little gremlin, who seemed to have taken up permanent residence on her shoulder, was going to do to her next. It wasn't long before she found out.

She heard the crack of the branch as she followed the footpath into the tangled scrub, which skirted the edge of the cliffs for 100 yards or so before emerging on to a gorse heath. The path wound its way through waist-high gorse and among stunted wind-blasted trees, which had taken the shape of the gnarled old men of children's fairytales, and in the moonlight they looked almost alive. She froze, using the sleeve of her jacket to wipe away the self-pitying tears which had started brimming in her eyes, and peered through her smeared mascara at the path snaking away ahead of her. The sound had come from somewhere to her right, a few yards ahead of her, she was sure of it. A fox? Maybe a badger? Hardly. Not out here anyway, and this had been a heavy 'crack', like a shoe or boot inadvertently stepping on a fallen branch rather than the wrong-footed move of some nocturnal predatory animal.

She shivered and gripped the torch she had brought with her more tightly in her hand before moving off again, her eyes darting left and right, looking for the slightest sign of movement. There was nothing and the alarming sound was not repeated. Maybe she had been mistaken? She was already over-wrought and imagination could easily play cruel tricks in such circumstances.

The derelict engine-house appeared suddenly as she rounded a curve in the path, its attendant chimney stack reaching towards the face of the moon like an accusing finger. She stopped short, swallowing hard. She had passed this relic to Cornwall's tin-mining past so many times in the weeks she had occupied The Beach House without giving it too much thought, but that was until now.

Silence, but for the murmur of the sea at the foot of the cliffs just yards away. She turned her torch around, so that the heavy end was held out in front of her like a weapon, and advanced slowly towards the ruined building. Nothing. The moonlight peered myopically through the empty windows, illuminating them like jaundiced eye-sockets, and a night bird of some sort rose with a startled cry from the tangle of ivy choking the door-less entrance.

Shaken at first by the panic-stricken flight of the bird, she now breathed a sigh of relief. There was more heath, extending for about 20 yards beyond the engine-house and then, 30ft or so further on, the path dropped away into a cleft leading to the cove and her bungalow. Nearly home, thank goodness. A reassuring thought – but it was then that she happened to glance behind her and wished she hadn't.

The dark figure had appeared suddenly from the scrub behind her, striding purposefully towards her along the track. A man, she felt certain, wearing a hooded coat, with the hood drawn up over his head. She stifled the sharp cry which rose to her lips and quickened her pace, heading past the engine-house, then out of the scrub and across the heath towards the cleft in the cliffs and the path down to the cove.

She risked another glance over her shoulder. The man seemed to be walking faster too and actually gaining on her. She tripped and almost fell, reached the cleft, and practically threw herself into it, stumbling once before breaking into a run down the steep slope towards the sea. She thought she heard footsteps behind her, thudding on the parched earth. But then she was out in the open again, sticking to a narrow line of shingle bordering a jumble of rocks to her left, conscious of the surf now licking at her shoes after the in-rush of the tide a few hours before.

The wooden bungalow stood on a ridge several feet above the beach, accessed by a flight of steep wooden steps anchored into the sand by the supporting posts of twin handrails. She caught her knee on the left-hand post as she went for the steps two at a time. The pain almost made her falter, but the thought of what was behind her drove her on regardless. She made the decking at the top with a gasp of relief, then yanked her key from her pocket and rammed it into the lock of one of the French doors with a force which threatened to remove it from its hinges.

Slamming the door shut behind her, she locked up again and leaned against it, drawing breath into her starving lungs in long agonised gasps which set her chest on fire and brought a metallic-tasting bile up into her throat.

Closing her eyes tightly in suppressed panic, she waited for her pursuer to reach the door and try to force it open – listened for his heavy footfalls on the wooden decking. But all she could hear was the sound of the sea, and as her breathing normalised and the shakes in her legs grew less and less, she edged her way along the wall to peer out of the living room window.

Moonlight still flooded the cove and the only sign of life was the black silhouette of what looked like a freighter of some sort way out on the horizon, displaying the usual glittering navigation lights. Her pursuer had completely disappeared.

Frowning, she tip-toed to the small square hallway at the front of the bungalow, picking up a heavy iron doorstop on the way. There was no sign of anyone on the patch of lawn which served as her front garden or on the track leading up to the main road, past where her silver Mercedes car was parked.

She checked the house thoroughly after that, satisfying herself that the front door was tightly bolted and the kitchen and bedroom windows were securely fastened. Then she returned to the living room and peered through the window to ensure no one was lurking out there on the decking. But there was no sign of a soul.

'Silly cow!' she breathed, pouring herself a gin and tonic from the assortment of bottles on the sideboard. He was probably just a late-night walker or jogger. Nothing more.

She gulped down some of the spirit and shivered, her fears returning in a rush. So maybe he was, but then what had he been doing lurking about in the copse in the first place? Yeah, and why had he come after her the way he had? She glanced at the luminous dial of her wristwatch – 11.30pm. What was a walker or jogger doing on the cliffs at this time of night anyway? And if he wasn't a walker or a jogger, exactly what was he? A mugger or sexual pervert maybe? Perhaps something even worse? Remembering the warning from Detective Chief Inspector Benchley about the terrorists who could still be looking for her, she shivered again, her imagination conjuring up all sorts of horrific possibilities.

It was past 1am before she managed to pluck up sufficient courage to climb into bed. Even then she lay there for a long time, turning the night's events over and over in her hyped-up brain and wondering what to do about them.

At first, her run-in with the character in the hooded coat took pride of place in her disturbed ponderings. Yet, as the initial panic gradually subsided and common sense began to prevail, she found herself looking at the incident in an entirely different light. Frightening though it had been at the time, was it possible that her own imagination had coloured things to the point that neurosis had taken over? There was really nothing to say that the hooded man had actually pursued her. She had only assumed he had, thought she had heard his footsteps pounding after her.

Despite all her previous suspicions, misgivings – call them what she would – she had absolutely no evidence to back them up. She had met a hooded man on a lonely clifftop late at night and had assumed he was up to no good. Yet he had said nothing to her, had made no attempt to assault her, and in the end had disappeared before she had reached home. Surely, if he had been up to no good, he would have done something unmentionable to her before she had got away from him? She was over-reacting, letting her imagination rule her head. It was a balmy night. Why shouldn't he be out for a walk, just like her? Yes, the more she thought about it, the more stupid her fears seemed to be, and in the end she found herself dismissing the whole incident as another non-event.

Alan Murray was a more difficult proposition, however. She had reacted like a fool to a perfectly innocent gesture and had probably put him off her for good. So, what did she do to rectify the situation? Go and see the man in the morning and apologise or just make out the spat had never happened in the first place and hope that he would come around again eventually?

Going for the apology option was certainly the obvious course, but it was not as simple as it appeared. After all, what would she say to him? "Sorry I behaved like an idiot last night, Alan, but I thought you were trying to screw me." She snorted. Oh, that would really sound good, wouldn't it? Probably result in her digging an even bigger hole for herself than she had already.

She frowned at the lamp-lit ceiling. On the other hand, she couldn't just bury the whole thing, could she – try and make out it had never happened? What would he think of someone who had insulted him in his own house, then run off into the night like a naive schoolgirl after her first petting session? Somehow she had to make amends and no matter how embarrassing that was, she would have to do it.

She was still thinking of his lithe tanned body and ready smile as she finally succumbed to the rhythmic swish of the sea below her bungalow and fell asleep.

CHAPTER 6

The rap on the front door came at precisely 11am next morning, just as Lynn finished dressing. Opening up, she found a very fat bejewelled Freddie Baxter, dressed in one his usual flamboyant outfits, standing on the doorstep with another man, wearing a polo-necked sweater and jeans. Damn it! With all the night's excitement, she had completely forgotten that they were coming.

'Hi sweetness,' Baxter smarmed, openly appraising her trim figure in the beige shorts and white T-shirt. He waved a podgy hand in the direction of his companion. 'Thought I'd bring along my business associate who you'll be working with on set.'

'On set?' Lynn said, frowning as she ushered them through into the living room. 'What are you talking about, Freddie? I thought you had a modelling job in mind?'

The fat man fell on to the settee beside his companion like a sack of cement, mopping his florid face with a brilliant yellow handkerchief. 'So I have – in a manner of speaking,' he replied, then added, 'Any gin on that little sideboard of yours, sweetness? Need a large one.'

Lynn's mouth tightened, but she went to the sideboard and did the honours anyway, adding the contents of a small bottle of tonic to the tumbler.

'And what about Mr … er …?' she queried, nodding in the direction of the other man as she handed over the glass.

Baxter's companion declined a drink with a shake of his head. 'Vernon,' he said in a soft lisping voice. 'Vernon Wiles. Everyone calls me Vern.'

Well, they would, wouldn't they, she mused? She studied the pinched white face, long thin nose and restless brown eyes, thinking uncharitably of how much he reminded her of a weasel.

'Lovely spot, my dear,' Baxter continued between slurps, 'but too damned hot for me right now. Talk about an Indian summer—'

'So, what's this job you're offering then?' Lynn cut in, irritated by the small talk and anxious to get this odious little man out of her house so she could head over to Alan's place to sort things out.

Baxter grinned, exposing a mouthful of gold fillings. 'Sort of filming, sweetness. Vernon here is a film producer, aren't you, Vern?'

She sat down carefully in the armchair opposite, staring briefly at her bare feet and wishing she had put more nail polish on her toenails. 'A film producer?' she repeated, unconvinced. 'A film producer with who?'

Wiles smiled. She wished he hadn't, for he exposed a rack of crooked teeth which looked none too clean. 'Small company,' he answered for Baxter. 'We call ourselves "Verniscope" actually.'

'Verniscope? Never heard of you.'

'No ... er ... probably not. We provide entertainment for a select niche market.'

Lynn's eyes narrowed. 'And why are you interested in me?'

Wiles shifted in his seat a little uneasily. 'We need a new lead actress.'

She laughed bitterly. 'What, for a horror film? You can see the scars on my face. I've plenty more. All over.'

He held up a slender white hand. 'Oh please, our audience wouldn't mind that. They like the unusual.'

Lynn started, gripping the chair arms so tightly as she leaned forward that the whites of her knuckles showed through the skin. 'Exactly what sort of films are we talking about, *Vernon*?' she grated.

He smiled again, then shrugged. 'Romances mostly—'

'You mean porn, don't you, you dirty little moron?'

Wiles looked decidedly uncomfortable now and he threw a swift pleading glance at Baxter. The fat man sighed. He didn't embarrass so easily. 'Oh come on, Lynn, you're not some naive teenager. You've taken your clothes off before.'

She sprang to her feet so suddenly that Wiles nearly jumped off the settee.

'Yes, Freddie,' she blazed, 'but not to satisfy the perverted appetites of the dirty raincoat brigade. I was a model – a damned good one – and with your lucrative agency business, I'm surprised that you have involved yourself in this kind of filth.'

He grinned. 'Just a little side-line, I assure you,' he replied. 'Meeting the needs of the market and all that – just like you were doing when I first found you in that bar, pole-dancing. Forgotten that, have you?'

'That's a whole lot different to the sort of filth you're talking about. How can you even think that I would stoop so low as to … to—?'

'Money,' he cut in. 'A lot of it. It's a business that pays top-notch salaries. Vernon is prepared to make you a very good offer.'

Lynn was quivering with anger now, her fists clenched tightly by her sides. 'I don't give a damn what this little creep is prepared to offer me – now get out, the pair of you!'

Baxter's near permanent grin faded. Switched off like a neon sign on a rundown city street. 'It's only a friggin' movie,' he exclaimed in exasperation. 'You wouldn't actually have to do anything, just pretend. And it's not as though we're talking about snuff – only a bit of simulated Rumpy-pumpy.'

'I said, get out!'

Baxter scowled and hauled himself to his feet with much panting and wheezing. 'I come all the way down here to help you and this is all the thanks I get,' he grumbled.

Lynn snorted. 'You came down here, Freddie, because of the cut you thought you were going to get out of the porn films, nothing more. Well, now you can go back disappointed, can't you? Life's a real bitch, isn't it?'

The fat man's face twisted into a vindictive mask and he waggled a podgy finger a few inches from her nose. 'You'll find out just how much of a bitch life can be if you cross me,' he snarled. 'Just remember that the press – not to mention the scumbags who planted that bomb – have no idea where you have gone to ground at present and the celebrity tabloids in particular would just love to get a few hot shots of the famous Lynn Giles, post-incendiary. It would make brilliant dramatic visuals for the glossies – you know the sort of thing, "Top Model, then and now". Maybe I should give them a bell?'

'You wouldn't dare.'

'Wouldn't I? Now you listen to me, Miss! Those scars of yours cost me a bundle. Not only did I have to pay you that extortionate severance bonus, but I was on the verge of clinching a serious contract for you that would have set me up for life. Now the whole lot's gone to rat's shit.

Well, you're going to make it up to me, whether you want to or not, and you'd better believe it!'

Waddling to the door after Wiles, he turned and stabbed a finger in her direction. 'You know my mobile number,' he finished, 'and you've got 24 hours to agree terms. After that, things are likely to get pretty nasty.'

Then he was gone and as the sleek black BMW pulled away from the house with a swirl of gravel, Lynn stared into the mirror through her tears and saw the end of the world.

****

'Anyone in?'

Lynn had not heard the knock on the front door and she swung round quickly. Alan Murray was feeling his way through with his stick, a large bunch of flowers clasped awkwardly in the same hand, preceded by an enthusiastic tail-wagging Archie. She hesitated, taken aback by his sudden appearance, her head still reeling over her run-in with fat Freddie. Then recovering quickly, she stepped forward and took his arm.

'Alan, what – what a nice surprise,' she said in a low halting voice as she guided him towards the settee. 'I … I wasn't … er …'

'Expecting me?' he finished for her, sitting down heavily and patting the black Labrador's head as the animal dropped obediently on to the floor beside him.

She bit her lip. 'Well, we hardly parted on the best of terms last time, did we?' she commented wryly.

He gave an equally rueful smile, his face turned slightly away from her. 'That's why I'm here,' he said. 'I've come to apologise.' He thrust the bunch of flowers out in front of him with a grin. 'A peace offering. I hope the florist picked the best and the taxi driver didn't damage them.'

She took the flowers and laid them across the coffee table, feeling her embarrassment mounting. 'They're … they're beautiful, thank you … but it's me who should be apologising. I behaved like a silly schoolgirl—'

'And I behaved like a chauvinist pig,' he cut in, waving her to silence. 'No excuses. I was right out of order. I can only ask you to forget what happened and give me a chance to make amends.'

'Make amends?'

His boyish grin returned with a vengeance. 'Another dinner date perhaps?' he suggested. 'There's a little place I know in Lizard Town that I'm sure you would like.'

'I have a better idea,' she said on sudden impulse. 'Why don't you let me cook for you this time? It's the very least I can do. Shall we say here, at 8pm tonight?'

He raised an eyebrow. 'That's hardly me making amends, is it?'

She took a deep breath. 'Let's just put all that behind us and move on,' she said, then emitted a soft chuckle. 'And I promise I won't hire Tremanny Enterprises to prepare dinner.'

Now he laughed. 'Touché,' he replied, 'and hopefully you won't send me packing quite as quickly as you did your earlier visitor. He nearly ran me down in the lane.'

She grimaced, remembering fat Freddie like a bad taste. 'Just someone from a previous life,' she said. 'Best forgotten.'

He nodded, but obviously didn't want to leave things there. 'Must have left half an inch of rubber on the road though,' he said, his curiosity very evident. 'Could do with an anger management course, don't you think?'

Lynn had no intention of entering into a discussion about her former boss and abruptly changed the subject. 'Would you like a drink or something? Whisky, wine—?'

'Lord, no,' he interjected again. 'Not at this time of the day and also, I've a novel to get on with. I hardly think alcohol would be much of a cure for writer's block.'

'Tea then, or coffee?'

He stood up with a shake of his head. 'Thanks anyway. I must be off. Only came to apologise – and to give Archie a walk, of course.'

Lynn snorted. 'Oh thanks,' she retorted and bent down to rub Archie's ears. 'Just don't spoil things by telling me who was your priority.'

He gave another chuckle as she turned towards him. 'Archie naturally,' he said. 'See you at 8pm then.'

She was still smiling as she watched him make his way up the lane towards the main road, Freddie Baxter and his threats as far from her thoughts as they could possibly be. Suddenly life was beginning to look promising again. Suddenly for the first time since the bomb blast, she felt a surge of optimism for the future.

She would not have felt quite so good about things had she known about the big black BMW parked in a gateway further up the lane and the two men in the car, who had witnessed Murray's brief visit and his slow hesitant departure as he felt his way past them with his white stick, aided by the ever-patient Archie. Freddie Baxter's grin could not have been broader as he started the powerful engine and pulled away. 'Well, well, well, Mr Wiles,' he commented to his companion in the front passenger seat. 'Seems our little girl has an admirer – a blind pillock, no less. What is it they say? There's none so blind as those who cannot see? Now that could be very useful to us, very useful indeed.'

****

The public car park in Mullion village was virtually empty when Lynn pulled in close to the exit and got out of her Mercedes. She was determined to give Alan Murray a dinner he would never forget – for the right reasons – but as she walked briskly into the tiny village, her excitement was mixed with trepidation.

What if she couldn't get all the ingredients for her ambitious menu? After all, Mullion only had a few small shops. Maybe she should have gone into Helston? That was the trouble with living in the back of beyond – choice was limited. Okay, so the crab salad starter should not pose a problem. Seafood was pretty plentiful in this part of the world. But the fillet steak entrée she had in mind might prove elusive. Then what? Beans on toast? And another thing, what if it all went wrong that night or Alan failed to turn up? She started to feel sick, wondering if her offer of dinner had been a mistake. Well, it was too late for second thoughts now.

She need not have worried, however. She managed to get everything she wanted – including a premium Italian red wine, a bottle of Chardonnay and a nice slab of Cornish Yarg cheese to follow her planned lemon meringue sweet.

Elated by her successful shopping trip, she headed back to her car with a spring in her step. But her elation didn't last long. A man wearing a dark hooded anorak was crouching by the front wheel of a small jeep a few yards from where she had left her Mercedes, ostensibly checking one of his tyres. She was immediately suspicious. What was he really doing there? Waiting for her to return perhaps? She noted the thin, angular build and the hooded coat and swallowed hard. It could easily have been the same man she had encountered on the headland the previous night, but as it had been dark at the time, it was difficult to be sure.

Who the hell could the guy be and what did he want? Press? Possibly, but he didn't seem to be carrying a camera of any sort. Furthermore, she didn't recognise him from her days with the agency and she prided herself on knowing by sight most of the "rat-pack", as the celebrity press were called. But if not press, then what? She shivered, keen to steer her thoughts away from the dark place to which they were heading and making every effort to focus her mind on her evening with Alan instead.

But it was almost impossible. Even as she quickened her step, forcing herself to resist the temptation to cast another glance in the direction of her suspected stalker, she prepared herself for the moment when he would suddenly spring to his feet and sprint towards her in an attempt to cut her off before she could reach the driver's door of her car. But he did nothing of the sort, and unable to stop herself throwing him a covert glance across the roof of the Mercedes as she flicked her remote and threw the door open, she saw to her surprise that he had not moved from his crouched position by the front wheel. In fact, he was apparently still engrossed in his examination of the tyre. Nevertheless, she suspected he was watching her out of the corner of his eye as she climbed into the driver's seat – or was she just being paranoid again?

Cursing through gritted teeth, she stalled twice before she managed to pull away and she was trembling fitfully as she accelerated along the narrow road out of the village, gunning the powerful car to a reckless 60mph as the exit road opened up before her. Thinking her suspected stalker might come after her, she glanced in her rear-view mirror, but there was no sign of the vehicle. Instead, what she was presented with was the single blazing headlight and flashing blue lights of a police Traffic motorcyclist. Seconds later the warbling note of the siren forced her to pull over to the side of the road.

'Bit of a hurry, weren't you, ma'am?' the bearded policeman said, peering in at her, his grey eyes sweeping round the interior of the car.

She winced, feeling totally stupid and searching for an excuse. 'Sorry, officer, but I … I was trying to get away from a man who's been stalking me.'

Deep down, she now felt sure that the character with the Jeep had not been stalking her at all, but was just some ordinary motorist her imagination had seized upon to satisfy her rampant paranoia, but the blurted explanation was out before she realised what she had said.

The policeman removed his sunglasses and studied her with renewed interest. 'A stalker, you say?' He turned to stare back along the empty road. 'I don't see anyone.'

Lynn inwardly cursed herself for a fool. This was the last thing she wanted – arousing the curiosity of one of Cornwall's finest and drawing unwanted attention to herself. 'I've probably lost him now anyway.'

He grunted. 'What did he look like, this stalker?'

Shit! She had done it now. Might as well just run with it. 'Thin build, wearing a hooded coat. That's all I could see. His face was obscured. But he ... he was driving a jeep.'

He produced a pocket book in a battered wallet and a pen. 'Index number?'

'I didn't get it. I'm afraid.'

He frowned. 'Seen him before, have you?'

She nodded. 'Yes, he followed me home on the headland above Bootleg Cove, where I live.'

'What in a jeep?'

'No, no, he was on foot.'

'How do you know it was the same man if you couldn't see his face?'

She shrugged. 'Same build, same coat. Bit of a coincidence.'

'And why would he be stalking you?'

'I don't know. Probably a perv.'

His eyes narrowed. 'Would you step out of the car for a moment, ma'am.'

Hell's bells! Why couldn't she just have accepted the speeding ticket? She'd have been on her way by now.

Climbing out of her seat, she forced a smile. 'Really, it was probably my imagination.'

He didn't answer, but she could feel his eyes studying her with a new intensity.

'Don't I know you, ma'am?'

She laughed unconvincingly. Surely cops weren't into fashion mags? 'I wouldn't think so. I haven't been living down here long.'

Another grunt. 'Licence?'

The sudden change of tack took her by surprise and she simply stared at him. 'Driving licence?' he said.

Her heart sank. Now her cover really would be blown. Reaching into the glove compartment she handed it over, watching for his expression to change when he saw the name 'Lynn Giles'. But it didn't and he handed the licence back after a cursory glance, obviously more interested in its validity than anything else.

'Well, Miss Giles,' he said, returning his wallet to his pocket, 'I'm going to give you the benefit of the doubt this time. If I catch you speeding again, I'll throw the book at you, do you understand?'

She nodded eagerly. 'Yes, yes, thank you.'

'And this stalker,' he added drily as he turned away, 'I suggest you come up with a better excuse than that in future, eh?'

He treated her to a brief smile. 'Nice car, though. Take care of it.'

She breathed a deep sigh of relief as he roared off. No speeding ticket and her cover still intact. How lucky was that?

Not that lucky, as it turned out. When she got home, she found that the French doors of The Beach House had been forced open – and if that wasn't enough, the sudden thud of a cupboard door or drawer being closed indicated that the intruder was still inside.

CHAPTER 7

The bar of The Blue Ketch Inn was half full when Freddie Baxter ushered a reluctant Vernon Wiles through the door and all conversation stopped for a few seconds as the regulars gave the visitors the customary once-over.

Wiles inwardly cringed. He hated being the centre of attention, much preferring the anonymity of the shadowy backstreet world of heaving flesh and sweaty film sets, which had been his life for 20 years. Now that Lynn Giles had so forcefully turned down the offer to "star" in one of his films, he couldn't wait to shake off the indecently clean, salty tang of Cornwall and the sound of waves breaking on the shore, and get back to London's poisonous cocktail of pollutants and the rumble of heavily congested traffic. At least then he would be on familiar territory. Not stumbling around some gorse-covered wilderness, up to the ankles of his new suede shoes in cow shit and being bitten half to death by sand flies – or whatever else the creepy-crawlies which seemed to infest the heathland scrub were called.

The trouble was, his business partner and financial backer seemed in no hurry to leave and, as always, he called the shots.

'Fresh air, Vern,' Freddie Baxter had said with an extravagant wink, 'that's what we need – clear out the old lungs.'

It was obvious that fat Freddie was up to something and it didn't take the IQ of a genius to work out that whatever it was, it centred on Lynn Giles. Baxter was one of the most vindictive men Wiles had ever met and from past experience he knew it was a big mistake to cross him. The flamboyant entrepreneur would do practically anything to get even with someone who opposed him and spotting the blind man heading for The Beach House seemed to have sent his vengeful scheming mind into overdrive.

What nasty little plan he was hatching, Wiles had no idea. Freddie rarely confided in him. But it was an even bet that lunch at The Blue Ketch was an essential part of it.

Baxter's bulging wallet hit the bar counter with just about the right amount of force and the thin cadaverous man on the other side slid off his stool like a serpent and slithered over to him, his snake-eyes eyes glinting. 'Couple of double whiskies,' Baxter said with an affected gasp.

Snake-eyes nodded. 'No problem, sir,' he said in a thick Cornish accent and turned towards the optics. 'Any partic'lar one?'

Baxter took another deep breath and shook his head. 'No, no … a Grouse will do.'

The barman took his time pouring the two whiskies and slid them across the counter with an attempt at a smile, raising an eyebrow as the fat man drained the glass in a single gulp. 'Looks like you needed that, eh?' he commented, his question hanging in the air.

It was the cue Baxter was waiting for and he went for it. 'Damn right, I do,' he retorted. 'Nearly killed a man out there.'

Conversation in the bar abruptly died and the barman leaned forward across the counter. 'You don't say?' he breathed. 'On the road, was it?'

Baxter tapped his glass, ignoring Vernon Wiles' astonished stare. 'Stepped right out in front of me,' he went on. 'How I missed him, I just don't know. Really shook me up, I can tell you. Damn fool with a black Labrador. Must have been blind.'

'Maybe he was,' another rough voice chimed in.

Baxter turned to look at the man standing a few feet away. His bearded weather-beaten face and woollen hat suggested he was either a farmer or a fisherman and the hand holding the nearly empty pint glass was calloused and dirty. 'What do you mean?' he replied, playing him along.

'Didn't 'ave a white stick with him, did 'e?' the man continued, without answering the question.

'Yes, I believe he did have a stick, come to think of it. Don't know whether it was white or not, though.'

There was a murmur of understanding from the other drinkers. 'Alan Murray,' another voice piped up. 'Lives up at The Old Customs 'Ouse on the 'eadland.'

'Says 'e's a writer,' the barman came back in, 'though we got our doubts about tha'. Bit of a mystery is our Mr Murray, I reckon. Al'ays wanderin' about with 'is dog, talkin' to hisself on one of them tape things.'

Baxter pushed his glass across towards him, nodding in the direction of the optics. 'Well, he's a bloody menace, that's all I can say.'

'What d'ye expect from an Emmet?' someone else chortled and there was an answering roar of laughter from the rest of the drinkers.

'Emmet?' Baxter queried with a frown.

'Vis'tor,' Snake-eyes replied. 'That's what we calls 'em down 'ere. In Devon it's Grockles.'

'Which, I suppose, makes me and Vernon here Emmets as well?'

Snake-eyes hesitated, obviously not wishing to upset customers. 'S'pose it do really,' he agreed carefully.

And fat Freddie laughed too, nodding his understanding. He could afford to laugh. After all, he had got what he had come for, hadn't he? Now he could sit down with Vernon and enjoy a nice lunch.

****

Lynn froze on the patio decking, staring in open-mouthed astonishment at the splintered frame of one of the French doors. If she had entered The Beach House via the front door as usual, she would have been unaware of the break-in until she'd reached the living room and would have been totally unprepared for anyone lurking inside.

Gently setting her shopping bags down against the wall, she swallowed hard. Yes, but now she was aware, what did she do about it? The sensible course was to call the police on her mobile, but that would mean attracting unwanted attention – maybe even result in a leak to the press about her whereabouts – and that was one thing she couldn't afford. Then what? Quietly vanish and come back when it was safe to do so? But how long would that be and what if the intruder was waiting for her return anyway? Then there was the curiosity thing. Who was her burglar? Why had he picked her bungalow of all places? She just had to find out.

Seeing a small hand-fork projecting from a patio planter beside the open door – she had been using it a couple of days before to pot a shrub – she carefully retrieved it, conscious of the fact that her heart seemed to be pounding almost as loudly as the breakers on the beach behind her. Then gritting her teeth, she pulled the damaged French door open a few more inches and stepped over the threshold into the living room, straining her ears for the slightest sound which would reveal her unwelcome visitor's whereabouts.

Silence. The floorboards creaked slightly as she crossed the room and she froze again. Damn it! Her intruder must have heard her car drawing up and the sound of her footsteps on the decking as she'd arrived. He would now also know she was actually inside The Beach House.

She waited for him to make a move, but there was nothing, save a fly buzzing irritably against one of the living room windows. Wincing in anticipation of further creaks from the floorboards, she advanced a few more steps, stopping again when she passed through the connecting doorway into the hall.

There was the sudden screech of a seagull from directly overhead and she heard something land on the roof, claws scrabbling on the sloping tiles. More thuds from above, then the sound of flapping wings – and a return to silence.

Thrusting the little fork out in front of her, she pushed the right-hand door open with her other hand and peered into the spare bedroom beyond. Even from where she was standing she could see that the room was empty. But through the crack between the door and the frame she noted that all three drawers of the single wooden chest just behind it had been pulled out, their contents strewn across the floor.

What the hell was the arsehole looking for – jewellery perhaps? Or maybe some loose cash?

She checked her own bedroom directly opposite and saw much the same story. Open drawers gaping at her from a corner chest and the door of the single wardrobe leaning outwards on one hinge, clothing apparently pulled from the hangers and spilling through the gap on to the fitted carpet.

Then she noticed the window. It was wide open, the corner of one of the curtains ripped from the rail and the curtain itself pulled through and hanging down the exterior wall.

Striding over to it, she leaned out, staring up and down the narrow passageway which connected the front garden to the back steps of the decking. There was no sign of anyone.

Wheeling around, she ran back into the living room and out on to the patio again. Shielding her eyes against the glare of the sun, she studied the cove and the path leading up to the headland. Her gaze met only a jumble of rocks and shingle at the foot of the steps, giving way to an empty beach. She was too late. Her intruder had flown, leaving her with the burning unanswered question – why? Somehow she sensed that this was something she really wouldn't want to know.

****

Vernon Wiles shook his head vigorously, spilling some of the wine in his glass down his sweater as he did so. 'No way,' he said. 'I'm not getting involved in your madcap scheme. I'm going back to the Smoke.'

Fat Freddie smiled, but there was no humour in it. 'Be my guest, Vern,' he said quietly, 'but I'd have to hang on to my car and it's a hell of a long walk from here. 'Mind you, I suppose you could always hitch or try to catch a train from somewhere?' He sat back in his chair. 'And of course, I would have to reconsider my partnership with someone who ran out on me, which would mean no more financial investment in your little business.'

Wiles gaped at him. 'Come on, Freddie, you wouldn't do that? It would ruin me.'

Baxter sighed, pausing briefly as a young waitress set some cutlery before them both. 'Sorry, Vern,' he went on as she withdrew, 'but back-scratching is a two-way thing, you know.'

The big man leaned forward across the table. 'Listen,' he said earnestly, 'I need to find out what that Giles bitch is up to. Then maybe I can force her to play ball. One night's stay here, that's all I'm suggesting and then it's back to your beloved shithole.'

Wiles frowned. 'I don't like it.'

'You don't have to like it. All you've got to do is to come with me when I drive out to that blind tosser's place and wait with the car while I have a nose around.'

'And what do you expect to find?'

'Hell, how should I know? But any guy who takes a girl flowers has to have the hots for her, so it's worth taking a closer look at him.'

Wiles chewed his lip. 'Then tomorrow it's straight back to the Smoke, is that what you're saying?'

'You've got it, Vern.'

The little porn film man took a deep breath. 'I just hope you know what you're doing,' he said.

Baxter beamed. 'What could possibly go wrong?' he said, raising a hand towards the bar to indicate they were ready to order their meal. 'You worry too much.'

Wiles made a face. Maybe he did, he mused, but something inside him told him that this time he had good reason.

****

Lynn sat down heavily on the edge of her bed, her open jewellery case beside her and a brandy in one trembling hand. An inspection of her bedroom had revealed that around £50 had been stolen from a top drawer of her dressing-table. A small amount of jewellery, including a distinctive gold necklace, diamond ring and matching earrings, had also been taken from her jewellery box, the empty red felt interior of the box now leering up at her in a mocking grin.

She took a deep breath, downing some of the brandy in a gulp. Walking in on the intruder had understandably shaken her and losing her best jewellery should have added to the trauma. Yet although she felt angry about the theft of her property, in a peculiar way she also felt relieved that it was missing. The fact that money and jewellery had been stolen suggested that the break-in had been motivated by simple gain rather than by something more sinister.

The point was what to do about it? She had already made up her mind not to inform the local police. In a low crime area like this such an incident, involving someone like her, would arouse a lot of interest if the details got out and that would very quickly bring the celebrity press racing down to Cornwall from London to scupper her anonymity. Furthermore, the culprit was unlikely to be caught, whatever happened, and if she informed her insurance company of the break-in, they were likely to insist on her contacting the police before they did anything, which took her back to square one. She did consider confiding in Alan Murray – more as a means of reassurance than anything else – but then dismissed the idea as a non-starter. In the first place, she didn't know him well enough yet and secondly, if she did tell him, he was also bound to put pressure on her to contact the police. As for Alan himself, in his condition he wasn't in any position to offer her physical support for the future should her burglar come back, so why involve him at all? No, maddening though it was, she had no option but to swallow her pride and her loss, forget what had happened – and get her locks changed, of course.

Draining her brandy glass, she set about clearing up the mess her intruder had left behind before concentrating on the special dinner she had to prepare for the evening.

And as she bustled around the bungalow, the same hooded figure, which two days before had watched her from the clifftops, crouched among the rocks that bordered the beach, once more studying her every move through a pair of binoculars while munching on a small red apple.

****

Vernon Wiles could not help fidgeting in the driving seat of the Mercedes as he stared through the fly-spattered windscreen into the dying day. It was as if the sea had been set on fire, creating a fierce orange glow tinged with liquid gold which seemed to be reaching further and further up into the heavens as the sun began its slow descent into oblivion. It would be a while yet before it was completely dark, but the little man took no comfort from that fact. With the departure of Freddie Baxter over two hours before, he had suddenly felt a growing sense of unease in the empty car park. His business partner had promised he would only be gone about an hour, so he was well overdue and that put him on edge. Whatever Freddie was up to, Wiles knew that he himself would be seen as a part of it all if things went wrong, and he didn't like that one little bit.

He'd never wanted to come to rural Cornwall in the first place. He hated the countryside – any countryside – with a vengeance. All those fields, hedges and woods did his head in and the coast had an even worse effect on him. Who in their right mind would want to live on the edge of a cliff, miles from anywhere? It didn't make any sense. He couldn't wait to get back to the mean dirty streets of the city he knew so well. In London, with all its noise and almost claustrophobic closeness, he felt safe and secure, but out here, in this empty wilderness, there was nothing solid to hold on to, nowhere to hide, and that infected him with a sense of isolation and agoraphobic vulnerability.

What made things even worse was the fact that he was only still in this god-forsaken place because he had once again allowed himself to be intimidated by Freddie Baxter, and he was still seething over the other's threat to withdraw his investment in his business if he didn't play ball. Seething not just over the threat itself, but the fact that Freddie had felt confident enough to make it. Baxter obviously felt secure in his belief that weak, spineless little Vernon was totally dependent on him and that made Wiles feel subservient, humiliated and very angry. Deep down, he had always hated his so-called partner and his constant bullying and intimidation, which he had had to endure for so many years, and he longed to break away from him and go his own way. He knew that finding another financial backer wouldn't be that difficult in his line of business. But Baxter made a formidable enemy and he was acutely conscious of the fact that, if he ever had the temerity to openly go against him, the fat man would, without the slightest compunction, do his level best to destroy him, just like he was planning to do with Lynn Giles if she continued to defy him.

Wiles was determined not to let that happen, but as he sat there in the gathering gloom, his hatred for Freddie Baxter eating away at him like a cancer, he knew he only had two options available to him. He could swallow what fragments of pride he had left and sit in the car and wait, as he had been told to do, or for the first time in his life he could make a stand and drive off and leave him. Unless, he thought vindictively, Freddie were to take the decision out of his hands altogether by falling off a cliff and breaking his flabby neck. But there again, that was just too much to hope for …

CHAPTER 8

The taxi had drawn up in front of The Old Customs House with a swirl of gravel and Murray and Archie were already waiting outside when it arrived.

From his concealed position in a patch of scrub just yards away, Freddie Baxter lowered the binoculars he had been using and watched with a sense of excitement as they left. Heavily overweight and in poor physical condition, Baxter had found the half hour spent crouched in the undergrowth a real endurance test, but driven by a vindictive determination to "fix" Lynn Giles, he had stayed the course and now had come the reward he had never expected. He had already satisfied himself from his uncomfortable stint of surveillance that there was no one else in the house and with Murray and the dratted dog now conveniently out of the way – no doubt for a substantial period if Lynn's new boyfriend was using a taxi – he was presented with the ideal opportunity to get up close and personal with the place. Maybe even take a look inside.

He waited some time before he made his move, then hauling himself up off his knees with much panting and wheezing, he lumbered across the short expanse of heath to the front gate, smirking when he saw the sign, "Private. Beware Land Mines". So, Mr Murray was a bit of a comic, was he, he mused? Be interesting to see what else the dickhead was.

He rang the front doorbell first, just to make sure there was no one inside – ready with a plausible "lost motorist" excuse if anyone opened up – but the bell jangled on emptiness and satisfied after a couple of minutes' wait, Baxter waddled down the side of the house and mounted the short flight of steps to the patio.

Absolute stillness. Even the sound of the sea seemed to have receded into the gathering dusk. He cupped his hands and peered through the wooden patio doors, noting a living room sparsely furnished with a fully upholstered three-seater settee and some rather shabby dark wood furniture. He studied the eaves of the house. No sign of wires or an alarm box. He grunted and gently tried one of the doors – feeling a thrill when it gave slightly. 'Careless boy,' he muttered and pulling it open, stepped inside, freezing a moment to prepare himself for any burglar alarm activation. Nothing happened and a quick glance around the room with the aid of his torch revealed a total absence of anything resembling an infra-red sensor. He couldn't believe his luck. The place was wide open. Now all he needed was a 20-minute nose around to see if he could turn up anything of interest on Mr Alan Murray. As it was, he found it in 15 minutes.

****

Lynn was tired and edgy. She desperately wanted her special evening to be a success and although all the necessary preparations had been made, she couldn't help checking and re-checking to make sure she hadn't forgotten anything. With the strain getting to her, she finally decided to take some time out to relax with a drink, but it wasn't to be. Clutching a glass of Chardonnay in one hand, she had only just deposited herself on the settee and taken a sip when the telephone rang, forcing her to set the glass down on the coffee table while she got up to answer the call instead.

'Hi, sweetness,' Freddie Baxter's sneering voice greeted her.

'Piss off, Freddie,' she grated. 'And the answer is still no.'

There was a soft chuckle. 'Now, that's no way to speak to an old friend,' he said. 'Quite hurtful actually.'

She tutted impatiently. 'What do you want, Freddie? I'm busy.'

There was a heavy sigh. 'Well, you know, I was just sitting on this clifftop seat in the setting sun, looking down into your little cove, and I got to thinking that the only thing missing on this balmy evening is the company of a pretty girl and a nice bottle of wine.'

She snorted. 'Then call up one of your slimy boyfriends.'

Baxter ignored the remark. 'So you wouldn't care to join me then? We could sit and watch the sun go down together.'

She released her breath in a short, irritable sigh. 'Do me a favour, Freddie, just sod-off back to London, will you?'

Another chuckle. 'Oh. I'm in no hurry to do that, luvvie. Actually, Vern and I have already booked rooms at The Blue Ketch Inn. Might stay a few days.'

'Why don't you just jump off the cliff instead. Do everyone a favour?'

'Oh, your little teeth are so sharp today, aren't they, sweetness? And just as I was about to give you the SP on poor old Blind Pugh too.'

Baxter's analogical reference to the fictitious character in Robert Louis Stephenson's *Treasure Island* seemed to amuse him and his throaty chuckle almost ended in a choking fit.

Lynn frowned, her senses sharpening at the heavily loaded remark. 'And who's Blind Pugh when he's at home?' she queried, trying to sound as casual as possible.

Baxter laughed again. 'Oh come on, my dear. No need to be coy. And I have to admit Alan Murray is rather dishy, in spite of his disability. I quite fancy him myself, in fact.'

She swallowed hard. 'I don't know what you're talking about.'

'Don't you, luvvie? Well now, that does surprise me, seeing as he brought you such a nice bouquet. He's got a lovely home too. Just had a recce.'

Lynn felt a mixture of anger and indignation surface in a rush. 'You broke into Alan's house?'

There was a feigned gasp. 'Broke in? *Qui, moi*? As if I would do a thing like that. But if good old Alan chooses not to lock his patio doors, well, who am I to pass up such an opportunity.'

'I don't believe you.'

'Your prerogative, sweetness, but it was a very illuminating visit, I can assure you. Discovered some rather interesting things.'

Lynn was gripping the telephone receiver so tightly that she heard the plastic make a sharp cracking noise. 'Like what, for instance? Alan is a nice, thoroughly decent man. A respected thriller-writer too.'

'You sure about the writing bit, sweetness? Never heard of him myself, nor has anyone in the village apparently, and you won't find any of his thrillers on the internet or in the library, of that I'm certain. I mean, what do you really know about him? And more importantly, exactly what does he know about you? See, I'm in a bit of a dilemma. Do I tell you what I've learned about nice, thoroughly decent Alan, or do I tell him what I know about not-so-nice you? For instance, is he aware of your rather unsavoury past or that he has actually latched on to damaged goods?'

Lynn's teeth were clenched tightly as she snarled back at him. 'You're sick, you know that, don't you? A complete waste of a skin – it could have been given to someone else.'

'Of course,' Baxter continued, unabashed, 'my dilemma could be overcome quite easily by a simple "yes" to a certain contract. Then all the little secrets you and I share could remain as … er … well, secrets?'

'You can rot in hell,' Lynn threw back at him.

The menace was back in his tone now, low and deadly. 'Maybe I will, sweetness, but not before I wreck what future you have left in this world.'

'Go screw yourself!' she snarled, and before he could say anything else she had slammed the phone down on him.

****

Freddie Baxter had certainly struck gold and he'd hardly been able to contain himself after carefully closing the patio door of The Old Customs House behind him and making his way back to the front gate. Okay, so the whole thing had taken a lot longer than he'd intended and poor old Vernon would be worried sick by now, but one find had led to another and he hadn't been about to quit while he was ahead. Coupled with which, he didn't give a jot about Vernon's feelings anyway.

Stopping by the wrought-iron seat on his way back to the car and giving the Giles bitch a ring had been a spur of the moment thing, motivated by malicious glee. But while the call had only been short, it had been oh so rewarding. As a result, he was on a real high as he made his way through the gorse and scrub, which had previously sheltered him, following the narrow path towards the derelict engine-house. Once on the heath which lay beyond the last few yards of scrub, he had intended heading for the car park where he'd left Vernon and the BMW, but then suddenly he saw the figure in a hooded coat approaching him, head down, along the footpath. He scowled angrily. The last thing he wanted was to be seen coming away from Murray's house. Fortunately it didn't look as though the person had seen him, so at least he had time to hide. After a second's hesitation, he stepped off the track into the undergrowth choking the empty doorway of the engine-house. Then fearing he could still be seen, he pushed right through a tangle of ivy into the evil-smelling gloom and froze as he waited for the approaching walker to pass by.

But fat Freddie was in for a big surprise. As he stared through the doorway with mounting alarm, the figure turned sharply towards him and headed straight for his hiding-place.

****

Alan Murray was very late. Lynn, dressed in a long blue dress and high heels, frowned at the clock on the bookshelf and sighed heavily. She was sure she'd told him 8pm. Yet it was now after 9pm and he still hadn't turned up. The annoying thing was, she'd geared the meal to 8.30pm, to give them time for a pre-dinner drink and a chat. Now, not only would that be out of the question, but the lettuce leaves on the artistically arranged crab salad were already beginning to look sad and limp and from the smell wafting out of the kitchen, she knew that it wouldn't be long before the dauphinoise potatoes and mangetout she had prepared to accompany her fillet steaks were ready.

Damn! Damn! Damn! Where was the man? For the umpteenth time she crossed to the window to peer out into the evening gloom, but there was still no sign of anyone in the moonlit lane at the front of The Beach House and she thought that with his disability Alan would hardly come the back way, via the headland and the beach.

But she was wrong. The sudden tapping on the French doors sent her back into the living room in a rush. The tall figure seemed to be leaning against the wall to one side of the doors and it was only when she opened up that she realised something was very wrong. Alan Murray was muddy and dishevelled and he staggered into the room like a drunken man, grabbing at her arm to steady himself as she led him to the settee. As he fell into the seat, rather than lowering himself into it, she saw that there was blood on his forehead, and although his dark glasses seemed intact, his face was dirty and the front of his jacket was torn.

'Good grief!' she exclaimed. 'Whatever's happened?' She threw another swift glance through the open doorway. 'And where's Archie?'

He directed a tired smile over her shoulder at the wall. 'Poor old Arch,' he said. 'Bit of a coward, I'm afraid.'

'What do you mean?'

He sighed. 'Someone ran into me up on the headland. Probably a jogger who didn't see me in time. Anyway, whoever it was, they knocked me flat. Must have frightened Archie to death, though. He took off like a rocket.'

'And they didn't stop?'

He shrugged. 'Why would they? I couldn't see who they were. Anyway, I managed to make it here on my own in the end, using the sound and smell of the sea as a guide, but I lost my stick in the gully down to your beach and tripped over a couple of times on the pebbles, hence the state of me. Good job I know this area so well, otherwise I'd still be lying up there on the heath.'

'Alan, for goodness sake, why did you come across the headland in the first place,' she breathed. 'You could have gone over the cliff edge. As it is, you look absolutely dreadful. I'll call a doctor.' She hesitated. 'And the police, of course.'

He fumbled for her hand and grabbed her wrist with surprising firmness. 'You'll do no such thing,' he said. 'I'm fine, really I am, just a bit shaken, that's all. As for the police, it isn't a matter for them.' He smiled again. 'I expect the jacket's ruined, though – just like your bloody dinner – and I dropped the bottle of bubbly I went all the way into Mullion to get for us too.'

She snorted. 'Forget it. You're okay, that's all that matters. Look, do you want to clean up in the bathroom? Use the shower, if you want. I'll pour you a drink.'

He nodded. 'Very kind. Whisky would be lovely. Can you … er …?'

She helped him up and guided him out into the hallway, then into the bathroom, hovering uncertainly in the doorway as he began to unbutton his shirt. 'Do you want me … er … I
mean …?'

He grinned. 'No, I'll be fine, honestly. I'm used to finding my way around unfamiliar places.'

She reddened. 'I'll get … I'll pour you that drink.'

He gently pushed the door closed. 'Look forward to it.'

She heard the shower going as she fumbled for the whisky glasses and took a deep breath to steady her racing heart. 'Get a grip, girl,' she muttered to herself, but it took a double brandy to calm her down. Her carnal feelings for Alan were almost on the pain level and she only hoped he hadn't noticed. Seeing him injured and vulnerable only stimulated her desires even more and she retreated to the kitchen and the ruined dinner to give herself something else to think about.

She turned the oven off and put her steaks under the grill before returning to the living room 15 minutes later to find him barefoot, wearing just his trousers – plus, rather incongruously, the ubiquitous sunglasses – and bending down in the middle of the floor fondling

Archie's ears. The black Labrador must have entered the room through one of the half-open French doors and was crouching there, panting heavily.

Murray seemed to sense her approach and turned slightly. 'Heard him whining as I was dressing,' he explained. 'Nice to have the old chap back and he seems fine, thank goodness.'

Lynn bent down beside the dog and Archie licked her hand. He was spattered with mud, but showed no signs of injury. 'He must have been telepathic to know you would be here,' she said.

Murray grunted. 'Probably remembered he'd been here before or just followed my scent.'

She nodded. 'Whatever. Now I suggest you get your shirt on and we'll eat.'

Murray grinned and straightened up. 'Another whisky first, eh?' he said boldly.

'I'll drink to that,' Lynn replied, appraising him with an answering smile. 'And on second thoughts, don't bother about the shirt.'

CHAPTER 9

Tessa Jarvis paused on the clifftop path and leaned on her walking stick to watch a pair of red-billed choughs flying low over the scrubland in front of her. Seven o'clock and lunch at the next B&B still to look forward to. What could be better than lungful's of clean Cornish air on a beautiful autumn morning like this?

Tessa had been coming to Cornwall since she was knee-high to a pisky, and throughout her childhood her love of the sea and the beach had earned her the name "Shrimp" in the family. Not that that was the only reason for the nickname. Even now, she was less than 5ft in height. 'Nice things come in small parcels' her late husband always used to say, and standing there in the early morning sun, listening to the murmur of the sea far below, she smiled sadly as she thought of him and of the ten years that had passed since his death. Now 68, her thin frame slightly stooped and her once flaming red hair tied in a bun under her woolly hat, she thought of her youth. Those halcyon days rock-pooling on Cornwall's wonderful beaches and the damp smell of the caravans and cottages she had stayed in with her late mother and father at Kynance Cove, Kennack Sands and Coverack.

'Dreaming again?' her portly friend snapped as she caught up with her, panting and wheezing.

Tessa laughed. 'You should pack in the smoking, Marjorie,' she advised. 'Then you wouldn't find these walks so hard.'

Marjorie Lantern grunted. 'Thanks for the advice,' she retorted, sweeping strands of grey hair back from her chubby face, 'but at 67, I'm not about to give up the habit of a lifetime.'

Tessa shrugged. 'Your life, Marj,' she acknowledged drily and watched with a grim smile as the other stomped across the heath to a wrought-iron seat parked a couple of yards from the edge of the cliff, and slipping out of the straps of her haversack, dropped on to the seat with an explosive gasp.

Tessa joined her, shaking off the straps of her own haversack as she did so. 'Time for some breakfast, I think,' she commented, unzipping the haversack and thrusting a hand inside.

'Good of you to buy the sarnies,' Marjorie acknowledged, taking the greaseproof package from her and tearing open the wrapping. 'Ah, salmon. What a star you are.'

Tessa dumped the heavy haversack on the seat and wandered to the cliff edge, peering over the drop to the rocks beneath. 'Lovely spot,' she said. 'But I wouldn't like to—' and she broke off with a sharp intake of breath.

Marjorie carried on devouring her sandwich, not really listening. 'You don't want to go too close, Tess,' she warned. 'You could slip.'

Tessa turned slowly, her face suddenly ashen. 'Marjorie,' she said slowly, 'would you put down your sandwich and come here a minute?'

'What?' Her friend gaped at her. 'Whatever's the matter?'

'Just do it, will you?'

The sharpness of her tone had more effect than the command itself and Marjorie put down her sandwich and walked over to where Tessa was standing.

'Do you have your mobile with you?' Tessa asked, her voice now shaking as she spoke. 'Look … down there.'

Peering over the edge with one hand gripping her friend's arm, Marjorie's eyes bulged. There was a shape lying on the pile of broken rock at the foot of the cliff, just out of reach of the creamy surf. It looked like a discarded tailor's mannequin, dressed in very bright flamboyant clothing, and its limbs were twisted from the fall into a kind of grotesque artistry.

'I think we'd better call for an ambulance,' Tessa gasped. 'I think it's a man.'

She was right about that too, but quite wrong about the ambulance. Freddie Baxter's smashed, bloodied body was well beyond any form of medical treatment.

****

Vernon Wiles had been sick three times, although whether just from the sight of fat Freddie's grisly remains or something more, it was difficult to say.

The police had been searching the rocks for two hours, lowered down the sheer cliff-face on ropes with a local rescue team as it was impossible to get a boat close to the scene. They had brought Baxter up in a canvas sling in the end as roughening seas had raised the risk of the corpse being swept away before the forensic pathologist, who was an hour-and-a-half from them at least, could get there. A local doctor had certified death, though no one would have needed medical qualifications to arrive at that diagnosis. The entrepreneur's body was smashed to pieces, with bones even projecting through the clothing, and the back of the skull had caved in completely.

'Looks like a nasty accident to me,' the uniformed police sergeant explained in a thick Cornish accent to his plainclothes colleague. 'Or maybe a suicide. 'Tain't the first time someone's fallen or thrown themselves off these cliffs and it certainly won't be the last.'

The young detective constable nodded, bowing to the experience of his much older colleague. 'The two biddies who found him got quite a shock,' he said. 'I'll have another chat with them later just to finalise things, but I've sent them on to their B&B in the meantime.' He frowned as his gaze focused on Vernon Wiles perched on the nearby police car's open hatch. 'Who's the creep?'

The skipper emitted a hard laugh. 'Dunno. Says he's a film producer and a close friend of the stiff and was out here with him looking at locations. When this Baxter feller didn't come back to the car after a couple of hours, he got windy and reported it to the local nick. Funny little feller. Looks like a perv to me. But apparently the stiff hasn't any relatives, so at least he was able to carry out the necessary ID on him.'

The DC nodded. 'We'll do a check on him anyway.' He shrugged. 'But unless the pathologist comes up with anything later, I reckon this job's a dead end.'

And they both laughed at his cruel pun.

Vernon Wiles didn't hear the remark, but even if he had, he wouldn't have thought it was funny anyway. After Freddie's violent death he wasn't feeling particularly jocular. He had too much on his mind for that.

****

Detective Chief Inspector Mick Benchley had taken the call at home while he was finishing a late breakfast. It was his own DI, Moira Angel.

'Don't choke on your cornflakes, Guv,' she said, 'but I've just popped into the office and I thought I should ring you.'

Her boss glanced at his watch and grunted. 'Thought you were off today? Shit the bed or something?' he retorted, unimpressed by her apparent dedication.

A soft chuckle. 'Not exactly. Left my personal mobile behind yesterday, so popped in for it. Thing is, some results have apparently come in for you on the stiff in Islington. Didn't know whether you would be in this morning as it's Sunday, so I thought I would ring you at home.'

Benchley put down his spoon with a scowl. 'Cheeky cow,' he threw back.

Another chuckle from the other end, 'I'll leave the reports for you on your desk before I go.'

He shook his head unnecessarily. 'No, let me have the details now?'

There was a slight pause and Benchley heard the rustle of papers at the other end of the phone. 'Okay,' Angel continued slowly, obviously reading, 'Weapon. Ballistics believe it was a .32 automatic. Possibly a Beretta. Small, but deadly evidently. Hollow nose round. PM result – single shot right between the eyes. Elevation suggests the killer was standing up when he fired – and at close range.'

'And that's it?'

'Not quite. Re the part thumbprint found at the scene of the bombing, confirmation that there's a 75 percent likelihood of a match with our deceased.'

'How did Forensics manage that? There wasn't that much flesh left on him.'

A short humourless laugh. 'Apparently the big toe on one of his feet wasn't quite as ripe as the rest of him. Good airtight boots, it seems.'

Benchley made a grimace. 'So he *was* our bomber?'

'Looks like it.'

'What about his ID?'

'Ah, now there's a thing. Nothing on our DNA database, but as you know, we also circulated his DNA profile and the pic from one of his passports to Europol and guess what?'

Benchley took a deep breath. 'What do you think this is – a bloody quiz?'

Another soft laugh. 'If it was, Guv, we'd be up for the million dollar prize. It seems that our friends from across the water got all twitchy when they received the info from our liaison chap and they came back with a pretty rapid response. Turns out that our man is one Goran Petrović, a Serb wanted in connection with the Srebrenica massacre back in 1995 and now believed to be footloose and fancy-free, fulfilling bombing contracts for whoever will pay the asking price. He was apparently offering his services on the Dark Web and he is suspected of being behind several botched hits in Europe and the Middle East. Not very good at his job, it seems. Which figures after the bomb blast at the club and what SO15 said about his kit.'

Benchley swore under his breath. 'So how come we knew nothing about this character before?'

'He must have somehow managed to slip under our radar.'

'Either that or our Euro colleagues have been a lot more coy than usual. 'Problem is, who stiffed him and why?'

'A dissatisfied customer maybe?' Angel suggested tongue in cheek.

'Or if he didn't actually plant the device, the perp who paid him to make it, as we've said before. Going by what the pathologist said at the scene in Islington, he was stiffed round about the same time as the blast – around three months ago – so very likely just before or just after the device went off.'

'Which adds weight to our original assumption that he was killed simply to shut him up because he knew too much.'

Benchley gave a disparaging snort. 'Yeah and that means all we have to do now is to find the shooter, eh?' he said in a tone laced with sarcasm, and he stabbed at the soggy mass in his dish with his spoon. 'Only a few million suspects to consider, if we just stick to London.'

She laughed. 'I should finish your cornflakes before you start, then, Guv,' she said. 'Could be a bit of a labour-intensive process.'

****

Lynn was awakened by loud knocking on her front door. Glancing at the bedside clock, she saw it was after 11pm. She winced as she sat up, the room swaying in front of her and spear-points of pain eroding the inside of her skull. The knocking resumed, even louder this time. Throwing a bleary-eyed glance at Murray sleeping beside her, she pulled on her robe and headed in the direction of the sound, holding her head on as she went.

It had been a heavy night and she had the mother of a hangover. The meal had been a big disappointment. Much of it had been ruined by the time they'd sat down. But Archie had enjoyed the leftovers and in the end she couldn't have cared less anyway, as her appetite had been satisfied in a much more spectacular fashion.

The wine had released in her what inhibitions she had so far managed to keep in check, and Alan had succumbed to her aggressive advances with little protest. Both of them were completely naked even before she'd led him away from Archie's crooked grin, kicking the bedroom door shut in the Labrador's face as the animal made to join them. What had followed was a lustful, no-holds barred intimacy, which lasted for several hours and left them both exhausted at the end of it.

In spite of the pain in her head, her lurid recollections of the night's fun and games brought a smile to her lips as she crossed the hallway, but the smile quickly died when she opened the front door and was confronted by the uniformed police officer on her doorstep.

The policeman scratched his nose and grinned when she appeared and to her embarrassment she suddenly realised her robe had come undone, exposing almost as much as she had displayed during her years as a model.

'Sorry to disturb you, ma'am,' he said, glancing away from her as she quickly fastened the ties. 'But there seems to have been a nasty accident up on the headland.'

She squinted at him out of the corner of one eye as waves of nausea hit her with a vengeance. 'An accident?'

He nodded. 'Feller fell off the cliff near the old engine-house. Dead, I'm afraid. We're doing house-to-house inquiries in the immediate area to see if anyone saw anything.'

She shook her head, trying to clear away the fug. 'No, we ... I ... was in all night.'

His grin returned. 'Heavy one was it?' he queried, chancing his arm.

She made a face. 'A little, yes. Do we know who the man was?'

He consulted the notebook in his hand. 'Feller named Baxter. Been identified by a friend who was with him.'

Lynn gaped at him and before she could stop herself, she blurted, '*Freddie* Baxter?'

The policeman tensed. 'You knew him?'

Lynn's mind was racing. She was angry with herself for coming out with Freddie's name like that, but there again, there was no point in trying to deny she knew him. After all, the police would find that out eventually anyway. Coupled with which, Vernon Wiles might already have told them.

'I used to work for him in London,' she said. 'He – he came down here to offer me a new contract with his modelling agency.'

The policeman frowned and she could feel his eyes on her face. No doubt studying the scar across her forehead and down her right cheek where the glass fragments from the bomb had embedded themselves. 'It … it was to do some body-parts modelling,' she added quickly.

'Body parts?' he echoed.

She nodded. 'Hands, feet, eyes, that sort of thing.' She forced a smile. 'We don't only model swimsuits, or do centrefold spreads,' she said, conscious of the fact that she sounded almost defensive.

He cleared his throat and relaxed. 'Sorry, ma'am, I didn't mean—'

Her smile was bitter now. 'Forget it, officer. I am aware of the scars – quite used to them by now actually.'

There was an awkward silence and he avoided her gaze, finding it necessary to study his notebook again. She felt almost sorry for him.

'And when did you last see this Freddie Baxter?' he asked suddenly.

She thought a second, trusting in Vernon Wiles' discretion to keep his mouth shut about the real reason for their visit. 'Yesterday morning. He came here to see me and went back to finalise the contract details.'

'Went back where?'

'I haven't the faintest idea.'

'And you haven't spoken to him since.

Lynn thought of the telephone call and took a chance. 'No,' she lied.

The policeman looked a little perplexed. 'See, ma'am,' he said, 'Mr Wiles – his friend – says they were here looking at film locations. That's why they were both up on the headland when the accident happened.'

Inwardly, Lynn tensed and she felt a spurt of acid in her stomach. 'That was probably part of it,' she agreed, compounding her lie. 'You know, girl on a beach, showing off ankle jewellery or toe-nail polish.'

He seemed far from convinced and she cut in before he could come up with any other difficult questions. 'Look, officer, as you've already observed, I've had a heavy night and unless you have anything else to ask me, I would very much like to get back to bed.'

He straightened up, nodding apologetically. 'Yes, ma'am, of course. If I could just confirm your name for our records.'

The acid was back, but she had no choice but to level with him. 'My professional name is Lynn Giles,' she said wearily, 'but locally I go by the name Mary Tresco. I would like it kept that way too, if you don't mind – publicity reasons.'

Another firm nod. 'No problem, Miss Gi—, Miss Tresco. Thanks for your help.'

She breathed a sigh of relief as he walked back to his car in the lane. But closing the door, she was faced with another problem. Alan Murray was standing in the hallway, wearing just his dark glasses and a tight grimace, and it was obvious he had heard enough to make things difficult.

'Lynn Giles?' he echoed slowly. 'So why would you call yourself Mary Tresco, eh? I think you owe me an explanation.'

****

Vernon Wiles was scared. Not just nervous in the way he had been when parked up on the headland, waiting for fat Freddie, but scared almost to the point of being terrified.

To be fair, the little porn film producer was someone whose daily fears bordered on the paranoid anyway. He was scared of the dark, lonely places, deep water, heights, spiders – even visiting the dentist or the doctor. In particular, he was frightened of the well-heeled punters who patronised his unsavoury business and their likely reaction should he fail to meet their perverse expectations or was less than discreet about their identities. And he was frightened of being targeted by the Met Vice Squad, who were always looking for an excuse to drag people like him before the courts, whether it was to do with the explicit nature of the films produced or the ages of some of the so called actors and actresses starring in them.

In short, Vernon Wiles was scared of his own shadow and he took the pills to prove it, but he reckoned he had reason to be really scared now.

Although at the moment the local police seemed to be treating Freddie Baxter's death as an accident, he was pretty sure that that would change once a link was established between the agency boss and the bomb blast at The Philanderer's Night Club in London. They were bound to suspect foul play then, maybe launch a full-blown murder inquiry, with all the in-depth probing such an inquiry would entail. As Freddie's friend and the last person to see him alive, he would be at the centre of all the resultant heat and it wouldn't take long for them to discover what he did for a living. Once that particular cat was out of the bag, he would really be in the cart. In a place like this gossip would spread with the speed of an Australian bush fire and because of his shady background he would soon find himself vilified and treated as some sort of pariah by all and sundry. Perhaps even attract the attention of the dreaded Met Vice Squad and be subjected to an investigation into illegal snuff movies, which he had always denied knowing anything about.

And there was something else too, something he hadn't told anyone about yet – the hooded man he had seen on the clifftop. Who was he and what had he been doing there? Had the man seen him walking back to the car after he had gone in search of Freddie? If he had, was he likely to come forward to tell the police, raising even more difficult questions? Questions like: where had Freddie's so-called business associate been before returning to the car on his own, and why hadn't he admitted to going to look for his partner when they had questioned him before? Alternatively, had the hoodie been up to something in that lonely spot, which precluded him from coming forward, and if that was the case, did that mean Vernon Wiles was at risk as a potential witness?

Wiles shivered. He didn't like the direction in which his thoughts were heading.

Sitting on the edge of the bed in his room at the local inn, he shivered uncontrollably, despite the heat of the day, jumping at every sound in the corridor outside and periodically going to the window to study the street below. Looking for he knew not what. He desperately wanted to get back to London, but the police had asked him to stay on for a while, if only until after Freddie's post mortem – just in case they needed to speak to him again, they'd said. Of course, they had no power to force him to stay. He had done nothing wrong as far as they were concerned. But he'd agreed anyway. It would have looked mighty suspicious if he'd refused and something dodgy had then been discovered at the PM after he had bolted back to the Smoke. He just prayed he would be gone before they found out about The Philanderer's Club bombing and he vowed to keep a low profile until he was able to make a safe departure. Maybe even skip meals or invent some excuse so that they could be brought up to his room. Yes, shock, that was it. He'd had a terrible loss, hadn't he – his good friend, after all? It was reasonable for him to want to be left alone to grieve. And he treated the mirror to a shaky smile. 'Poor old Freddie,' he muttered, then gave a cracked laugh. 'Couldn't have happened to a nicer arsehole.'

CHAPTER 10

Alan Murray's face was grim, his sunglasses adding to the severity of his expression, and now fully dressed, he sat sipping his cup of coffee on the settee for several minutes without speaking. A shower had not improved his mood. And also fully dressed, this time in a skirt and blouse, Lynn gnawed at her lip in the armchair opposite, waiting for him to break his silence.

It had not been easy telling him the truth about herself. Who she really was. The bomb at the fashion show. What it had done to her. In mentioning Freddie Baxter, though, she had omitted any reference to the real nature of the contract he had offered her or her pre-model life as a pole-dancer, and she sensed a burning resentment in Murray's demeanour over her failure to level with him before. What was he thinking, she wondered? What sort of scars had she got? Whereabouts were they? Was her face badly disfigured? Had she come on to him because she couldn't attract a sighted man? Even in death, Freddie Baxter had won, wrecking another part of her life as effectively as he'd threatened to do when he was alive.

'Alan, I'm so sorry,' she finally blurted, unable to stand the silence any longer, 'I didn't mean to upset you.'

He gave a thin smile and shook his head. 'It isn't about being upset,' he said quietly. 'It's just that you seem to have thought so little of my integrity that you couldn't bring yourself to trust me.'

She stared at the floor, embarrassed and ashamed. 'I … I thought,' she stammered, 'I thought if … if you knew I had been scarred by a bomb, you would lose interest in me. I … I didn't know what to do.'

'People who trust each other don't keep secrets like that,' he said simply.

She met his sightless gaze, angered by the self-righteous censure in his tone. 'We all have our secrets, Alan,' she snapped back, thinking of what Freddie Baxter had intimated and also now beginning to feel more than a little uneasy about the way he himself had turned up in such a dishevelled state the previous evening. Had Archie really run off or was there more to it all than that, she wondered, feeling a sudden chill?

'I bet you're not so lily white either,' she said aloud, without thinking.

He started, his tone hardening. 'Oh? What makes you say that?'

She almost bit her tongue. To have repeated what Freddie Baxter had said about him would have meant opening up a whole can of worms, revealing not only that Baxter had broken into his house, but that she had actually had a phone call from him just before he'd met his death, even though she'd already told the police she had not spoken to her odious former manager since the morning before. 'Big mouth,' a voice sneered inside her head.

'Just one or two secret mutterings I picked up,' she replied lamely. 'Gossip is what keeps places like this going, and you are an Emmet after all, same as me.'

He ignored her attempt to make light of things. 'Gossip about what?'

'Oh, nothing specific, only that one or two of the more inquisitive souls don't reckon you are all you pretend to be,' and she forced what became a hollow laugh, adding, 'Nudge, nudge.'

He considered her reply for a moment and although it was obvious that he was not entirely satisfied with her explanation, he abruptly relaxed and treated her to a rueful smile. 'Well, maybe I can hazard a guess as to what they could have been implying and since this now seems to be the moment for baring souls, let me add my own confession to yours.'

'Confession?'

He shrugged. ''Fraid so. In short, as I said before, I'm a bit of a fraud – and not only with regard to cooking either.'

Lynn felt her heartbeat quicken, wondering what was coming next, but she said nothing and waited for him to continue.

'Fact is, I am not the professional novelist I've claimed to be and maybe someone in the village has checked and found that out.'

She thought better than to enlighten him on the internet inquiries she had made at Helston Library and said instead, 'So, if not a professional novelist, what are you then?'

'Well may you ask. A dismal failure would probably be a good description. You see, when I told you I'd had three books published, that was a total fib. I am not even close to being mid-list – more likely lurking at the bottom of the slush pile. I'm another *Walter Mitty*, you see, a total wuzzit.'

She stared at him in astonishment. 'And that's your confession?'

'Well, it's a pretty big thing for someone like me to admit.'

She gave a short laugh, more relieved than she cared to admit to herself that Freddie's insinuations must have been about nothing more than this. 'Not to me, it isn't. I thought you might be a paedophile or a wife-beater.'

He also laughed. 'Heaven forbid. Nothing so exotic.'

Then, with a weary sigh, he climbed to his feet, Archie jumping up expectantly beside him. 'Anyway, I must be off. Things to do and all that.'

She stood up too, smoothing her skirt in a nervous gesture. 'Will I be seeing you again?' she queried, expecting the worst.

He smiled again, this time with something that seemed more akin to genuine humour, although it was difficult to tell what was going on behind those dark glasses. 'After the hospitality I received last night, how could I keep away?' he replied, adding mischievously, 'The meal wasn't that bad either.'

And he was still laughing as Archie led him up the lane towards the main road, seemingly unaware of the worried gaze she directed after him as she thought again about his alleged encounter with the jogger the very night Freddie Baxter had died, and finding herself wondering whether there could be any connection.

****

Lynn Giles sat for a long time in her armchair after Alan Murray had left, the gin and tonic she had poured herself still on the arm of the chair and hardly touched. Alan was something of an enigma and she was still unsure as to whether he had told her everything about himself. Maybe there were other skeletons in his cupboard that he had decided to keep quiet about and maybe, just maybe, Freddie Baxter had unearthed them during his visit to The Old Customs House.

She picked up her gin and tonic and took a thoughtful sip before returning it to the arm of the chair. She was probably being stupid, but she had to be sure Alan was not hiding something even more important from her. After all, she had been open with him – to a point anyway. But as burglary was not one of her skills, she baulked at the idea of doing a

Freddie on his home. No, there was an easier way. The thought of making further contact with Vernon Wiles didn't exactly fill her with relish, but there was a possibility that Freddie had told the little turd something before he'd taken his dive off the cliff, so it was worth a try.

She didn't bother with her car, but decided to walk the couple of miles to the village, anxious to clear her aching head in the Cornish sunshine, and she was relieved to see Baxter's BMW parked outside The Blue Ketch Inn when she arrived. At least that meant Wiles was still there and not on route back to the Smoke.

The bar was almost empty when she pushed through the door and the snake-eyed barman behind the counter gave her the usual once-over as she approached.

'Vernon Wiles,' she said. 'I gather he's staying here.'

The barman nodded, pushed himself off the barstool where he had been reading the local newspaper and picked up a telephone. 'Not answering,' he said, setting the receiver down again. 'You might as well go up. Room is called Coverack, after one of the Cornish coves.'

She knocked several times on Wiles' door without any response and it wasn't until she actually called out to him that he opened up, peering at her myopically around the door as if to satisfy himself it was really her before throwing it wide.

'And what do *you* want?' he queried as she followed him inside.

'Now that's not a very nice welcome, Vernon,' she replied. 'And I've come all this way, just to see you.'

'You know about Freddie?' he said quickly.

'Who doesn't?' she retorted, pulling up a chair and dropping into it. 'You didn't push him off the cliff by any chance, did you? He certainly wasn't a candidate for suicide. Too much of a coward.'

He looked horrified. ''Course I didn't,' he exclaimed. 'He ... he slipped and fell. Police said so.'

'They were there at the time then, were they?'

He shook his head irritably and propped himself on the corner of the bed.

'Look, why are you here?' he said. 'It's too late if you've decided to accept the contract. That's all out the window, now Freddie's dead.'

She emitted a short laugh. 'Oh, I haven't come about your porno film, Vernon, you can be rest assured on that point, and I hope that now Freddie's snuffed it, we can forget he ever broached the subject, eh?'

'Not my idea anyway,' he said sullenly, 'so I'm not likely to tell the police about it, if that's what's worrying you.'

'Oh, it's all right telling them he had come down here to offer me a contract,' she replied. 'I told them he wanted me to do body-part modelling – though not the sort of body parts your mucky little business is into, of course. That rather surprised them, because you had evidently said you were both here looking at film locations. Still, hopefully, we can tie the two things together if their curiosity starts getting the better of them. You know the sort of thing – girl on a rock in her bare feet showing off an ankle chain.' She gave a bitter smile. 'No scars on my feet.'

He nodded. 'Okay by me. I don't want any heat from Old Bill, and that's a fact.'

She studied him intently for a moment. 'Noble sentiments, Vernon, noble sentiments indeed. But tell me, what was it you and Freddie were really doing on the headland when he had his accident?'

Wiles squirmed. 'Looking at locations – as I told the Old Bill,' he said.

She smiled sweetly. 'Balls, Vernon. You see, Freddie rang me after he had broken into Alan Murray's house and told me what he had done.'

Wiles gaped at her. 'He broke in?' he gasped. 'I didn't know that. He said he was just going to watch the place.'

Lynn sighed. 'Oh come on, Vernon, don't treat me like an idiot. Just tell me what Freddie found out about Alan, will you? I need to know.'

Wiles shook his head several times. 'Honest, he didn't tell me anything. I didn't even know he had broken in. I just waited in the car when he went off. It's the truth. I never saw him again after that.'

Lynn frowned, not convinced. 'So you saw and heard nothing?'

Wiles licked dry lips, glancing at the window. 'Keep your voice down, will you?' he said. 'Someone might hear us talking.'

Her frown deepened as she noted the shadow of something in his restless brown eyes. Guilt or fear, she wondered? 'Why would that be a problem, Vernon? You say you don't know anything?' She shot forward in her chair. 'You do know something don't you, you little shit? What is it?'

He lurched to his feet, still shaking his head furiously. 'No, no, I don't,' he protested, the tone of his voice rising a couple of octaves. 'I … I just sat in the car. No one said anything to me. Didn't see a soul.'

'Which means you saw someone,' she snapped back. 'Who did you see, Vernon? Where did you see them?'

More head shaking. 'You have to go,' he said. 'I had nothing to do with it.'

'Nothing to do with what?' she echoed. 'Are you saying Freddie's death was not an accident?'

He seemed to be having difficulty swallowing. 'No, no. I know nothing about it,' he whispered. 'Please, just go.'

She shook her head firmly and sat back in her chair. 'Not until you tell me what you saw.'

He was really trembling now, like someone in the grip of flu spasms. 'I didn't see a thing, honestly – just someone in a hooded coat, going into the old engine-house.'

She felt her mouth start to dry up as her mind flashed back to her own encounter with the hooded man on the headland. 'Hooded coat, you say?' she breathed. 'Did you see his face?'

He shook his head several times, as if trying to shake an image loose. 'It … it was just a hooded figure.'

'You sure about this? Did you tell the police about it?'

His eyes widened. 'No, not the police. I wouldn't tell them anything. I just want to keep out of it.'

'Out of what?' she persisted. 'You think Freddie was murdered, don't you?'

'No,' he gasped, still darting glances at the window. 'No, I don't. Look, I'm going back to the Smoke first chance I get tomorrow. I've got nothing to say to anyone.'

Her eyes narrowed. He was either putting on a very competent show or he was actually very frightened and playing to the gallery in case someone was listening in to their conversation. Whichever it was, she sensed she would not be able to get anything further out of him. Climbing slowly to her feet, she gave him a contemptuous look and turned for the door. 'Freddie would be really proud of you, wouldn't he?' she snapped sarcastically and threw open the door. 'Don't forget to lock up after I've left, will you?'

And she smiled grimly as she heard the bolt shoot home the moment she stepped back out into the corridor.

'Everything okay?' the barman queried when she passed through on her way to the street.

'Couldn't be better,' she lied, 'but I think someone should take Mr Wiles up a drink – a stiff one.'

****

Felicity Dubois had received the call from Carol Amis, Freddie Baxter's PA, in the middle of a photo-shoot and she muttered her irritation as she snatched the phone from the choreographer.

'And what the hell do *you* want on a bloody Sunday?' she snapped in her customary polite manner.

Well used to the arrogance and rudeness of the posh ex-public school girl, Amis just took a deep breath. 'I'm calling from home, Felice,' she replied. 'Terrible news, I'm afraid. Vernon Wiles has just telephoned me in a bit of a state. Freddie Baxter is dead. Fell off a cliff in Cornwall apparently. I'm ringing round to let everyone know.'

Dubois' expression changed dramatically during the brief conversation and she turned, gaping and wide-eyed, towards the choreographer as she handed the phone back to her.

'Bloody hell, Jane!' she gasped, her dark brown eyes suddenly moist. 'It's Freddie Baxter … he's … he's dead. Took a dive off a damned cliff in Cornwall.'

Jane Purnell's hand shot to her mouth in a gesture of horror. 'But that's awful.'

'Isn't it just?' Dubois exclaimed. 'But Cornwall? What on earth was he doing down there in the first place?'

'I know,' Purnell replied. 'He's always hated the sea.'

Dubois took a deep breath. 'Poor old Freddie. He didn't deserve to go like that. And he was such a nice guy too.'

She shook her head at the photographer as he adjusted the backdrop he had been using for the photographic session. 'Sorry, Clive, I can't do this now. Much too upset.'

'Quite understandable,' Purnell soothed. 'Look, you go home, Felice. We'll fix up another shoot tomorrow. I'm sure our clients will understand.'

Dubois nodded. 'Yes, I think that would be best,' she agreed and grabbing her robe to slip over the brief bikini she had been modelling, she headed for the little changing room and carefully locked the door behind her.

Once there, her demeanour quickly changed. The sorrow in her expression was abruptly erased, as if wiped away by an invisible hand, and leaning against the wall for a moment, she tilted her head back slightly, with her eyes partially closed in thought.

So fat Freddie was actually dead, was he? The best news ever. And both Jane and Clive would have been astonished to see the gleeful smile, which was suddenly born on those full red lips, in place of the shock she had affected just a moment ago.

Dressing quickly, she made her way down in the lift to the basement car park, resisting the urge to run, and flicked the remote control of her sleek, maroon BMW. Sliding behind the wheel, she studied her face in the rear-view mirror for a moment, adjusting the mirror to admire the delicate brown skin and the haughty, finely chiselled features she had inherited from her West African mother. Smoothing the black dreadlocks away from her high cheekbones, she winked at her reflection. 'Well, Freddie, hon,' she drawled, curling her lips into a vindictive sneer. 'I always said you would hit the rocks one day. And you've certainly done it this time.'

Then starting the car's powerful engine she roared out of the car park with all the exuberance of someone who had just won the National Lottery.

CHAPTER 11

The offices of the New Light Modelling Agency stood on the edge of the square mile covered by the City of London Police, but just inside the Metropolitan Police District's boundary. Occupying a corner of the first and second storeys of a large business complex, the place was accessed by a lift from a shared car park directly underneath, and was nothing short of a design statement in itself. Mick Benchley raised an eyebrow as he entered the plush foyer with DI Angel on a bright Monday morning. The DI, who had been to the premises previously as part of the bombing investigation, gave him a nudge. 'As I said earlier, Guv,' she commented, 'We're in the wrong business.'

Benchley grunted and approached the long reception desk with his warrant card already in his hand.

'Detective Chief Inspector Benchley and DI Angel, Metropolitan Police,' he snapped at the blonde girl behind the desk and frowned as he noted her puffed eyelids and pale face, which suggested she had been crying. 'Here to see Mr Baxter.'

For a moment the girl just gaped at him and visible tears started running down her face. 'Freddie?' she echoed. 'But … but you can't.'

For a second both Benchley and Angel simply stared at her. 'What do you mean can't?' Benchley rapped. 'Just ring him, will you?'

She released a little whimper. 'I … I'll get his PA,' she said and picking up the phone beside her, dialled a number, cupping her hand around the mouthpiece as she whispered into it.

Carol Amis was down in the foyer within minutes, her face also pale and drawn and strands of dark hair straying out of the tight bun which usually held them in place. Drawing the detectives to one side after introducing herself, she dropped her bombshell. 'I'm afraid Mr Baxter is … is deceased,' she said.

'Deceased?' Benchley exclaimed, visibly shocked. 'How on earth did that happen?'

'He … he apparently slipped on the edge of a cliff in Cornwall and fell on to the rocks.'

'Cornwall? And when did this happen?'

'Saturday evening, I understand. I've been off for a few days. A business colleague, Vernon Wiles, who was in Cornwall with him, rang me at home yesterday to give me the terrible news. The press have only just found out and they have been plaguing us non-stop all morning. I think there is going to be a major story on it tonight. Freddie was quite a celebrity in the fashion world, you see.'

'But what was Mr Baxter doing in Cornwall?'

She shook her head. 'I have no idea. He didn't confide in me.'

Benchley released his breath in a long sigh. 'Well, we're sorry for your loss, Miss Amis,' he went on, his mind racing ahead of him now, 'but we do need to talk to you.'

She nodded. 'My office would be best.'

Minutes later, seated opposite the diminutive little brunette in her smart white blouse and very short black skirt, Benchley said, 'I'm investigating the bombing incident at The Philanderer's Night Club three months ago.'

Amis looked surprised, her brown eyes narrowing behind the large, full-frame spectacles. 'Is that still going on?' she exclaimed. 'I thought the case was closed? You didn't catch anybody, did you?'

Angel shook her head. 'We never close an undetected case, Miss Amis,' she replied, 'and certainly not after only three months.'

'We have a few more routine inquiries to make,' Benchley went on. 'I've just been to The Philanderer's Club again, and we would be interested in speaking to the models who were there at the time of the incident. Perhaps you could let me have their current addresses.'

Amis looked puzzled. 'But the girls were all interviewed at length by your officers soon after the incident.'

Benchley's face twitched irritably. 'I'm well aware of that, Miss Amis, but we would like to speak to each of them again anyway.'

Amis sighed her own irritation. 'Well, there were six girls in all. They were modelling evening wear for three different designers.'

'And where are they now? Working?'

Amis shook her head. 'I had to ring round everyone personally with the bad news and they've all been told to take some time off until we decide what our next steps will be. I have the company solicitor coming to see me later this afternoon and there's bound to be a board meeting soon.'

'And Felicity Dubois, where is she now?'

'Felicity? Why do you want to know about Felicity?'

'Is it a problem answering our questions, Miss Amis?' Angel put in tartly.

The PA cast her a daggers look, but ignored her and addressed Benchley directly. 'She was sent home from a photo-shoot yesterday after she heard the news. I expect she is still at her apartment.'

'Models work on Sundays then, do they?'

'In special circumstances, yes. Felicity had had the Friday and Saturday off, so it was necessary for her to work on the Sunday to keep a client happy.' She treated him to a waspish smile. 'Modelling is not all about fashion shows and glitzy cat-walks, Chief Inspector,' she added. 'Our models represent a whole variety of clients in all kinds of areas, including catalogue, film and television advertising. It can be very demanding work, requiring a 100 percent commitment. Weekends are not sacrosanct and many of our models endure long, unsociable hours.'

Benchley grunted, apparently unimpressed. Then he came in again on a completely different tack, as if he hadn't heard her. 'Do you know why the dressing rooms of Felicity Dubois and Lynn Giles at The Philanderer's Club were changed at the last minute?'

Amis shrugged. 'No idea. Freddie dealt with all the arrangements there. I had nothing to do with them. In fact, I remained here during the set-up of the fashion show, fielding calls and so forth.'

'Felicity and Freddie get on well, did they?'

Amis looked surprised by the question at first, but then gave a little twisted smile. 'Oh yes. Felicity and Freddie got on extremely well,' and the bitch in her surfaced in a rush. 'In fact, you could say they were very close.'

'You mean they were lovers?' Angel said.

Amis laughed without humour, her contempt now only too apparent. 'Lovers? Hardly. Freddie was bi-sexual. He was incapable of that sort of normal relationship. He simply liked sex – any kind of sex. Felicity was just one of a long line of affairs – with both men and women.'

'Like who, for instance?'

'Well, his more recent conquests included our esteemed publicity and advertising manager, Cate Meadows – I think he liked a bit of rough on occasions – but that was probably his shortest sexual foray and their parting was anything but sweet sorrow. I think she would have put metal filings in his coffee if she could have managed it.'

Benchley was immediately interested. 'And where is this Cate Meadows now?'

'On her hols, I believe. She's taken a couple of weeks off.'

'You say his more recent conquests included her. So who else did he sweep off their feet?'

The PA considered the question for a moment. 'Well, poor old Cate was actually dumped for our former salon manager, Julian Grey—'

'Julian?' Angel cut in.

Amis gave another tight smile and nodded. 'Must have been a bit humiliating for her to be dumped for a man, but that was Freddie. Julian was a nice-looking, athletic lad, though. Gay, of course, but there you are. Rather sweet on Julian, was our Freddie – before he was distracted by Felicity, of course. Then he just dropped him like all the others.'

'Others?' Benchley queried.

'Oh, I could give you a whole list.'

'Perhaps you would do that,' he said. 'And how did this Julian take to being dropped?'

'Not very well at all. There was a flaming row. Most embarrassing too, as it all happened in Freddie's office next door while I was sitting here. Julian left us after that, I'm afraid, but said it wasn't over and that Freddie should watch his back in the future.'

'What did Julian mean by that, do you think?'

'No idea, and Freddie himself was too besotted with Felicity to care.'

'And where is this Julian now?'

'North London. I don't know exactly where.'

'Would you not have his forwarding address on file?'

'Probably.'

Benchley took a deep breath, his irritation barely concealed. 'Be most helpful if you could dig it out for me, Miss Amis. Before we leave, eh? But back to Freddie. From what you are saying, he seems to have been a bit of a Don Juan. What was his secret, do you think? Some sort of natural talent or charisma?'

Amis gave another short laugh. 'Hardly. Freddie was one of the least attractive men I have ever met and being bi-sexual, his relationships were always physically intense, but emotionally shallow and short-lived.

Felicity was a lot more sexually versatile than the others. That's what probably attracted Freddie to her in the first place, though after the bomb blast, if he had known she'd also started having it away with Lynn Giles' boyfriend at the same time as she was pleasing him, maybe he would have thought differently. In any event, I don't suppose her fling with him would have lasted much longer, even if he had not fallen off the cliff.'

'And how come you know how versatile Felicity was?' Angel cut in again.

Amis snorted. 'How do you think? He wasn't exactly discreet about his affairs and, as his PA, I was pretty close to the action.'

'You're saying he was doing the business at work?'

'Most nights after he thought I had gone home actually.' She waved an arm in the direction of Baxter's office. 'On the sofa, the floor. Maybe even in his leather chair. I reckon all options and positions were open.'

'Did that annoy you?' Benchley asked mildly.

'Why should it? What they got up to was their own affair. But I knew what Felicity was after.'

'Oh? And what was that?'

'Well, Freddie was well connected, wasn't he? He could open doors others couldn't.'

'So you're saying Felicity was selling her favours for a leg-up in the modelling business, if you'll pardon the expression?'

'Something like that, yes.' Amis began sorting through some papers on her desk. 'Now I really must get on.'

But Benchley had no intention of letting her off that easily. 'And did Felicity get the leg-up she was after?'

The PA was suddenly re-animated. 'No way. Freddie was much too cute to be had over by someone like her. Lynn Giles was always his favourite, even though she would never succumb to his charms. Lynn got most of the good contracts as a result and Felicity even lost out on a really big opportunity at The Philanderer's Club after the bomb blast.'

'How so?'

Amis smiled again, plainly enjoying recounting Dubois' woes. 'Freddie had been negotiating a lucrative new modelling contract with a top fashion house and their scouts were all at the club that night. When Lynn was quite literally blown out of the running, Felicity thought the contract would ultimately be hers, but instead it went to a new model, Melanie Jones, who was picked at another fashion show.'

'That must have really pissed Felicity off, eh?' Angel said.

Amis tensed, as if she feared she had said too much, and glancing quickly at her watch she said, 'Look, I've got the company solicitor here in ten minutes. I really must ask you to leave.'

For a moment Benchley just stared at her and Angel thought he might be about to refuse until she answered his question. But instead he gave a frosty smile and stood up. 'Fine. Thank you for your cooperation.' Then on his way to the door, he half-turned and snapped his fingers. 'Oh, yes, there's just the matter of Julian Grey's address. If you would be so kind?'

****

Minutes later the two detectives were seeing themselves out through the big glass doors of the foyer. 'Reckon we touched a nerve back there?' the DCI remarked, pausing by the lift.

Angel laughed grimly. 'We certainly touched something,' she agreed.

He nodded. 'Certainly no love lost between Amis and Dubois anyway.'

'Maybe a touch of the old green eye?' she suggested. 'But why are you so interested in Dubois in particular?'

He shrugged, then told her what he had learned from Wilfred Kent about the change of rooms at The Philanderer's Club on the night of the bombing.

She listened in silence and nodded slowly. 'Hence your question to Amis about it,' she acknowledged with a rueful grimace. 'Nice of you to tell me beforehand.'

'You were off this weekend, so how could I?'

'You spoke to me yesterday.'

'Okay, okay, point taken. Anything else you would like to know?'

She treated him to her sweetest smile. 'No, that should about do it, Guv, thank you. And now I have the full SP, I can see that you suspect Dubois might have been a party to the bombing?'

He nodded and pressed the lift button. 'I certainly think she has some questions to answer and it would be remiss of us not to give her the opportunity of answering them. Giles was originally the favourite for that top modelling job and it's clear Dubois desperately wanted it, so the sudden last-minute change of rooms could be very significant.'

'If Giles was the target and not Baxter.'

'Maybe both of them then. You know, catch two birds with one stone. Get rid of the competition and punish Baxter at the same time.'

Angel thought about that for a second. 'Feasible, but equally, the perpetrator could be someone else. Baxter could have been the real target and Giles just collateral damage. He seems to have made enough enemies and from what Carol Amis said, Cate Meadows and Julian Grey might be worth talking to as well.'

He grunted. 'Grey especially, in view of his alleged threat to Baxter. He might also have an angle on Dubois. After all, he was dumped for her, so he can't feel particularly well disposed towards the young lady and might be ready to deal some dirt on her.'

'But Cate Meadows had a pretty good motive too, don't you think? She must have felt humiliated beyond measure to be chucked for a man.' She hesitated. 'Of course, having said that, there is the possibility that we are complicating the whole thing unnecessarily. Maybe Lynn Giles *was* the target and Dubois is the one we want. Simple as that.'

'And Baxter's death in Cornwall?'

'Just an unfortunate accident, as has been said up until now?'

The lift arrived with a soft *ping* and Benchley ushered Angel in ahead of him. 'That would be one hell of a coincidence,' he said, pressing the button for the car park. 'Three months ago someone sets off an explosive device at a club where Baxter's holding a fashion show, scarring one of his models. Now he himself ends up as brown bread after falling off a cliff in Cornwall. More than a bit iffy, I would suggest.' He hesitated, then added, 'Especially as Cornwall is where Lynn Giles, our amnesiac witness, has chosen to retire to, away from public view.'

'I didn't know she'd gone to ground down there?'

'Nor did anyone else. I kept her address to myself for her protection, but I suspect she must have passed it on to her former employer anyway, against my advice, which means there's every chance Baxter was paying her a visit when he died.'

The lift doors opened once more and Benchley followed his DI out into the basement car park, talking to her over his shoulder as he walked towards their car.

'The thing to bear in mind is that, whether Baxter was the principal target or not, Lynn Giles saw something the night of the bombing which might give us all the answers we need, if and when her memory returns, so she is a key witness. That means she is very much at risk from the perp who planted that bomb and who may also have pushed Baxter off the cliff—'

'A perp who could have followed Baxter to Lynn Giles' address,' she finished for him.

His face was grim as he climbed into the car. 'Exactly, which is why I intend ringing her as soon as we get back to the nick,' he replied. 'Let's just hope she answers the bloody phone.'

But Lynn Giles didn't answer the phone, and although Benchley tried several times that morning there was no reply. He considered leaving a message, but then thought better of it. What could he say? "Sorry to bother you, Miss Giles, but I think that someone might be on their way to kill you." That would have gone down really well, wouldn't it? And anyway, on reflection, maybe he was jumping the gun by ringing her in the first place. Despite his own suspicions, there appeared to be no suggestion at present that Freddie Baxter's death had been anything other than an accident. Even if it had been a case of murder, the killer had had ample time to waste Lynn Giles already, but apparently hadn't or he would have heard about it by now. No, common sense dictated that he liaised with Devon and Cornwall Police as to their take on things before he acted on what at this point in time amounted to nothing more than a hunch.

As for his own investigations, while Felicity Dubois certainly had questions to answer regarding the last-minute change of dressing rooms on the night of the bombing, so did Julian Grey and Cate Meadows. Until he had interviewed them all or had dug up something more substantial from another quarter, he had nothing substantial to go on and putting the fear of God into Lynn Giles by warning her she might be at imminent risk could be regarded as a mite premature, to say the least.

He stretched in the battered swivel chair behind his desk, then glanced at his watch. The sound of the traffic in the street below his window had lessened considerably after two hours of smoking, honking congestion and he was suddenly conscious of the fact that his stomach was rumbling. Pulling out a packet of cigarettes, then changing his mind and returning them to his pocket, he called to his DI in the next office. 'Come on, Moira, lunch – and I think it's time you bought me that pint.'

****

Detective Inspector Maureen O'Donnell had almost half a packet of extra strong peppermints in her mouth as she stood in the little mortuary just outside Helston, reflecting grimly on the fact that, as the holidaymakers flocked to Cornwall in their thousands, few realised that as well as sun, sea and sand, such gruesome tasks as post mortems were being carried out on a regular basis just yards from the holiday routes they were using.

O'Donnell was not Cornish, which was pretty obvious when she opened her mouth to voice her thoughts or criticisms in her soft West of Ireland brogue, and she often asked herself what the hell she was doing working in a British police force when she could have been idling her time away with the Garda in Connemara or Galway. The trouble was, if she had stayed in the land of her birth, she wouldn't be a detective inspector, but still a uniformed constable waiting for a dead man's shoes, whereas now she was not only a senior CID officer serving in a major British force, but a rising star with an enviable future to look forward to if she played her cards right. So maybe that answered her own question.

The call for someone to attend the mortuary had originally come from the coroner's officer. 'The Emmet who fell off the cliffs,' he'd told the local detective sergeant who'd first attended. 'Pathologist isn't happy about cause of death. Suggests it could be sus.' The result had been a swift buck-passing job, which O'Donnell had ended up with.

Now studying the gutted carcass of Freddie Baxter lying on its back on the dissecting table, she waited as the police photographer took some close ups of the dead man's skull while pathologist, Hector Morey, washed his hands in the stainless steel sink opposite. The last thing O'Donnell needed was for this to be a dodgy death. She was due to go on leave to Corsica in two days' time and she knew only too well that once involved in a crime investigation, it was almost impossible to pass the job on to someone else.

'Finished then?' the pathologist snapped at the photographer, turning back towards the corpse and drying his hands on some paper towelling. The other nodded, grinned briefly at O'Donnell, then headed for the exit, whistling loudly. Cheerful sod, she thought grimly,

'Take a look, Inspector,' Morey invited, beckoning her over.

O'Donnell grimaced and joined him at the head of the corpse. 'Some nasty damage,' Morey went on. 'Death would have been instantaneous.'

'Sure, but he fell off a cliff, did he not?' the DI commented in her distinctive Irish brogue. 'Probably about 40ft.'

'Indeed,' Morey agreed, but correct me if I am wrong, wasn't he found lying on his back?'

O'Donnell nodded. 'Aye, that's true enough.'

The pathologist nodded. 'And the multiple injuries he sustained are certainly consistent with such a fall, but look at this.' He pointed to a distinctive narrow indentation within an oval of what looked like heavy bruising at the right side and towards the front of the skull. 'This is something quite different – an injury which is very unlikely to have been caused by impact with a rock, especially as the rest of his head injuries are to the back of the skull.'

O'Donnell's spirits sank and she sighed heavily. 'So you're saying someone gave him a quare crack on the head before he went over the edge?'

The pathologist gave an icy smile. 'No, I'm not saying that at all. I cannot confirm absolutely that he was attacked, but he certainly got a "quare crack on the head" from something at some stage before his death,' he said, gently mocking her colloquialism. 'And even if he was suicidal, unless he was both a masochist and a contortionist able to inflict the injury on himself, yes, I think that could be one conclusion you could reach, Detective Inspector. Though whether this injury has anything to do with his fall is unclear.'

'So a more detailed check of the scene would be in order?'

He shrugged. 'Well, that's your call, but it might be a good next step.'

'And what should I be looking for?'

Morey pursed his lips for a second. 'Something long and thin,' he said, 'like a length of metal pipe.'

Holy Mary, O'Donnell thought, goodbye to that beach in Corsica.

CHAPTER 12

Lynn saw the flashing blue lights on the headland above the cove when she was pulling the curtains in The Beach House as dusk was closing in. Going out on to her patio, she shaded her eyes with one hand against the dying rays of the sun and frowned. What the hell was going on? Surely not another body on the rocks?

Grabbing an anorak, she closed and locked the door and headed along the shingle towards the track leading up on to the cliffs. She could hear the voices as she emerged on the green swathe at the top, but came to an abrupt halt, blinking in the pulsing, eye-twisting glare of a parked police car's flashing light bar just yards before the scrub and the old engine-house. A white Ford Transit was parked on the heath a few feet to one side of the police car with its rear doors wide open, and a blue and white "Police" tape had been drawn across the track between the car and the Transit, barring her passage. Lynn could just see a knot of uniformed and plainclothes figures on the path in front of the derelict building.

'Can I help you, madam?' a voice queried, and she started as a uniformed policewoman emerged from beside the police car, one side of her face tinged blue in the light of the flashing strobe.

'Er ... no,' Lynn replied quickly, feeling nosy and rather silly. 'I ... I just wondered what was going on.'

'Nothing to worry about,' the policewoman replied curtly. 'We're simply checking the cliffs after the death of a man on Saturday. Local, are you?'

Lynn nodded and waved a hand vaguely in the direction of The Beach House, suddenly wishing she had kept her nose out of things. 'I live down there in Bootleg Cove.'

Immediately the policewoman's attitude changed. 'Do you, now? Well, it's possible our DI might like a word with you, if you don't mind.'

Before Lynn could say anything else, the policewoman had lifted the tape. 'Come on through.'

Now cursing her stupidity, Lynn ducked her head under the tape and followed the officer along the track to where an auburn-haired woman in a trouser suit was standing a few feet in front of the Transit. Instinctively hanging back while the uniformed officer had a few words with her senior colleague, she noted that there appeared to be spotlights of some sort set up in and around the old engine-house. Then she jerked her gaze away and forced a smile as the trouser-suited woman approached her, with her hand extended.

'Detective Inspector Maureen O'Donnell,' the woman said in a strong Irish brogue, her voice warm and friendly. 'And you are?'

'Lynn ... I mean Mary Tresco.' As soon as she'd spoken, Lynn regretted it. She should have given her real name. What if this DI happened to check with the officer who had called on her about Baxter's death earlier and found out that she had given him the name Lynn Giles? Hells bells, why was she so stupid?

'You live around here, do you now?' O'Donnell went on.

Lynn nodded, but couldn't think of anything else to say.

'You'll have heard about the tourist who was killed near here then?' O'Donnell queried.

'Yes, I did hear about it.'

The DI thought for a moment, then went on. 'Ever seen anyone up here, have you? Sleeping rough in the engine-house maybe?'

Lynn thought of the hooded man, but shook her head. 'No, never. Not many people get up here – bit out of the way.' She hesitated, then blurted. 'Do the police think ... I mean, suspect– ?'

'Sure, it's early days yet, so it is, but we're considering all possibilities and we have a lot more inquiries to make to establish what actually happened here.'

Lynn swallowed hard. 'Oh, I ... I see.'

'Perhaps we could talk again – maybe tomorrow? You are one of the closest people to the spot after all. Could be helpful, so it could.'

'Yes, only too pleased.'

'That's grand. I'll be letting you get off home then.'

Inwardly, Lynn breathed a sigh of relief, turning back towards the crime scene tape, anxious to be on her way. But her relief was premature. A familiar gruff voice stopped her in her tracks before she had gone more than a few feet: 'Just a minute, Miss Giles.'

Out of the corner of her eye she saw the DI stiffen and cast a swift glance in her direction as the Traffic cop who had stopped her outside Mullion village strode over to her. 'Well, if it isn't Miss Speedy,' he chuckled. 'And how's that lovely car of yours, me'dear?'

She winced. 'Fine, thank you. Look, I have to be getting back—'

'Giles?' the DI queried, now at her elbow. 'And there's me thinking you said your name was Tresco ... Mary Tresco?'

Lynn took a deep breath. 'It is, but—'

'Done some homework on you,' the Traffic policeman butted in again. 'Used to be a top model, didn't you? Saw your pic in one of our old mags at the nick and it all clicked.'

'Giles?' O'Donnell murmured thoughtfully, then snapped her fingers. 'I remember ... Lynn Giles. Sure, you were the wee lady who was badly injured in that bomb blast in London?'

So the cat really was out of the bag now and Lynn closed her eyes in resignation. But she was thrown an unexpected lifeline. O'Donnell was a lot more perceptive than most.

'Using another name to escape the press, are you, love?' the DI said quietly, and there was more than a hint of sympathy in her tone.

Lynn nodded again. 'They ... they will hound me if they find out where I've gone to ground,' she said. 'I just want to be left alone.'

The Traffic cop shuffled his jack-booted feet, his embarrassment obvious, and the DI flicked her head at him, her unspoken instruction unmistakable. As he lumbered away, O'Donnell put her hand on Lynn's wrist. 'Now, you be getting off home,' she said. 'Sorry to have put you on the spot.'

With a renewed sense of relief, Lynn thanked her and headed back the way she had come, conscious of her legs shaking as she walked. She had got out of that one by the skin of her teeth, but she knew it was only a temporary thing. When the DI eventually made the connection between her and Freddie Baxter, as she surely must sooner or later, there would be a lot more difficult questions to answer. And with the loose-mouthed Traffic cop now also aware of who she was, it wouldn't be long before the press got to hear about it and descended on the place in their droves. Not only the press either, she thought, remembering Detective Chief Inspector Benchley's warning about the terrorists who had planted the bomb.

Suddenly she needed Alan Murray more than she had ever needed anyone and crossing the car park where Vernon Wiles had sat in Freddie Baxter's BMW the night of his death, she headed along the main road towards The Old Customs House.

****

Felicity Dubois waited until she saw Carol Amis' blue Mazda MX5 leave the underground car park of the New Light Modelling Agency building late in the evening before she drove in herself, blatantly parking her BMW in Freddie Baxter's own bay, next to the lift. So what, she thought callously as she got out and locked the car doors with her remote? The fat man wouldn't be needing a parking space again, would he? Not this side of hell anyway.

Dressed in skin-tight black trousers and a matching leather jacket, she grinned as she pressed the lift button, feeling a bit like a female James Bond when she thought about what she had come here to do. Well, she couldn't have done it when Freddie was alive, could she? No way, José! No one crossed the fat man — he knew too many people — and being caught in the act by her vindictive boss would have been tantamount to career suicide.

Doing nothing up until now had been a real bitch though. Not naturally blessed with an equable, patient disposition – and despite her privileged upbringing in a ladies' finishing school – the tall black model had a fiery, strong-willed temperament and was prone to a degree of volatility, which made her a formidable adversary when she lost control. But for months on end she'd had to keep a really tight rein on her natural inclinations, forcing herself to sit on her hands and wait for the right moment instead of rushing in. But now the waiting was over – and she could hardly contain herself.

The place was alarmed – Freddie had always been careful about security – but Dubois was hoping that it would not present any problems tonight. After Baxter had found out about her less-than-respectable past – forcing her to dump Lynn Giles' pathetic boyfriend and give herself to him instead or face ruin when he released certain photographs and documents to the media – she had put a lot of effort into pleasing her boss in any way she could. Baxter had always been bi-sexual and Felicity Dubois had had a lot to offer a man of his deviant tastes. It had all paid off too. In less than two months her sexual favours had won her privileged status and though this still hadn't persuaded the fat man to give up the dirt he had on her, it had enabled her to gain unrestricted access, not only to the building itself, but to Baxter's inner sanctum as well. It was this that she was counting on netting her the prize she sought most of all – provided there were no unforeseen hiccups with the alarm.

Unlocking the heavy glass door, she gritted her teeth as the system activated, producing its familiar high-pitched whine, and quickly tapped the four-digit code into the keypad just inside. Nothing happened and in sudden a panic she jerked the door back open, ready to take to her heels. If the thing went off and she was caught on the premises by one of the security officers patrolling the business complex, she knew she would have one hell of a job explaining what she was doing there. But then abruptly the alarm's warning note cut off and the keypad registered the deactivation message. Shutting and locking the door again, she took a deep breath and gave a shaky laugh. Close, she mused – too damned close!

The building was now deathly still, the silence descending immediately the heavy glass doors were closed, shutting out the murmur of the London traffic. The tap of her high heels on the polished woodblock floor of the front foyer sounded unnaturally loud as she strode past the now deserted reception desk and into the short, thickly carpeted corridor beyond.

On both sides, the glint of stainless steel and polished wood, with the ubiquitous office rubber plants and giant ferns in big ceramic pots occupying shallow alcoves and gilt-framed pictures lining the Sanderson papered walls. Stupid bastard, she gloated, musing that Freddie may have invested a whole lot of time and money in creating the right company image, but the glitzy effect he had so painstakingly put together wasn't much good to him on a mortuary slab, was it?

Passing interview rooms, a large photographic studio and a couple of administrative offices, she mounted a flight of steel stairs to the upper level. More rooms now, including a reception lounge, conference room and another small studio. Then the corridor she was following ended abruptly before a panelled mahogany door signed "Carol Amis, Personal Assistant".

The door was locked, as she had expected, but she knew the security code for it too and punched the numbers in with renewed confidence, stepping into a cool, thickly carpeted room with an imposing workstation on one side and a row of steel cabinets on the other. Baxter's inner sanctum was directly opposite and again the locked door with its security keypad was no obstacle. After all, she was a privileged member of staff and fully trusted.

She smiled as she cast her gaze around the room, taking in the ornate gilt desk with its bank of telephones, the black leather chair set behind it and the brown leather sofa in one corner. That sofa had often borne the brunt of so much action between Freddie and herself after Carol Amis had gone home that she was surprised it was still intact and she had to admit that on such occasions she had always found the gilt-framed portraits on the walls a bit off-putting, imagining that the faces in them were watching the sexual spectacle beneath with rapt, voyeuristic attention.

She wondered if the old men leering from the frames were watching her now and on sudden impulse, she directed an obscene finger sign at each of them in turn as she crossed the room to Baxter's desk and dropped into the chair behind it. There was a small steel safe bolted to the floor underneath the desk and she stared at it for a moment. Freddie had always boasted it was force-proof and only he knew the correct combination – he had apparently not even entrusted his PA, Carol Amis, with that information. This could not have suited Dubois better. The last thing she needed was for Amis to be any the wiser than she already was, besides which it was commonly accepted that there was no honour among thieves, so why break with tradition? More importantly, though, it meant that what she had come here to retrieve should still be inside the safe. Provided – and she felt sick at the thought – that Freddie had not changed the combination since she had lifted it from his electronic tablet one night while he was showering in the adjacent en suite.

Taking a deep breath, she bent down and slowly manipulated the dial, listening for each tell-tale click. She completed the sequence and turned the door handle, but it didn't move. Shit! The bastard must have changed the combination after all. Now what? She sat back in the chair for a few seconds, thinking hard and trying to keep calm. So maybe she had just made a mistake with the number sequence. Try a second time, girl. What have you got to lose? Gritting her teeth and conscious of the fact that her fingers were trembling with the tension, she started again, carefully turning the dial left and right, as required. Once more the handle resisted her efforts and she felt a stab of panic. But then a sharp *clonk* and the heavy metal door swung open. The thing had just been stiff, that was all, and she emitted a shaky, relieved chuckle as her heartbeat began to return to normal.

Getting down on her knees, she peered into the safe and saw a stack of £10, £20 and £50 notes resting on top of an A4 size black leather wallet. Feeling a thrill of excitement, she lifted the lot out and placed them on the desk in front of her. First the money. There had to be at least a couple of thousand pounds there. Well, alleluia! Reaching into her pocket, she tugged a couple of plastic supermarket bags free, chuckling repeatedly again as she stuffed the notes into them and tied the handles in secure knots. Well, why not? Freddie wouldn't be needing the money, would he? And it would pay for all the weeks of misery she had suffered at his hands.

Next the wallet. It was equipped with a zip, but not locked in any way, opening easily when she pulled on the tab. There were several A4 envelopes inside and the top one had the name "Dubois" printed in thick, black pen in the upper right-hand corner. Picking up a gold-coloured paper-knife from the desk, she slit open the flap with shaky fingers and emptied the contents out on to the desk top, then immediately closed her eyes in a brief prayer, even though she didn't believe in a god – or anything else for that matter. Everything about her dodgy past was there including photographs, addresses and some very incriminating documents. All dynamite if they had got to the tabloid press. The only place they would be going to now, though, was into a shredder. She was in the clear. After all this time she could finally get her life back.

Returning the whole lot to the envelope with a grim, satisfied smile, she slipped it inside her leather jacket, mouthing a brief 'Up yours, Freddie' at a framed photograph of Baxter on the corner of the desk. But she made no immediate effort to return the wallet to the safe and lock up again, for her gaze had suddenly caught sight of something else – a second envelope in the wallet, bearing the name "Giles" on the front in the same thick, black pen.

'So what's this, hon?' she murmured. 'You have your own little file, eh?'

Slitting open the flap, as before, she emitted a low whistle as she leafed through the documents and revealing photographs clipped together inside. '*Nice*,' she murmured with a soft throaty chuckle. 'So, he had the dirt on you too, did he, sweetheart?' Then, a second later, she started as a hastily scribbled note fell out of the clutch of papers on to the desk. It had obviously been torn from a spiral-bound notebook and she recognised Freddie Baxter's neat hand immediately: 'New Name, Mary Tresco,' she read aloud, 'The Beach House, Bootleg Cove, Near Mullion, Cornwall.

Staring across the room at glossy portraits of six of Baxter's models, including herself, which were displayed in a neat line on the far wall, she focused on Lynn Giles' seductive, smiling face and treated her to a hard stare. 'So, that's where you've gone to ground, is it?' she said softly. 'Cool new name, too. Well now, I think it's about time you got a visit from an old friend – and I don't think you'll be too happy about that.'

Sniggering at her own private joke, she tucked the second envelope into her leather jacket with the first before zipping the wallet up again and putting it back where she had found it – showing no interest whatsoever in the other envelopes inside. Then re-closing the safe and picking up her bags from beside the desk, she blew a kiss at one of the portraits on the wall and headed for the stairs, closing and securing both office doors behind her.

Minutes later, she was swinging out of the car park on to the main road, a triumphant grin on her face.

'RIP, Freddie,' she sneered as she joined the traffic heading out of the city. 'You have a nice death now.'

CHAPTER 13

Lynn awoke late to the sound of heavy rain on the bedroom windows. She could hear Alan banging about in the kitchen and she stretched with a slow relaxed smile. It was great to have a man in her life again, to know he was there if she needed him – and she'd certainly needed him the previous night.

He'd been more than a little surprised when she had appeared on his front door step, but he had detected the anxiety in her tone and his welcome had been warm and genuine. After a light supper, bed had been the eventual and delicious consequence and now lying there staring into the grey overcast day, remembering his tender love-making just a few hours before, she couldn't help feeling guilty over her earlier doubts about him.

'Doing eggs and bacon if that's all right,' he called suddenly from the bottom of the stairs. 'If you want to shower first. Be about 15 minutes.'

She shook her head in disbelief. Cooking eggs and bacon without being able to see a thing? The man was incredible. Then she took a deep anticipatory breath as the aroma of frying fat drifted up into the room to stir her stomach juices. Swinging her legs over the edge of the bed, she stood up and stretched again. The en suite shower beckoned and she headed for it, closing her eyes in ecstasy in the steam of the big tiled cubicle and feeling the muscles in her arms and back relax with the heat. But everything changed the moment she stepped out on to the bathroom floor and started towelling herself down. There was a large mirror above the wash-hand basin and despite the partially clouded glass, she could see her slim body relatively clearly and the tracer-like scars down her face, breasts and stomach seemed even more pronounced than before.

Sobbing bitterly, she returned to the bedroom and dressed herself – covering up the "damage" as quickly as she could before sitting on the edge of the bed, towelling her hair and staring out of the window into the grey day, which was once again in keeping with her own mood.

The scars would never fade, deep down, she knew that. They were there for the rest of her life. But what about the scars inside her head?

Were they going to be permanent as well? Would she ever be able to lead a normal life again or was she doomed to spend the rest of it in lonely isolation? Alan was her last chance. If it turned out that he was treating this as just a casual fling, she couldn't bear to go on. She needed commitment and a future, but it was far too early to ask that of him. She could only wait and hope.

The sound of someone knocking loudly, followed by Alan's yell, 'You decent, Lynn? Can you get that? ' abruptly shook her out of her self-pitying mood. Jumping to her feet, she headed barefoot down the stairs to the front door, still towelling her hair as she went.

Detective Inspector Maureen O'Donnell raised an eyebrow in surprise when she opened up. 'Ah, Miss Giles,' she said, wiping some rain drips off her nose. 'Just been around to your place. Didn't expect to find you here.'

The remark sounded almost like a criticism and Lynn stiffened. But then O'Donnell's eyes sparkled and she grinned as Alan appeared in the doorway behind Lynn, shirtless and clutching a spatula. 'Who is it, Lynn?' Murray snapped, obviously irritated by the intrusion.

'A police officer,' Lynn replied. 'An Inspector O'Donnell.'

'Just making a few routine inquiries, sir,' O'Donnell explained, eyeing him up and down. 'The body of a tourist, a feller named Freddie Baxter, was found at the bottom of the cliffs near here on Sunday morning, not far from the old engine-house. We are treating the death as unexplained. Just wondered if you saw anyone about near there at between—'

'He's blind!' Lynn cut in brutally. 'It would have taken a miracle for him to have seen anything.'

Immediately O'Donnell's smile vanished and she winced. 'Sure, I'm terrible sorry, so I am – I didn't realise. We're rather short staffed at the moment and I was trying to follow up on a few things meself. I'll … er … leave you in peace.'

Lynn felt embarrassed at the way she had treated the detective and gnawed her lip as she watched her hurry back to a colleague who was waiting for her in a plain car parked at the front of the house, then drive away without a backward glance.

'You were rather rude, young lady,' Alan commented, adding insult to injury. 'She was only trying to do her job.'

Lynn nodded, more to herself than anything else, and closing the door, followed him back inside. Yes, she thought, not only rude, but bloody stupid. It never paid to antagonise police officers, especially one investigating a possible suspicious death, and she had a feeling that she hadn't seen the last of the friendly Detective Inspector O'Donnell.

****

Vernon Wiles had finished packing Freddie Baxter's suitcase to take back to London with him and was hauling it along the narrow corridor to his room when he was confronted by Maureen O'Donnell.

'Ah, Mr Wiles,' she said with an engaging smile. 'You're not leaving us already, sure you're not?'

Wiles quickly shook his head. 'No, no, no,' he said, 'just packing up Freddie's things to take with me when I do go. Haven't done mine yet.'

'I'll warrant you can't wait to say goodbye to Cornwall?' she said. 'Especially after all that has happened?'

He gave an insipid smile. 'I prefer the city – but no offence,' he said. 'It was Freddie's idea to come here.'

She nodded with apparent understanding. 'Have you time for a wee chat?' she said, pushing his door open so he could go ahead of her into his room.

He swallowed. 'Yes, yes, of course. I was waiting for the police to let me know the result of the post mortem anyway before I left. I ... I did agree to stay on until then, you know.'

'Ach, but that's very good of you, Mr Wiles,' she said, staring out of the window. 'But I'm afraid we have no option but to treat the death as unexplained.'

Wiles dropped the suitcase and nearly pitched over. 'Unexplained?' he gasped. 'I thought it was an accident?'

'Aye, so did we, Mr Wiles, but the pathologist has suggested there could be another possibility.'

'What ... what sort of possibility?'

O'Donnell shrugged. 'Suicide maybe or ... er ... foul play.'

Wiles could feel a faint trickle in his underpants and realised to his horror that he had just wet himself. 'Foul play?' he whispered, dropping on to the end of his bed. 'Suicide? But ... but why?'

'Ah,' O'Donnell replied, 'y'see we were wondering if you could help us there?'

'Me? But I didn't do anything.'

O'Donnell laughed, but her eyes were hard and watchful. 'Ach, no one is suggesting you did, Mr Wiles. No, we were just wondering if you had any idea who might have had it in for Freddie Baxter?'

Wiles shook his head several times. 'No ... no one that I know of. Everyone liked Freddie.'

'Well that's real nice, so it is. Did you like him, sir?'

'Me? Er ... yes, we'd known each other a long time.'

She pursed her lips. 'It's just that one of the waitresses in the bar downstairs says she overheard a wee argument in the bar between the two of you the night Mr Baxter died – something about him withdrawing his financial support for your business?'

Wiles felt sick. 'Yes, but it was only in jest.'

'Not a threat then?'

'No, absolutely not a threat.'

O'Donnell's smile was undiminished, but she said nothing and waited for him to go on.

He licked his lips, something he knew she would notice and interpret as nerves, and inwardly he cursed his stupidity. 'Freddie ... we were discussing a forthcoming film,' he lied, 'and Freddie wasn't sure he wanted to support it, that's all.'

Her smile broadened. 'Ah, well, that sorts that out then, so it does? Thank you. What about suicide then? Do you think he might have had worries, which could have caused him to decide to kill himself?'

Wiles shook his head quickly. 'No ... no, Freddie would never have done that.'

She nodded again, thinking for a moment. Then, abruptly changing tack, she said, 'What sort of film business are you in, Mr Wiles?'

He gulped. 'Oh, romances mainly.'

She raised her eyebrows. 'Romances, is it? What *Gone With The Wind* sort of thing?'

'Not exactly.'

There was a slightly contemptuous curl to her bottom lip and he knew she was baiting him. 'D'ye think I'd like your films, Mr Wiles?'

He shook his head with a short cynical laugh, which he hadn't intended. 'I ... I don't think so.'

'What, too hot for me, are they?'

He could feel himself getting rattled and tried to keep control of his rising anger. Who was she to criticise what he did for a living? Bloody bimbo cop!

'You know what sort of films they are, Inspector,' he snapped.

She smiled again. 'What, pornography, you mean? Aye, Mr Wiles, I do know what sort of films they are, but what I would like to know is what you and Mr Baxter had planned to film on our lovely stretch of coast here?'

'We ... we were just looking at options, that's all.'

'And Lynn Giles, was she to be part of one of those options? Is that why you both came down here, to see her?'

So the truth was out. No point in denying the obvious. 'Yes,' he said. 'We offered her a contract, but she ... er ... declined.'

'Told you to piss off, did she?'

Wiles started, taken aback by her sudden crudity. 'More or less, yes.'

'But you were still going to go ahead with it, that's why you were on the cliffs?'

'There are plenty of other actresses about who would grab the opportunity.'

Her eyes gleamed. 'I'm sure there are. Good money in depravity, is there, Mr Wiles?'

He didn't answer but stared sullenly at his feet and after a pregnant pause she changed the subject. 'One final question, Mr Wiles. I know you've been asked this before, but when you were up on the cliffs the night Freddie Baxter was killed, did you see anyone on foot in the vicinity. Someone sleeping rough perhaps – maybe a vagrant?'

Wiles cleared his throat, conscious of the fact that he was sweating profusely. 'No, no one,' he lied. 'I didn't see a soul.'

For a moment she just stared at him and he shrivelled up inside. But then she turned for the door. 'Well, I must be getting on,' she said briskly. 'It's been grand talking to you, Mr Wiles, so it has – very interesting.'

'Can I go then?' he blurted.

She faced him again, looking puzzled. 'Go?'

'Yes, back to London?'

'Well, 'course you can, Mr Wiles,' and her eyes bored into him, 'though I have to say it would be most helpful to the police investigation if you could stay on for another couple of days, just in case any other questions come up—'

'Questions?' he interrupted. 'But ... but I've told you all I know.'

'Sure you have, but there will be an opening inquest very soon, which may prompt further inquiries, and it would be grand if you were still here should we need to speak to you again.' She shrugged. 'I have no power to detain you, though…' and that irritating smile returned '… unless, of course, I were to place you under arrest.'

And she laughed at the expression on his face. 'But that won't be necessary – unless we discover you've done something wrong – will it, Mr Wiles?'

Then she was gone, quietly closing the door behind her, leaving Wiles shaking in his shoes and her thinly veiled threat still hanging in the air.

****

Julian Grey lived in an upmarket first-floor apartment in Clapham and with Angel peering curiously over his shoulder, Benchley rang the front door bell at just after 7pm.

It had been a long trying day for him and his DI. He had had to make three phone calls to Devon and Cornwall's Helston police station about Freddie Baxter's death before he was finally put through to a detective sergeant in an incident room that was apparently in the process of being set up. Even then the sergeant, allegedly speaking for a Detective Inspector Maureen O'Sullivan who seemed to be permanently 'out', had not been that forthcoming. The DS had only been prepared to say that the death was being treated as 'unexplained' and that 'inquiries were still on-going,' although he'd promised to pass on Benchley's interest in the case to his boss when she returned. To be fair, the fact that an incident room was being set up in relation to the death was enough of a steer for Benchley, as it suggested that there were, at the very least, suspicious circumstances surrounding the death, but he was angry and frustrated by the sergeant's parochial attitude and his reluctance to come clean on what was going on – possibly because the man was unsure of his ground.

Attempts to re-interview the other four models who were at The Philanderer's Club the night of the bombing had then added to Benchley's frustration. Two of them – a Parisian and a girl from Rome – had been given leave by Carol Amis to return home while the affairs of New Light were sorted out. Of the other two, only one – Melanie Jones, the model who, according to Carol Amis, had won the key modelling contract over Felicity Dubois – was at her London address when the detectives called. But in Benchley's own words after the interview, she was about as much use as a 'clockwork orange'.

Tall and thin to the point of emaciation – no doubt a size 6, Angel had enviously commented later – she had the sort of finely chiselled features, Mediterranean tan and silky black hair which any woman would have died for, but it had soon became apparent that there wasn't a lot going on in her pretty little head. Frowning at nearly every question, then shaking her head in response, it was obvious that she would have had difficulty remembering what day it was, let alone coming up with any useful information about the bombing, so in the end they had given up and left.

Julian Grey was their last hope and Benchley's pulse quickened slightly when he heard a chain being pulled back from the front door. At least someone was at home, he mused.

The good-looking young man who opened up to them was nothing like either Benchley or Angel had imagined. Tall and muscular, with shoulder-length blond hair and sharp penetrating blue eyes, he was dressed in a white T-shirt, black baggy trousers and a pair of light blue trainers. But his smile seemed genuine, if a little wry, when Benchley showed him his warrant card, and he invited them in without hesitation.

Then, waving them to white leather armchairs in his luxuriously furnished living room, he leaned back against the fireplace and studied them curiously. 'I must admit, I am intrigued,' he said in a soft, slightly effeminate tone which was in direct contrast to his macho appearance. 'What is all this about?'

After Benchley had explained, Grey pursed his lips in thought for a few seconds, then shrugged. 'Well, I'm afraid I can't be of any help to you with regard to the bombing, Chief Inspector,' he said. 'As you probably know already, I had left the agency when that happened, though I did read about it in the newspapers. Poor Lynn Giles. Such a lovely girl too.'

'Can I ask you where you were on the night?' Benchley asked abruptly, watching Grey's face and anticipating an indignant response to the insinuation his question carried with it.

Instead, Grey emitted a low chuckle. 'Ah, I'm a suspect, am I, Chief Inspector, after my little contretemps with Freddie?' he said. 'How absolutely thrilling. But I'm afraid you're way off beam. I despised the man for the way he'd treated me, but I didn't try to kill him. And bombs?' he rolled his eyes dramatically. 'Horrible things and not my bag at all—'

'So may I ask you again where you were on the night of the blast?' Benchley interjected.

He shrugged. 'Do you know, I haven't the faintest idea,' he said. 'Probably partying somewhere, I usually am. Too long ago and too many vodkas in between for me to remember, though.'

'Yet you do remember reading about the incident in the newspapers?'

'Well, newspapers or the telly, yes. I worked at New Light for around two years and Freddie and I were an item once, so a news story like that does tend to stay in the old memory. As to what I was doing when I heard about it all, however ...' another shrug '... I can't help you, I'm afraid.'

Benchley got the distinct impression that behind the pleasant manner and ready smile, Grey was playing with him, so he changed tack. 'You do know Freddie Baxter is dead, don't you?' he said.

Grey nodded soberly. 'It's all over the city,' he said. 'Fell off a cliff in Cornwall, didn't he?'

'Pleased about that, were you, Mr Grey?' Angel put in provocatively.

An irritable sigh. 'No, Sergeant,' he said with emphasis. 'I wouldn't have wished that on anyone, not even Freddie, but I can't cry crocodile tears and say I'm sorry. Actually I'm quite ambivalent about it. Freddie, you see, turned out to be a rather unpleasant arse.'

Benchley gave a little cough, picking up on the pun and wondering whether it was actually intentional. 'So I believe,' he said. 'Lots of enemies, had he?'

Another laugh, this time with a hard cynical edge. 'Half of celebrity London, I would think, which makes your job rather difficult, I would imagine.'

'Why should it make my job difficult? I'm not investigating Mr Baxter's death and as far as we know, it was an accident anyway.'

Grey was unfazed by the DCI's attempt to catch him out. 'Of course,' he said smoothly, 'but you are investigating the bombing, aren't you? Since you are both here asking me questions about my relationship with

Freddie and if I am pleased he is dead, it's obvious you think he may have been the target of the bomber.'

'Did you see Mr Baxter again after you left the New Light agency?'

'You mean did I follow him to Cornwall and push him off the cliff after the bomb failed to snuff him out?'

Benchley gave a rueful smile. 'Something like that, yes.'

'Well, I'm sorry to disappoint you, Chief Inspector, but the answer is no. I never saw Freddie again after our bust-up, and if it helps to allay your suspicions I have never been to Cornwall in my life.'

'But you were obviously pretty pissed off when he dumped you for Felicity Dubois?'

'Well, I wasn't too happy about it, I must admit. As you already know, we had a row over it. But it was to be expected, I suppose. Freddie was easily distracted and I couldn't compete with that bitch's long legs and pert tits – oh, my apologies, Sergeant Angel, I was forgetting myself.'

Angel inclined her head in acknowledgement and treated him to a faint smile, without commenting on his crude remark, which she sensed had been deliberate anyway. Instead, she said, 'Strange that a pretty girl like Felicity would want to embark on an affair with someone like Freddie Baxter, though, isn't it? After all, he wasn't exactly the catch of the year, was he?'

Grey chuckled again. 'Well put, Sergeant, and one would suppose that she was after the same things as myself. You know, career advancement and financial gain, which I willingly admit to. But the fact is, she had no choice in the matter.'

'How do you mean?'

Grey's face was suddenly bleak. 'Freddie Baxter was a dangerous, odious man, Sergeant, and he was also an ace manipulator who had a knack for digging up the dirt on people and using it to get what he wanted—'

'You're saying he had a hold over Felicity?' Benchley cut in again, leaning forward in his seat and staring at him intently.

Grey nodded. 'And quite a few others, I believe,' he confirmed. 'He once boasted to me that he had dirt on half his staff. Probably an exaggeration, but I am sure it wasn't far from the truth.'

'And what was the dirt he had on Felicity Dubois?'

'No idea, Chief Inspector, but he intimated he had her over a barrel, if you'll pardon the expression, which is why she so willingly succumbed to his advances.'

'What did he have on you then?' Angel queried sharply.

Grey laughed again. 'Sorry to disappoint you, Sergeant, but the answer is nothing. My affair with Freddie was motivated by gain, purely and simply. I was after what his influence in the business could put my way, nothing more.'

'And did you get it?'

'Not from him, no, but I am doing very well with my own salon in the celebrity world anyway,' and he waved an arm around the room to indicate its opulence, 'thanks to my new partner, of course, who has all the connections I could wish for. Now, can I help you with anything else …?'

'Well, Guv,' Angel said to Benchley as they returned to their car in the street outside, 'what do you think about our Mr Grey? A possible?'

Benchley frowned. 'Could be,' he replied as they both climbed aboard. 'Too bloody self-assured for my liking, but after what he told us about Baxter, I reckon Felicity Dubois still has a lot to answer.'

****

Lynn heard the crunch of wheels in the gravel outside her bungalow as she was preparing a light supper for herself. She had left Alan's home shortly after doing the breakfast dishes and since an abrupt change in the weather had produced another warm sunny afternoon, she had spent it lying on the beach as usual. She had only just got back and she grimaced her irritation when she heard the hollow sound of footsteps on the patio decking as her visitor ignored the front door and came round the back.

Maureen O'Donnell wore her usual disarming smile as she poked her head through the open French door. 'Anyone in?'

Lynn forced a smile of her own from the hall doorway and drying her hands on a tea-towel, she beckoned her inside.

'Thought I'd pay you a wee visit before I returned to the station,' the DI said.

Lynn nodded, stepping into the room and indicating a chair. 'Would you like a drink?' she queried. 'I was just making some supper.'

O'Donnell shook her head and sat down. 'Sorry. You know the score. On duty and all that, so I'm afraid it'll have to be a no.'

'Tea? Coffee?'

'No, thanks, I'm grand, so I am.' The DI glance around the room. ''Tis a nice wee place you have here. Been in long?'

Lynn shook her head and sat down on the edge of the settee, still clutching her tea-towel. 'No, just a few weeks, since I was released from hospital.'

O'Donnell made a face. 'Desperate business, that. No one in the frame for it, I suppose?'

Lynn smiled faintly. 'You'd know that better than me, but no, not as far as I'm aware.'

O'Donnell leaned forward in her chair, her expression less relaxed. Now it's down to business, Lynn thought grimly.

'Been to see Vernon Wiles,' the detective began. 'Not a very nice wee man, I think.'

Lynn shrugged. 'Not one of my favourites, no.'

'I gather he's into porn films?'

Damn it! Lynn had guessed the police would find out sooner or later. 'So I believe.'

O'Donnell's gaze was fastened on her face now. 'He told me he and Freddie Baxter were down here to make a porn film and that they'd offered you a part in it?'

Lynn was expecting that and was ready with her reply. 'I told them both to go to hell.'

The detective's smile flickered back. 'Ach, I don't blame you. But ... er ... did it annoy you that they had thought of you that way after you had previously been a top model?'

'Not particularly.'

'Maybe they tried a bit of unwelcome pressure?'

Now Lynn smirked. 'You mean did I murder Freddie Baxter because he was trying to bully me into accepting his offer?'

O'Donnell was not put off by her directness. 'Aye, something like that.'

'Then the answer is no.'

'When did you last speak to Mr Baxter?'

Lynn hesitated very slightly. 'The morning before his ... er ... accident when he came to see me with Mr Wiles.'

O'Donnell's eyes narrowed. She had obviously picked up on the hesitation. 'What makes you think it was an accident?'

'Why would it be anything else?'

'Maybe he committed suicide?'

'Very unlikely. Freddie Baxter was a coward. There's no way he would have topped himself.'

'And you didn't see or speak to him after the morning before his death?'

Lynn shook her head. 'Why would I? I told him and Wiles to get lost and that's exactly what they did.'

'Sure, that was very accommodating of them, so it was'

O'Donnell paused for a second, studying her fixedly, then added with deliberate emphasis, 'Do you know any reason why anyone would want to kill Freddie Baxter?'

Lynn tensed inside, but tried not to show that the question had unnerved her. 'Dozens of them, I would think. He was not a particularly nice man either.'

'Have you anyone in mind?'

'No one specific. But he had a lot of enemies in the Smoke. People he'd shafted businesswise. Models he'd dumped. Bad people he'd crossed.'

'Open season on Freddie then?'

Lynn nodded. 'You should ask Vernon. He could probably name a few.'

'I have. He says everyone liked Freddie.'

'In his dreams.'

'Did he dump you after your injuries?'

Here we go, Lynn mused, back to motive again. 'No,' she said. 'He was very good actually. Gave me a generous pay-off.'

'But he still tried to use you after it had happened. Put you in one of Vernon Wiles' films?'

Lynn sighed heavily. 'Look, Inspector,' she said wearily. 'I never saw Freddie Baxter again after that one meeting in this room and I didn't push him off the cliff, if that's what you're implying. In fact, I had Alan Murray from The Old Customs House over here for dinner the evening Freddie died, so if you don't believe me, you can ask Alan. Furthermore, I have no idea how Freddie died, so I really can't help you anymore.'

O'Donnell nodded and stood up. 'One other thing,' she said. 'We found evidence in the old engine-house of someone sleeping rough. Blankets and a haversack containing dirty clothes. It's pretty old stuff, so could have been there a while, but on the other hand, it might be relevant to our inquiries. Ever seen anyone suspicious wandering about in that vicinity?'

Lynn thought of the hooded man and her recent burglary, but met the detective's gaze without flinching. 'You asked me that before, up on the cliffs, and the answer is still no,' she lied. 'But there are still some walkers using the cliff paths even at this time of the year.'

'The Traffic man who stopped you for speeding says you complained about a stalker?'

Lynn thought quickly. Oh this one was really on the ball, wasn't she?

'Yes,' she admitted, 'but it wasn't true. I was trying to avoid a ticket.'

The DI gave a sympathetic grin, apparently satisfied with her answer, and handed her a business card. 'Okay then, but if you think of anything that might help us with our inquiries, would you give me a wee ring me on this number,' she said. 'In the meantime, it might be a good idea to keep your doors and windows locked at night.'

Lynn showed her to the door. 'I always do,' she said and watched her pass the side windows on her way to her car at the front. Only when O'Donnell had finally driven away, did she relax and make straight for the bottle of white wine on the kitchen table. Why on earth hadn't she said about the hooded man, she asked herself? And why rubbish her story about the stalker? She'd had a golden opportunity to get O'Donnell and the rest of them off her back and had wasted it – or had she? No, girl, she thought as she sipped her wine, the last thing you want is involvement as a possible witness and the inevitable publicity churned out by the hyenas of the press. Done that. Got the T-shirt. Seen the video. And what good did it do you, except force you into hiding? So stay out of it all. Let the police play their little games and just keep schtum. That's what all good survivors did.

****

Felicity Dubois pulled up outside The Blue Ketch Inn in Cornwall at just after 6pm. 'What a hole!' she murmured to herself as she climbed out of the BMW and stared at the thatched, white-walled cottages huddled together in a half-circle around the pub, as if trying to shield it from prying eyes.

It had been a long frustrating drive from London, with heavy delays on both the M4 and M5 motorways, but now, finally in Cornwall, tired and hungry, the place she had booked over the phone for her intended overnight stay was a big let-down.

Like all the other models at New Light, she had managed to park her commitments for a couple of days while the agency's solicitor and the bank executers sorted out the legal position regarding the company, following Freddie Baxter's death. There were still important contracts to fulfil, but as far as she knew, the agency boss had not made any provision for someone to take over the reins in the event of his death, which meant that everyone was in total limbo – although to be fair, Freddie could not have known when he'd left for Cornwall that he would end up at the bottom of a cliff.

A hush fell on the crowded bar when the model pushed open the door and she felt all eyes on her as she stepped up to the counter, conscious of most of the gazes studying her legs and wishing she had put on a much longer skirt than she was now wearing. The snake-eyed bartender even bent over the counter for a closer look as she approached, but under her contemptuous stare, he gave an insipid grin and studied her face instead.

'You've got it, chaps,' she drawled, tapping one thigh. 'My pins go right up to my arse, okay?'

A faint titter of amusement rippled through the other customers and Snake-eyes coughed his embarrassment. 'What would you be wantin', Miss?' he queried. 'Drink, is it? We does good food 'ere too.'

'You should already have me booked in,' she replied. 'Name's Denise Cross. She nodded towards the same corner table, which unbeknown to her, Freddie Baxter and Vernon Wiles had taken the afternoon they had arrived. 'A glass of red wine and something to eat first, though. Then I'll see the room.'

Snake-eyes raised an eyebrow. 'No problem,' he said, reaching behind him to remove a key from the board on the wall by the optics, adding, 'Driven far today?'

'From London,' she replied, taking the key from him.

'Lon'on, eh?' he said and raised both eyebrows this time. 'Lots of folk comin' down 'ere from Lon'on lately.'

Dubois looked surprised. 'You have others staying?'

'Only one now,' he replied. 'Used to be two of 'em. Come down together, they did. Then one feller went and fell off a cliff.'

She knew he was referring to Freddie Baxter, but didn't seek clarification. 'That's awful,' she said. 'And the other one?'

'Still 'ere,' he said, pouring her a glass of wine and nodding towards the beamed ceiling. 'Got Coverack, my best room, too, else you could've 'ad it.'

'That's a pity.'

He nodded. 'Yeah, well, 'e decided to stay on till after the post mortem. Says 'e owes it to the feller what died. Friend of 'is apparently.'

'What a lovely thing to do.'

Snake-eyes shook his head slowly. 'Maybe, but 'e was all set to go. Then 'e gets a visit from the police and changes 'is mind.' He leaned forward, lowering his voice conspiratorially. 'Rarely leaves 'is room, you know – 'as all 'is meals sent up and left outside the door. Funny business, that. Like 'e knows more'n 'e's tellin', if you catch my drift.'

Oh, I catch your drift all right, she thought grimly, guessing that the man in question had to be Vernon Wiles. But she made no comment.

'You visitin' 'ereabouts then?' Snake-eyes went on, 'or just passin' through?'

Dubois took a sip of her wine and studied him thoughtfully for a moment. Obviously not much of what went on locally escaped the inquisitive barman, so odds on, he could fill her in on little old Lynn Giles. It was worth a try and updates were always handy.

'Calling in on an old school-friend actually,' she said after a pause. 'Lynn … er … Mary Tresco. You know her?'

He nodded. 'Lives out at Bootleg Cove,' he said. 'Not been 'ere long. Don't mix with local folk. Strange wench, I reckons.' He grinned. 'You'll be lucky to catch 'er at 'ome, though.'

'Why's that?' she asked casually, taking another sip of her drink.'

He leaned across the counter again. 'Got took up with another Emmett,' he replied. 'Writer feller livin' up at The Old Customs 'Ouse on the 'eadland.' He gave an extravagant wink. 'Be all accounts, shares 'is bed sometimes too.'

'Good for her,' she retorted sharply. 'Maybe he'll be able to find a friend for me.'

Then smirking at the shocked expression on the barman's face, she picked up her glass of wine and a menu from the counter and headed over to her table.

She ordered 20 minutes later – impressed when her lasagne and salad arrived within a quarter of an hour, but not so impressed when her fork discovered the soft squidgy filling. Grimacing, but very hungry, she forced the meal down nevertheless and ordered another couple of large red wines to wash away the greasy cheese taste.

Then sitting back in her seat, she watched the bar gradually fill up with locals until it became so crowded that even the counter was almost hidden from view. Time to go. Collecting her overnight bag from her car outside, she headed for the stairs leading to the upper floor where she guessed the bedrooms would be located.

The corridor at the top was poorly lit and smelled damp and musty, but the illumination was sufficient for her to find her way and she saw that there were only six rooms anyway. Three on each side, all individually labelled – unbeknown to her – with the names of different Cornish coves. The fob on her key-ring bore the name "Kynance" and she found the corresponding name on the first door to her right. The door was unlocked and moonlight flooded the room through the window opposite, revealing dark wooden furniture and a double bed smothered by a heavily patterned oversized quilt. 'Great,' she muttered sarcastically. 'Home from home.'

Switching on another ineffective light, she kicked the door shut with her heel and dumped her bag on the bed. From the bar downstairs she could hear raucous laughter and the clink of glasses. Then a car pulled up at the front of the place, rap music blaring out of its speakers, before the driver cut the engine and the noise ceased.

Crossing to the window, she checked to make sure her own car was still there, then pulling the curtains firmly across, she dropped on to the edge of the bed and sat there thinking for a few moments. More raucous laughter from downstairs and someone dropped a glass with a loud crash. She scowled. It seemed like it was going to be a noisy night.

Unzipping the bag she had dumped on the bed, she rummaged around inside and produced a small hip-flask. Unscrewing it, still with her face set in a thoughtful frown, she took several mouthfuls of the American rye whisky it contained. The spirit flowed through her like fire, drawing a sharp gasp from her before she resealed the flask and returned it to her bag. But it had been what she'd needed, and with the sleeping tablet she intended taking before turning in, at least it should ensure she got a good night's sleep. First, though, she had that other little job to do.

The corridor outside was deserted. She studied it for a moment in the smoky ceiling lights. A sign on the door of the room directly opposite said "Coverack" – Vernon Wiles' room – and there was a covered plate and clean cutlery wrapped in a napkin on a tray outside, cold to the touch and apparently ignored. She smiled grimly. If the lasagne she had just sampled was anything to go by, it wasn't surprising that Vernon had lost his appetite. Still, whatever the reason, it was time to find out what, if anything, the little creep might have chosen to keep to himself about Freddie Baxter's demise? After all, there shouldn't be any secrets between friends, should there? And she smiled grimly as she knocked on the door.

CHAPTER 14

Once again, Lynn Giles couldn't sleep and she finally got up to another warm, dry day. But after a shower and a leisurely breakfast, the azure ocean beckoned and she decided on a swim to cool off. Conscious of the fact that there might still be police activity on the clifftop by the old engine-house, this time she opted for a black one-piece bathing costume instead of her birthday suit. Not out of any sense of modesty in case some randy copper got an eyeful, but because, thin as the material was, it at least hid most of her unsightly scars.

Seagulls wheeled noisily overhead and tiny crabs scuttled away from her feet like little old men as she picked her way down the beach to the chuckling surf. It was an idyllic, peaceful scene and it seemed incredible that such a short time before, Freddie Baxter's corpse had lain broken and bloodied on the rocks at the foot of the cliffs a few hundred yards from where she now stood, ankle deep in the surf.

Poor old Freddie. What an ignominious end for him. Especially as he'd always hated the sea. Rather ironic really and she gave a bitter smile. Still, she couldn't honestly say she was sorry. He had been an absolute arsehole to her since he had plucked her from the sleazy nightclub, where she had been performing as a nude pole-dancer a few years before, and had then threatened her with the release of explicit photographs of her act to the press if she didn't do exactly as she was told. In her opinion, he had deserved all he'd got and she had no intention of shedding false tears over what had happened.

Striding into the surf, she threw herself forward when it got to her waist and pulled away from the beach in a confident crawl, heading towards the gap between the two arms of the cove and the open sea, the sun pricking her shoulders and salt stinging her lips with each stroke. She'd had no intention of swimming out of the cove this time. The water seemed a lot more choppy than usual and she knew enough about Cornwall to avoid taking any liberties with the old man of the sea. So, within a few yards of the jagged mouth, as the water became choppier and the current increased its pull on her slender body, she performed an arc and turned back towards the shore. And it was then that she saw the dark figure creeping along the decking at the rear of The Beach House, apparently peering in through the windows. Her burglar was back to turn over the place again, the cheeky sod! Well, this time he had made a big mistake.

Controlling her inner fury with an effort, she resisted the temptation to increase her speed, maintaining the same long measured strokes she was so used to. An extra push would have created more water disturbance and risked attracting attention. Coupled with which, she wanted to catch her man in the act this time, and not arrive on her doorstep gasping for breath before he'd actually gained entry.

The shingle bit into the soles of her feet as she emerged from the sea and she went for a direct approach to The Beach House instead of sticking to the patches of soft sand. Ordinarily the sharp jabs would have brought her to a stop with a cry of pain, but she kept going in silence, her teeth gritted with determination and her gaze never leaving the decking. The intruder had disappeared – possibly around the side of the place – and she prayed he hadn't seen her and already taken to his heels. She needed to at least catch a better glimpse of the bastard after all this.

The wooden steps were hot on her bare feet, but again she put up with the discomfort, deliberately taking her time climbing up to the patio, creeping rather than walking to the top, then pausing to listen. But all she heard was the murmur of the sea. Even the gulls seemed to be holding their breath.

She turned left, leaving wet foot-prints on the decking, and paused at the corner of the house to peer along the sideway – and immediately found herself staring into a pair of mocking brown eyes.

****

Detective Chief Inspector Benchley and DI Angel paid a visit to the luxury apartment block Felicity Dubois called home at just after 9am.

'You've missed her,' the security man on the desk said after they had been buzzed into the public foyer and had stated their business.

'How so, Mr ... er ...?' Angel encouraged.

'Dolby, Miss. Terry Dolby. She went off somewhere yesterday – for a few days, I reckon. Had a suitcase with her when I picked her up on the CCTV camera going down to the basement car park, and I saw her motor leave a few minutes later.'

'What kind of motor?'

'Maroon Beamer ... 7 Series.'

'Don't suppose you got the registration number?'

Dolby smirked. 'Didn't need to. We keep the regs' of all the residents motors here.'

'Jot it down for us, would you?'

Dolby frowned. 'Dunno 'bout that. Confidential, see. What's she done?'

Angel frowned. 'We can get it soon enough from the DVLC.'

Dolby thought a moment before nodding and tapping the keys of his computer. Then, tearing off a strip from a small notebook, he wrote the number down and handed it to her.

'No idea where she was going?' Benchley queried.

Dolby gave an apologetic shrug. 'Haven't the faintest,' he said.

The detective treated him to a thin smile. 'No, I suppose being just the janitor here you wouldn't get to know much about your residents.'

Dolby scowled. 'Oh I know more than you think,' he said, puffing out his chest and adding, 'And I ain't no janitor neither. I'm a security officer.'

'Of course you are,' Benchley patronised, and turning towards Angel flicked his eyes towards the entrance door and handed her the car keys. 'Nip back to the car, will you?' he said. 'See if there are any messages on the radio for us.'

The DI cottoned on immediately. Her boss was obviously about to do something naughty and didn't want to involve her in whatever it was. It wouldn't be the first time he had done that either, she mused, as she took the keys and headed for the door. His unorthodox approach to police work was almost legendary.

The security man watched her go and nodded approvingly. 'Good idea to keep in touch with the old control room,' he said, puffing out his chest again, plainly oblivious to what was actually going on. 'I have to do the same, you know.'

Benchley smiled again. 'No chance of me popping up to Miss Dubois' apartment, is there?' she queried mildly.

Dolby shook his head. 'Sorry, ain't allowed, but I could take a message up for you for when she gets back.'

Benchley made a face. 'Not possible, I'm afraid. Police business. Confidential and all that, you know.'

Dolby nodded and tapped the side of his nose with a forefinger. 'Comprenez-vous,' he said, reminding Benchley of David Jason in the television series *Only Fools and Horses*. 'In the same business, ain't we?'

Benchley let the wallet displaying his warrant card flip open in his hand as it rested on the desk, revealing a back pocket stuffed with £10 and £20 notes. 'Helping the police with their inquiries is part of it all too, isn't it?' he said innocently.

The policeman saw Dolby lick his slack lips and his piggy eyes fastened on the wallet with a greedy intensity, then darted a quick glance around the small room.

'And such public-spirited cooperation is always deserving of recompense, don't you think?' Benchley went on, pushing the wallet towards him.

Dolby threw another glance around the room, then reached forward and deftly removed three £20 notes. He would have made a return trip, but Benchley beat him to it and slipped the wallet back into his coat pocket.

'Number 30, third floor,' the security man muttered, scanning the foyer for the third time, before turning to unlock what turned out to be a key cabinet beneath the desk. 'Master key,' he added, pushing a pamphlet about the premises across the desk towards him with the key inside, 'and I want it back. You savvy?'

'No problem,' Benchley murmured, smiling as he carefully picked up the pamphlet, folded it over the key and slipped it into his pocket. 'But it would be helpful if your security camera was pointing another way while I'm up there, if you follow me?'

Another scowl. 'You won't say I let you in?'

'Absolutely not. I would be in the shit too then, wouldn't I?'

That seemed to satisfy the little man and seconds later Benchley was in the lift and heading for the third floor, wondering how the hell he was going to make a case for recovering his bribe from the department's informant's fund when he got back.

Apartment 30 was at the end of a short, thickly carpeted corridor and the security camera had been electronically swivelled to focus in the opposite direction by the time he stepped out of the lift. He knocked a couple of times to ensure the apartment was actually empty, then stared up and down the corridor to make sure he was alone. It was deserted, but maybe not for long. Quickly pulling on a pair of gloves, he slipped the key in the lock, stepped through and closed the door quietly behind him.

Safely inside, he stopped to listen for a few moments, but there was nothing. The place was as still as his own departmental archives on a Sunday.

A quick check revealed a beautifully appointed bedroom, a marble bathroom and a kitchen shimmering with stainless steel. But it was the living room he was interested in and he studied it from the doorway for a second before stepping through.

In the street below, the muffled drone of traffic only just penetrated the triple glazing and the sharp *ping* of the lift in the corridor outside froze him for a moment as he waited with pounding heart for the sound of a key turning in the lock of the external door. But nothing happened and he relaxed with a heavy sigh.

Pictures of Felicity Dubois in a variety of poses crammed one wall of the living room and the leather sofa was strewn with fashion magazines and more revealing photo shots of her. The walnut cocktail cabinet had been left open, a dirty crystal glass and a half-full Vodka bottle occupying the flap, and the big wide-screen television was on standby.

Benchley frowned, thinking that maybe Dubois didn't intend being away for as long as the security man had thought, or alternatively had left things the way they were in anticipation of a cleaner calling, which meant he would have to work fast.

The policeman had no idea what he was looking for, but the model had achieved such a level of prominence in the investigation that much closer scrutiny was certainly called for. To his mind, that justified recourse to the old unofficial "Ways and Means Act", so often used by CID officers to get a result. But embarking on what was plainly an illegal entry and search, he had no illusions as to what the outcome would be if he were to be discovered and he tried not to think about what incarceration in Wormwood Scrubs prison might be like.

Consigning that thought to the back of his mind, he sifted through a pile of papers – mostly bills and receipts – dumped on a coffee table, but found nothing of interest. Carefully putting the correspondence back exactly as he had found it, he turned his attention to a small corner bureau, but it was locked. He frowned. Bugger it! In his experience, a locked drawer or bureau in a suspect's home often held guilty secrets – or at the very least some nice confidential material which could be of value to a police investigation. All he had to do was find the bloody key. That was, providing Dubois didn't have the only one with her on her key ring.

Turning round to scan the room again, he tried to spot where a key might be hidden. But although it was a modern apartment, there were so many likely places and he just didn't have the time for a thorough search. Dubois might have forgotten something and decide to come back or that cleaner might turn up any minute to clear up the mess the model had left behind.

Yet he couldn't just leave the place without making an effort. There were several vases in various places around the room and he checked those first. Nothing, not even underneath. The stainless steel standard lamp was clean too and a cursory examination of the television and an expensive-looking music system also produced a big fat zero. His frown deepening, he was about to turn his attention to the bedroom, when the cocktail cabinet caught his eye again.

He shook his head. Surely no one would be stupid enough to hide a key in something like that?

He was wrong. It was under the ice bucket. The right key too. A second later he had the lid of the bureau open and was peering inside, and he didn't have to look far before he found something of interest. The gummed seal of the A4 envelope which lay on top of a pile of papers had been torn open and he glimpsed what looked like a photograph inside. Turning the envelope round so that the torn end was towards him, he eased it open a little further. Then inserting two fingers in the gap, he carefully pulled the contents out on to the now horizontal flap of the bureau – and with a sense of shock, found himself staring at a selection of really obscene black and white photographs involving a number of different naked men and women in various sexual positions, with Felicity Dubois occupying centre stage.

'Well, well, well,' he breathed, his heart now pounding. 'You dirty little cow!'

He didn't need the wisdom of *Hercule Poirot* to appreciate the fact that if pictures like these were ever to fall into the hands of the media, it would be curtains for Dubois' career. So why had the model decided to hang on to them? Pretty obvious as far as Benchley was concerned and he smiled grimly as he thought of the envelope, which had obviously been torn open in a rush. Maybe it wasn't a case of Dubois hanging on to the photos at all, but rather that she hadn't yet had time to destroy them, which meant they had only just been received – or more likely retrieved.

Flicking through the photographs again, he came across the confirmation – a couple of unsigned typed letters, addressed to Freddie Baxter and headed "Re FD Pics", and asking for £1,000 payment.

He smiled grimly. 'So, nasty old Freddie's did have a hold on you, did he, Miss Dubois?' he murmured. 'Just like Julian Grey said. Point is, did you pay him off to get the pics or maybe come up with a more permanent solution?'

Gently sliding the prints and letters back into the envelope in the same order, he replaced the envelope in its original position before closing and locking the bureau and returning the key to its hiding place.

Then quitting the living room, he wandered into the kitchen for a final check before leaving, noting with unashamed envy the expensive-looking double oven, the big American-style fridge-freezer and the stainless steel work surfaces over what looked like solid oak cupboards. But there was nothing of interest there – apart from the obvious fact that Dubois was an untidy bitch. The work surfaces were cluttered with dirty cutlery and cups and plates, and a loaf of sliced bread leaning out of its plastic bag had tipped a couple of slices into the sink. Either Dubois had left in a hurry or she didn't have to worry about clearing up after herself anyway. Warning bells sounded in Benchley's head. As he'd suspected – a cleaner. There had to be. Time to go.

He returned to the hall, but stopped briefly by an ornate, gold-coloured telephone on a half-moon table. There was a memo pad on the table and he saw that it bore a scribbled note. Picking the pad up he scanned the two short lines quickly and his heart raced. "Blue Ketch Inn, The Lizard," it read and there was a telephone number underneath. The Lizard? That was in Cornwall – where Lynn Giles had taken refuge. It was more than likely that Dubois had been booking accommodation, which meant she could already be on her way to the South West. That didn't bode well at all, he mused, and he frowned as he turned to the door. But even as he reached for the handle, the sound of the key turning in the lock of the external door gave him an uncomfortable jolt. Shit! The cleaner had arrived and she had her own key with her. He had dallied much too long.

He just had time to dart back into the kitchen and conceal himself behind the door before the main apartment door opened and closed again and he heard the swish of clothing in the hallway. Now what? He was trapped.

Fists clenched and eyes closed tightly with the tension of the moment, he heard someone step into the kitchen and stop level with the open door behind which he was hiding. For a second he thought his presence had been detected and waited for the shout, which meant discovery. But instead he heard a muttered oath and the voice of what sounded like an elderly woman commenting, 'Lazy bitch,' as she evidently surveyed the mess on the work surfaces. Then through the crack between the door and the frame, he saw brief movement and heard the swish of clothes again as the woman went back into the hallway. The crack of a plug being inserted into the wall dividing the kitchen from the living room, then a vacuum roared into life.

Leaving his hiding place, Benchley crept to the doorway and peered around the frame. A thin, dark-haired woman was busy vacuuming the thick living room carpet and she had her back to him. Gritting his teeth, Benchley took a chance and made for the apartment door. His fingers fumbled with the catch, but then it was open and he was back in the corridor. Closing the door gently behind him, he took a deep trembling breath. Bloody hell, man, he thought, that really was close, but had the risk been worth it? He gave a fierce, humourless grin as he pulled off his gloves and headed for the lift to return the key to the desk. In the words of movie star, John Wayne, 'You betcha,' he breathed.

Angel was waiting expectantly and very nervously in the car park beside their car and she breathed a sigh of relief when he reappeared.

'Been a naughty boy again, have you, Guv?' she queried drily as she climbed behind the wheel.

He smiled grimly and settled into the passenger seat beside her. 'You could say that,' he said and told her what he had found.

She whistled, starting the engine. 'Dirty bitch' she exclaimed.

He nodded. 'My sentiments entirely. But it's beginning to look like she is a lot more than that,' he replied grimly. 'Which is what worries me. Especially as it sounds as if she's heading for Cornwall, where Lynn Giles is holed up.'

Angel's eyes narrowed. 'You really do think she was the one behind the bombing of The Philanderer's Club then?' she said. 'No longer just a possibility?'

He selected a cigarette from a half empty packet, lit up, then offered the packet to her, returning it to his pocket when she shook her head. 'We can't say anything for certain, even at this stage,' he replied, 'but think about it. Her boss almost certainly had a hold over her, just as Julian Grey claimed. That's why she had to let Baxter screw her. My money is on the dirty pictures, which she probably retrieved after his death. Seems to me that her apparent willingness to give him what he wanted had nothing to do with trying to gain a leg-up in the modelling business, as Carol Amis seemed to believe. She was forced into it and I can't think of a better motive for murder, can you?'

'It's certainly plausible.'

'It's a lot more than plausible. Think about the bomber's MO. It was known that Baxter would be supervising the fashion show from the lounge, which was right next door to the room Dubois then insisted on vacating. And we have forensic evidence to say that this was precisely where the bomb was placed. It was just the bomber's bad luck that Freddie was called to the other end of the building when the device went off, and Lynn Giles' misfortune that she happened to be in that room in place of Dubois at the critical moment.'

Angel nodded. 'And if Dubois was the one who planted the bomb,' she extrapolated slowly, 'it's more than likely she was also responsible for topping our bomb-maker in the Islington doss and pushing her boss off the cliff in Cornwall?'

'Very good,' he commented. 'We'll make a detective of you yet.'

She ignored the sarcastic remark. 'Okay, so it's possible she stiffed Petrović or arranged for someone to do it for her. But you forget that Carol Amis said Dubois was at a modelling shoot on the Sunday when Baxter's body was found, so she could hardly have been in Cornwall when he took his dive off the cliffs.'

Benchley nodded. 'And *you* forget that Amis told us Dubois was off work on the Friday and Saturday, which gave her plenty of time to get to Cornwall and back again via our excellent motorway system after the murder was committed.'

'In time for her photo-shoot on the Sunday?'

'Exactly.'

Angel engaged gear and pulled away. 'All nice and tidy then?'

He scowled. 'Far from it. At the moment it's all hypothesis. I can't prove a damned thing and I can't use the pics in Dubois' flat to establish a motive because my search was illegal in the first place.'

'What about asking for a search warrant?'

'On what grounds? Again, I haven't any evidence to put forward as a reason for one.'

'So what's our next move?'

'Well, you are going to get the team stuck into some background inquiries, not only on Felicity Dubois but also other key staff at the New Light Modelling Agency. Check out Baxter's jilted lovers and Lynn Giles' ex-boyfriend, Greg Norman, too. His address is in the file.'

'You are convinced that this conspiracy is an inside job then?'

'Aren't you? And I suspect there is more going on there behind the scenes than we at first realised. Let me know what you dig up.'

She gave him an old-fashioned look. 'And what will you be doing while the rest of us are slogging away at all this?'

He thought about that for a moment, then drew heavily on his cigarette. 'You know what?' he said. 'I think I might take a drive down to the Cornish Riviera to see how our country cousins investigate suspicious deaths. Maybe I'll even call on Felicity Dubois at The Blue Ketch too.'

CHAPTER 15

Lynn Giles stared at her "intruder" in astonishment.

Tall and slender and with a figure any woman would have died for, Felicity Dubois was wearing the sort of figure-hugging black leather trousers and tight white sweater, which accentuated her assets to a T.

'Felicity?' Lynn gasped, dripping water on to the decking. 'How the hell did you find me? No one but Freddie was supposed to know where I was.'

Her former rival shrugged, adjusting the long strap of the designer bag she was carrying over one shoulder. 'Does it matter? I'm here now anyway.'

'So *why* are you here?'

The glint in Dubois' brown eyes became even more pronounced. 'I wanted to see how you were doing.'

'You wanted to see how I was *doing*?'

Dubois nodded and took a step forward. 'Right on, hon. That was a bad thing you did, leaving us all without even saying goodbye.'

Lynn held up one hand in front of her as a signal for her to stay where she was. 'Yeah, I bet you were really cut up about it.'

'Sure was, hon. I missed you lots.'

Now Lynn laughed – a hard, humourless sound. 'Did you now? Was that during or after shagging my ex?' she sneered. Then before Dubois could reply she gave a long shiver as the cold from her dip started to get to her, and with a dismissive wave of one hand, she turned away from her visitor. 'Now I have to get dressed, so goodbye – and shut the front gate after you've left, will you?'

Throwing the patio door wide, she stepped quickly inside and closed it behind her, leaving Dubois standing on the decking, staring after her.

She heard the door open again a few moments later as she was towelling herself down in the bathroom and grimacing, grabbed her robe to stride back into the living room.

Dubois was standing by the settee, studying her with a faint, arrogant smile playing on her full, red-glossed lips.

'I thought I told you to go?' Lynn snapped.

The other nodded. 'So you did, sweetness, but we need to talk.'

'I have nothing to say to say to you. I thought I'd made that plain? Does my ex know you're here?'

'Hell, no – and it doesn't matter anyhow. Greg Norman and I are done.'

'You mean you dumped him after he dumped me for you?'

Dubois shrugged. 'He wasn't much of a shag, so I got bored – and he was only a distraction while I was screwing Freddie anyway.'

Lynn gave a short laugh. 'Freddie had more going for him in that department, did he?'

Dubois chuckled and dropped on to the settee, crossing her legs at the knee. 'Freddie – now there's a thought. Well, he was a lot more imaginative, I'll say that for him.'

'So what was it like? The shagging, I mean? Did he take you up against the wall or doggy fashion? I'd really like to know.'

Dubois chuckled again, unperturbed by her obscene innuendos. 'Every which way, hon, and you'd better believe it.' She produced a gold-coloured cigarette case from her pocket and flicking open the lid, selected a filter-tip. 'So how's the old memory these days?' she went on, changing the subject and lighting up with a matching lighter.

Lynn's eyes narrowed. 'Memory? What are you talking about?'

Dubois tapped her forehead with her forefinger. 'Still trapped in there is it? Who or what you saw the night of the bombing? Old amnesia still keeping it buried, is it?'

'How do you know about my amnesia?'

'Maybe a little bird told me.'

'So what's it to you anyway?'

'Well, think about it. If I can find you so easily, other people not as nice as me can do the same.'

'Don't tell me you're concerned for my safety?'

Dubois didn't answer, just blew smoke rings. 'Big mistake talking to Old Bill you know?' she said, her expression suddenly bleak.

Lynn snorted contemptuously. 'You won't get anywhere trying to frighten me,' she said.

'I didn't come all this way to frighten you,' Dubois replied, 'but after what happened to poor old Freddie, I'd be remiss not to point it out. I hear the police are treating his death as suspicious?'

'How do you know that?'

Dubois waved one hand airily. 'Local gossip, hon. It's all around the place.'

'And what has it got to do with me?'

Dubois studied her intently for a moment, as if trying to visually reinforce what she was about to say. 'Could be fat Freddie was the target in the first place,' she said. 'Maybe someone finally got to him down here, which means some very nasty people could already be on your doorstep?'

'So why haven't these so-called "nasty people" tried anything before now?'

'Possibly because of the heat generated by Freddie's death. They could be biding their time until things quieten down. Seen any dodgy strangers around lately, have you? Or had any suspicious things happen?'

Lynn thought about the hooded man on the clifftop and her recent break-in and felt a sudden chill crawl down her spine. 'Not so as I've noticed,' she lied. Then abruptly crossing the room to the patio doors, she indicated the still open door with one hand. 'Now, I have absolutely no idea why you came here, but I suggest you leave anyway.'

Dubois' smile this time was one of contempt and climbing to her feet, she deliberately stubbed out her cigarette on the polished top of the coffee table set to one side of the settee. 'Oh I don't think so,' she said softly and slid a hand almost casually into her bag, which was now back on her shoulder. 'Because, you see, I've got a little present for you.'

Lynn picked up the menace in her tone and stiffened, wondering after the model's sinister warnings exactly what she was about to pull out of her bag.

She never found out. The voice on the patio behind her put a stop to any further interaction between Dubois and herself.

'Miss Tresco?'

Lynn looked up quickly to see a young man, maybe in his mid-teens, dressed in faded jeans and a denim jacket, standing there awkwardly, clutching a large bouquet. She hadn't heard a vehicle arrive at the bungalow and for a moment was taken aback by his sudden appearance.

'For you, Miss,' he said, then added with a cheeky grin, 'Somebody loves you.'

As Lynn stepped out on to the patio to take the bouquet from him, Dubois quickly squeezed past her. 'Watch your back, hon,' the model breathed in her ear. 'See you again.' Then treating the gaping delivery boy to an extravagant suggestive wink, she disappeared round the corner of the building.

Lynn stood for a several minutes at the front window of the bungalow after Dubois' BMW had driven away in a cloud of exhaust fumes, followed closely by the old white Ford van of the delivery boy.

Fear was welling up inside her like a hungry beast. Why had Felicity come all the way down from London to see her? Why was the model so keen to find out whether she had recovered from her amnesia? Why had she been at such pains to suggest a possible connection between The Philanderer's Club bombing and Freddie Baxter's death, and to emphasise Lynn's vulnerability?

'Big mistake talking to Old Bill,' she'd warned. 'Watch your back.' What was meant by those words? Were they intended as a thinly veiled threat? In which case, was she somehow mixed up in The Philanderer's Club bombing and the death of Freddie Baxter? And what had she been about to produce from her shoulder bag before being interrupted? A gun? A knife? Did she have murder in her heart? It didn't seem plausible. Felicity had always been a "wild child" and intensely ambitious, which was why she and Lynn had become rivals. But murder and planting a bomb? Somehow that didn't fit. Yet her parting shot, 'See you again', had certainly sounded ominous and Lynn's first instinct was to make a point of checking round the bungalow to ensure the front door and patio doors were locked and all windows securely closed, just as she had after being followed home by the hooded man days before.

But then she realised that what she was doing was pointless. She could hardly shut herself away within four walls for ever. She would have to go out sooner or later. No, the answer was not to succumb to blind panic, but to maintain a sensible perspective and at the same time keep her wits about her. She couldn't do any more than that.

Then she remembered her flowers, which she had left on the window sill. Taking them to the kitchen in search of a vase she looked for a card. There wasn't one, but she knew instinctively who they were from and she smiled as she put them in water. Two bouquets in one week, Mr Murray, she mused. You really do know how to cheer a girl up.

****

Detective Inspector Maureen O'Donnell frowned as she got out of CID car in the parking area a few yards from the clifftop where Freddie Baxter had met his death. She didn't really know why she had decided to revisit the spot and she sensed that her cynical DS, Nick Halloran, who had driven her there under protest due to his own heavy caseload, thought she was simply wasting their time. After all, despite what the pathologist had intimated, the previous intensive police search of the scene had turned up nothing to suggest Baxter's death had been anything but accidental and her own inquiries had produced a big fat zilch. Yet the voice deep inside her head telling her to go back to the scene had refused to be ignored, and in the end she had succumbed to its insistent nagging.

It was mid-afternoon and the air was very still and humid as she sauntered towards the old ruined engine-house, with its attendant finger-like chimney stack thrusting grimly into the heavy grey sky above the gorse and tangle of stunted trees lining both sides of the footpath.

A strand of the blue and white police tape which had been put up across the footpath during the search of the scene now curled around a nearby gorse bush just feet from the crumbling building, and the tyre tracks of the patrol car and Ford Transit were still clearly visible in the soft grass.

She walked right past the engine-house to start with, following the footpath through the scrub to the gaunt skeleton of the wrought-iron seat close to the cliff edge. For a few moments she stood there, staring at the foot of the cliffs and the foam spewing over the rocks where Freddie Baxter had met his death. She could see nothing sticking out of the cliff face on which he could have struck his head as he'd pitched over, but there again, that was only one possibility the pathologist had put forward, and it was almost impossible to see all the way down the ragged drop because of the contours of the rocks and the clinging vegetation.

Sensing Halloran fidgeting impatiently behind her, she turned with a smile. 'Okay, Nick,' she said, 'let's just have another look at the engine-house. Then we'll head back.'

As before, a dank, urine-like smell greeted her when she approached the ruined building. She ducked her head through the doorway, shining her torch around the gloomy interior. But there was nothing to see – just a cleared area, where her colleagues had found the sleeping bag and blankets, and a couple of small heaps of rubble poking through a patch of undernourished nettles and weeds that strained towards the light filtering into the place via the doorway and the single high window.

So what had drawn her back here? In the past her hunches had proved to be worth following up, but maybe this time she had been misled. Perhaps she was finally losing it? Making something out of nothing. Sensing things that just weren't there. Everyone in the department seemed to be satisfied that Freddie Baxter had simply fallen off the cliff, so why didn't she just accept that as the most likely scenario and move on? Give herself and the rest of the team a break? Claim her leave and head for Corsica?

She was on the verge of doing just that as she turned to leave the engine-house – ready to drop the whole thing there and then and eat humble pie – when she heard Halloran's shout. Ducking back through the doorway, she was just in time to see her overweight 40-year-old DS charging across the heath after a slender figure in a short hooded coat. Halloran certainly had some bottle, but it was pretty obvious that his cigarette-weakened lungs left him little chance of catching his quarry. With an oath, she dug her toes into the soft earth and joined the chase.

Easily outstripping the DS, she homed in on the fleeing figure like a human torpedo and hurling herself at him in the last few feet, brought him down with a rugby tackle. It was only then that she suddenly realised she hadn't the slightest idea what her prisoner had done and why they were pursuing him.

'Great tackle, Guv,' Halloran wheezed, stumbling up to them. 'Shit-bag was making for the engine-house when he saw me and bolted.'

Bruised and winded, O'Donnell climbed to her feet, hauling her captive up with her by one arm. A thin florid face, with a long narrow nose and a straggly grey beard peered at her out of the hood. Pale blue eyes, one of them half-closed, studied her with a crafty half-smile hovering over the thin lips and a dirty bony hand clutched at the front of the hooded jacket, as if trying to pull it tighter in an effort to retreat inside it.

The man was obviously elderly – probably in his 60s – and from the state of him and the earthy unwashed smell which clung to him like a miasma, it was apparent that he was a vagrant.

'And who the devil might you be?' O'Donnell queried sharply, pulling away from him slightly to distance herself from his unpleasant odour. 'And why did you run away?'

To her surprise, the old man chuckled. 'Daniel Froggett at your service, madam,' he replied a little breathlessly and in a soft, cultured voice. 'As to why I ran, well, I sussed your companion was Old Bill and I'm not particularly fond of the police, you see.'

'So what were you doing here?'

He sighed. 'I left my worldly belongings in the engine-house a few nights ago and came back to retrieve them.'

'Did you now? But why leave them there in the first place?'

He shook his head slowly. 'Had to,' he said. 'I came back one evening to find police all over the place and my little doss sealed off, so I made myself scarce.'

'Do you know why the police were there?'

'I saw later in a newspaper that a poor fellow had fallen off the cliffs. Tragic.'

O'Donnell studied him thoughtfully for a few seconds, but for some reason decided not to pursue that line of questioning for the moment. Instead, she released his arm and nodded to Halloran. 'So let's see what you've got in your pockets, Mr Froggett – Nick, do the honours, will you?'

Halloran gave her an old-fashioned look. 'Me?'

She nodded. 'RHP, Sergeant—'

'That means rank has privileges,' Froggett patronised.

'I know damned well what it means,' Halloran growled, sliding one hand into the pocket of his hooded coat. 'Thing is, how do you know?'

'Oh, I know many things, Sergeant.'

'I'm sure you do,' O'Donnell agreed drily. 'But what sort of things would they be now?'

The old man chuckled. 'You'd be surprised,' he said. 'Maybe I'll enlighten you before the day is done.'

'Well, first off, you can enlighten us about these,' Halloran retorted, producing a pair of binoculars from the pocket of his coat. 'What have you got these for? Bird-watching? I wonder what sort of birds they might be, eh?'

Froggett said nothing, simply smirking at him.

Checking another pocket, the DS held up a pair of lace panties and held them aloft. 'And what about these? Where'd you get them? Marks and Spencer's?'

Froggett sighed. 'I succumbed to temptation in a moment of weakness,' he replied. 'I'm afraid I have no will power at all. Especially where ladies' fripperies are concerned.'

Halloran snorted and now held up a small plastic bag. 'Was this lot down to a moment of weakness too?'

O'Donnell's eyes narrowed when she saw the expensive looking necklace curled up in the bottom of the bag with some other jewellery. 'Well now, you're not just a dirty old perv then?' she murmured.

'Oh, no,' Froggett replied. 'I have hidden depths.'

She nodded grimly. 'Aye, and those hidden depths have now earned you a nice wee en suite room at the nick, so they have,' she said.

'On what charge?'

'Let's start with "on suspicion of burglary", eh?'

Froggett chuckled yet again. 'As good a charge as any, madam, I would agree. Two sugars with my tea, please and I would like a decent mattress in my en suite room, if you don't mind.'

****

'So, Daniel,' Maureen O'Donnell said, studying Froggett across the police station's interview room table following the obligatory caution, 'you intimated up on the headland that you knew things. Could one of those things be about the man who plunged to his death from the clifftop?'

The old man treated her to a crafty grin, his gaze switching briefly to the recording machine in the corner, which had been switched on. 'Perhaps, but there again, perhaps not.'

Seated beside his DI at the table, Halloran tensed. 'Did you see how it happened?' he snapped.

'Now, that's a question and a half, isn't it?'

Well, did you? Maybe you actually pushed him?'

Froggett chuckled. 'Why on earth would I want to do that? And how could a little old man like me heave a big lump like that off a clifftop?'

O'Donnell could feel the adrenalin surge inside her. 'How could you know he was a "big lump" if you hadn't seen him?'

'I never said I hadn't seen him.'

'Well, did you see him?'

'Might have done.'

'Either you did or you didn't.'

'That's very logical.'

'So what's your answer?'

Froggett sighed and looked down at the empty mug on the table in front of him. 'Could I have some more tea?' he said. 'I'm rather thirsty.'

Halloran exploded, forgetting that the tape-recording machine was running, 'Stop pissing us about, Daniel!' he snarled.

'My dear boy,' the old man chuckled, studying him through half-closed eyes, 'there's no need to lose your temper or be offensive.'

O'Donnell threw her DS a withering look. 'Of course I'll get you some more tea, Mr Froggett,' she went on, 'and I might even throw in a currant bun as well. But there are some questions to be answered first, so there are. To start with, did you or did you not see the man who went over the cliff?'

Froggett sighed. 'Oh I saw him all right. A nasty bit of work he was too. Walked right into my doss, he did, and when I challenged him he said he would feed me to the seagulls if I didn't get out of his way. Most rude.'

'That must have made you quare and angry?'

'Oh, I don't get angry these days, and I disregard Neanderthals like that anyway.'

'What happened after he left your doss?'

The crafty grin was back on the florid face. 'Don't you want to know about the jewellery and those nice panties?'

O'Donnell nudged Halloran sharply under the table with her knee when she sensed him tensing in his chair. She could see that their prisoner was playing with them. He was obviously well educated, probably with a very high IQ, and no doubt regarded the thrust and parry of interview as intellectually stimulating. He would not respond to threats or the kind of heavy-handed approach Halloran favoured and would only tell them what they wanted to know when he tired of the

153

game. So all they could do was to go along with him and hope he slipped up in due course and unintentionally revealed something significant.

'Okay, Mr Froggett,' she went on patiently, 'where did you get the stuff?'

'Well, I stole it, didn't I, Inspector? Broke into a house and lifted it.'

Halloran gaped at him, astonished by his sudden admission after all the prevarication. 'You what?'

'But that's what you wanted to hear, isn't it – my confession?'

'Sure it is, but which house?' O'Donnell queried.

'Froggett smiled and leaned forward slightly, his gaze now fixed on O'Donnell. 'Problem is, I'm a bit of voyeur,' he said, going off at a tangent. 'Always have been, you know. Cost me my career as a senior tutor at uni some years ago too. All those leggy things at play in the halls of residence after dark. Couldn't stop watching them.' He looked almost wistful. 'The old libido has never been much good, you see, so I've tended to go in for a bit of peeping. Passes the time, after all, doesn't it? And I do love ladies' perfumed fripperies too. Helps me to fantasize. Do you wear lacy underwear, Inspector?'

The DI smiled faintly. It was obvious that he was trying to shock and embarrass her and was getting off on it in the process. But he was going to be out of luck. She had been too long in the business to be shocked or embarrassed by anything. 'Which house, Mr Froggett?' she repeated, without turning a hair.

He still didn't answer the question. 'This beautiful young lady first attracted my attention when I saw her sunbathing in the neddy,' he rambled on. 'Made quite an impression on me and I even followed her home one night. Kept my eyes on her after that—'

'That's why you had these then, is it?' Halloran cut in harshly, producing a pair of binoculars which he slapped on the table in front of him.

Froggett raised an eyebrow. 'Well, they certainly weren't for bird-watching, Sergeant,' he said. 'Very powerful lenses they have too. Enabled me to see, even from a distance, that she had sustained some sort of dreadful injuries and was quite badly scarred.'

O'Donnell stiffened. She knew straightaway whose house he was referring to. It could only be that of Lynn Giles, the victim of the Islington bombing, but she said nothing.

'Well, I still found her very attractive – lovely tanned skin and all that – so I decided to take a look at where she lived. Place above the beach it was – lovely views. Anyway, when I went there, I found she was out, so being me, I thought I'd have a look around inside—'

'And then ransacked the place?' Halloran finished for him.

Froggett looked horrified. 'Ransacked? Good lord, no, I don't ransack, Sergeant, I … er … do a thorough search, but I'm always very careful not to damage anything. That's when I found the jewellery and some cash – and of course, those delightful knickers. I feel I know that young lady so well now, you know. Perfumed underwear is so personal, don't you think? It's like an extension of personality.'

Neither O'Donnell nor Halloran answered him and he smirked again. 'Naturally I felt bad. But …' and he shrugged again '… it's all about economics today, isn't it? So I took possession of the stuff, intending to sell it to an interested party, such as a pawnbroker or jeweller, on my travels.'

'Which house?' O'Donnell repeated quietly, seeking confirmation of what she had already guessed.

Froggett shrugged. 'I believe it's called The Beach House,' he said. 'Charming little bungalow. I spent many happy hours outside with my binoculars.'

'Saw a lot there then, did you?'

'Oh yes and it was most rewarding for someone like me.'

'For a pervert, you mean?' Halloran growled.

'Exactly so,' the little man agreed without the slightest embarrassment. 'Especially as the lady resident had a penchant for wandering around the place naked.'

'When was the last time you were there?' O'Donnell slipped in quietly.

Froggett thought for a moment. 'Must have been the night the fat man was pushed off the cliff,' he replied.

'Pushed off?' Halloran exclaimed, once more taken aback by another sudden unexpected admission. 'You're actually saying he was pushed?'

Froggett regarded him with his usual amusement. It was evident that he enjoyed making surprising disclosures out of the blue to wind up his interviewers. 'Of course, Sergeant. I had a ringside seat.'

'You saw it happen?' O'Donnell echoed.

Now Froggett had the bit between his teeth and couldn't wait to give up his information. It was his big moment – his brief moment of power. 'Oh yes. It was shortly after the fat man had made his threats to me and left. I followed him to see where he went and saw him sit down on the iron seat by the cliff edge. He appeared to make a call to someone on his mobile. Then just as he seemed to finish his call and get up off the seat, this figure appeared out of the scrub, went straight up behind him and hit him over the head with something – I couldn't quite see what – before pitching him over the edge. All rather dramatic.'

'Could you describe his assailant?'

He screwed up his face in thought. 'Tall, slender, long dark hair, wearing a beret of some sort and a short coat – it was getting dark, so I couldn't see a lot more.'

'So you didn't see the man's face?'

Froggett looked almost gleeful. 'No, I didn't see *her* face.'

'Her?'

'Precisely, Inspector. The fat man's assailant was a woman. Now, can I have my tea and bun?'

CHAPTER 16

Lynn Giles made the decision to call and see Alan Murray again when she reluctantly climbed out of bed at well after 11am the following morning. Felicity Dubois' sudden appearance and ominous warnings the previous day had certainly not helped her to get a good night's sleep and the humid atmosphere in her room, despite the close proximity of The Beach House to the sea, had only made things worse. In the end, she had spent the early part of the night sitting naked on the steps of her bungalow, letting what breeze there was fan her hot, perspiring body and for the first time since she had moved to Cornwall, not caring whether there were any press photographers hiding in the rocks nearby with their long night lenses. She had only returned to bed after her third gin and tonic at around 3am, exhausted and oblivious to everything save the need to achieve a few hours shut-down to recharge her batteries.

She was surprised, after the heat of the previous day, that there was no sun to greet her when she pulled back her bedroom curtains, and wandering out on to her patio sipping a mug of black coffee, she thought she heard distant mutterings of thunder somewhere above the heavy black clouds which now hung low over a grey uninviting sea. But it was almost as humid as the day before and after a light lunch, which she had to admit to herself she was using as a delaying tactic while she tried to pluck up the courage to do what she had decided to do, she got dressed, donning a pair of blue shorts and a skimpy top. Then carrying her sandals in one hand, she crossed the beach and made her way up the path to the clifftop, hoping that any rain due would stay away until she got back.

There was no one in sight as she headed barefoot along the cliff path. It appeared that the police had finished what they had to do on the headland and only the blue and white tapes remained just before the old engine-house, draped over the gorse bushes where a breeze had taken them.

She shivered as she passed the iron seat on the edge of the cliff, knowing that Freddie Baxter had telephoned her from that very spot just before his death, but she forced herself along the path to the end until The Old Customs House reared up in front of her.

Slipping through the side gate and around to the front of the house, she banged on the front door. There was no response and even after further knocking only the seagulls on the slate roof responded, uttering harsh cries as they swept away out to sea. She frowned. To be crude, she really needed sex – it was eating away at her like a kind of hunger – and it was just her luck to find that Alan was not at home. Where the hell had he gone? Maybe she should just find somewhere to wait until he returned?

Making her way round to the patio, she pulled out one of the plastic chairs and was about to sit down when she noticed the wooden patio doors. One was not shut properly – insecure just like fat Freddie had claimed. In an agony of indecision, she stood for a moment staring at the tiny gap, trying to resist the temptation that was growing on her.

She had been given a golden opportunity to take a look around inside while the place was empty to satisfy her curiosity and the reservations that had plagued her about Alan. But did she have the will to seize the moment? True, there was something about him that bothered her, especially after Freddie's mocking phone call. It was that which had first sown the seeds of doubt in her mind, and although she had desperately tried to bury her suspicions and just enjoy that beautiful bronzed body while she could, the nagging doubts always returned, regardless of what she did. But "doing a Freddie Baxter" was just not her style – and she was acutely conscious of the fact that if she found out something she didn't want to know, it could destroy everything she had ever hoped for in her relationship with Alan.

Yet fat Freddie's mocking words "What do you really know about him?" still echoed in her brain. Furthermore, she couldn't erase from her mind the memory of a dishevelled Alan turning up at The Beach House the night of Baxter's murder, with the unconvincing story about being bowled over by a jogger. Something just didn't add up about the blind novelist, who had even lied to her about his literary status, and she knew she wouldn't be happy until she found out what.

The patio door opened easily and she saw at once why it was insecure. The door was warped and the catch did not engage properly. It had probably clicked open again after being fastened. No wonder Freddie Baxter had been able to get in so easily.

The living room of the old house was cool and filled with the strong scent of the roses which occupied a tall glass vase on the window sill, and she felt the softness of the thick pile carpet beneath her bare feet. The clock in the hallway produced a peal of Westminster chimes as she approached the living room door, startling her for a second and giving rise to a rueful grimace as she recalled how it had also momentarily interrupted her previous night of passion with Alan.

Waiting for it to finish striking the hour, she couldn't help thinking of Freddie and the fact that he must have been in this same room maybe just an hour or so prior to his death. It was a sobering thought and she felt her skin crawl as she glanced quickly around her, half-sensing another presence close by, then dismissing the idea as totally absurd and moving on.

Going from room to room, she was struck by the tidiness of the whole house. It was as though it had had a woman's touch. Everything seemed to be in its proper place. Dishes washed and put away. The kitchen work surfaces clear of crockery and cooking utensils. Upstairs, the bed made and the bathroom scrubbed and clean. She had gained the impression on her previous visits to the house that Alan was a very fastidious man and the look of the place now certainly confirmed that fact.

But there was something not quite right about it all. At first she couldn't put her finger on it, but then it dawned on her. Being blind, how did Alan know when the house was untidy or needed dusting or vacuuming? As far as she was aware, he didn't employ a domestic of any sort. Yet the place was even cleaner than her own.

It was too clean in another way too, and the word "clinical" immediately sprang to mind. In short, it was completely devoid of anything of a personal nature. Anything to say who Alan actually was. There were no family photographs. No correspondence lying about. No credit cards. Not even a single bill or receipt with his name on it. So he was blind and wouldn't have been able to see these things anyway, but surely he would have wanted to display pictures of the wife he said he lost, even though he could no longer see them himself? Despite his disability, letters would still have arrived in the post too, if only junk mail, addressed to the occupier, and she supposed there would have been communications in braille from the blind associations and the welfare and support agencies.

Furthermore, surely there should have been some evidence to indicate his strivings as a writer? Rejection slips or letters from agents or publishers who were not aware of his disability maybe? A few reference books in braille? So he'd said he used a Dictaphone, which seemed to be missing now anyway, but there were not even any used tapes lying around to support his claim that he stored his manuscripts electronically. In short, it was as if Alan had no identity at all. That he didn't actually exist.

To think that she had had dinner with him. Had shared his bed and imparted confidences to him. Had trusted him completely. Yet, in the final analysis, she didn't even know who this handsome man really was.

Her misgivings were about to get a lot worse too. She saw the expensive-looking Rolex wristwatch lying on the bedside cabinet in the main bedroom, but didn't give it much thought at first. So Alan had forgotten to put it on when he went out. So what? But then the realisation hit her. It was quite conventional in style. Not a watch with a braille face that had been specially adapted for use by a blind person. The bedside clock was the same – bog-standard and unremarkable.

It struck her that she should have noticed these anomalies when she had shared Alan's bed. She gave a rueful smile. At the time she had been a little bit too preoccupied to notice what was on the bedside cabinet – or anywhere else for that matter – so maybe that wasn't so surprising. But were these the things that Freddie Baxter had noticed or had he found something more significant?

Her heart was thudding with a mixture of excitement and apprehension as she carried out a more thorough search of the room. Nothing in the built-in double wardrobe was of any interest except a steel cabinet in one corner, almost hidden behind a couple of coats, but this turned out to be locked. Making a grimace, she checked the drawers of the bedside cabinet to see if she could find a key.

There was no key. Just the usual handkerchiefs, underwear, socks and trouser belts, which were to be found in most men's bedside cabinets. But then she frowned as her nimble fingers located something hard under a pile of neatly folded underpants. She carefully lifted it out. It was a spectacle case containing steel-framed glasses. More significantly, there was an appointment card trapped under them, bearing the name of a Truro optician, with an appointment time of 3.30pm the following Thursday. That wasn't the last of her discoveries either. Pulling open a second drawer and delving into another pile of underclothes, she discovered a pair of small, but expensive-looking field glasses.

For a moment she just stood there looking at the "evidence", her brain clenched in an ice-cold fist and her legs beginning to shake at the knees. A blind man with a standard wristwatch and bedside clock was suspicious enough, but spectacles and field glasses? She dropped on to the edge of the bed, feeling sick and dizzy. What on earth had she uncovered? Who the hell *was* Alan Murray? And more importantly, *what* was he?

But she was given no time to try and work that one out. Hearing a loud whistle, she stumbled to the window and glimpsed Murray walking up the path to the front door, Archie trotting ahead of him off the lead. In a panic, she about-turned and raced back down the stairs, taking two at a time. She heard the key turn in the front door as she reached the living room and only just exited on to the patio in time. Archie saw her through the open hall door as she closed the patio door, she felt sure of it. But even as he bounded into the living room, she was across the patio and running barefoot down the path to the side gate.

It began to rain as she stumbled homewards across the headland and she was soon soaked to the skin. But she was hardly aware of her sodden hair or the water streaming down her arms and legs. She had other things on her mind. In fact, her thoughts were spinning around inside her head like some crazy kaleidoscope as she asked herself the question over and over again: what the devil did a blind man want with spectacles, field glasses and optician's appointments?

****

Mick Benchley turned up at The Beach House late in the afternoon in warm heavy rain, exactly four and a half minutes before Lynn Giles returned home from her clandestine visit to Murray's home. The policeman had left London at just on 7am that morning. He had stopped just once on route for lunch at a motorway services, and apart from being very tired after his long journey he was both disappointed and irritated by the fact that there was no response to the rap of his knuckles on the weathered wood of the front door and then the French doors at the back.

He decided to call on The Blue Ketch Inn immediately afterwards and he took an instant dislike to Snake-eyes. The barman's shifty manner suggested that he was someone who couldn't be trusted, and the mark of the schemer was clearly written into his crafty expression as the detective faced him across the counter of the empty public bar, holding his warrant card up in front of his face.

'Have you a Felicity Dubois staying here?' he queried.

The barman shook his head. 'No one 'o that name, no.'

'A black girl.'

Realisation dawned. 'Did 'ave, yeah. Gave 'er name as Denise Cross. Checked out sudden like yesterday afternoon'. From Lon'on. They's all from Lon'on.'

'They?'

'Yeah, Emmet what fell off the cliff an' 'is mate. Feller called Wiles. All from Lon'on.'

'Emmet?'

'Yeah, means vis'tor in these parts.'

'Is Mr Wiles still here?'

Snake-eyes nodded.

'Pop'lar feller, this Mr Wiles. Lots of folk hereabouts wants to see 'im lately.'

'Like who, for instance?'

Snake-eyes smirked. 'Well, there's that detective woman. Oh yes, and the Emmet staying over at Bootleg Cove. Mary Tresco I think she calls 'ersel'.' They's both been 'ere.'

'So which room is Mr Wiles in?' Benchley snapped.

Snake-eyes sighed. 'Tha's confidential.'

Benchley could see what the man was after, but he was in no mood to barter for the information. Thrusting his face across the counter to within an inch of the barman's pointed nose, he rasped, 'Room number, mister, before I really lose patience with you.'

Snake-eyes flinched and the Adam's apple in his scrawny throat visibly jumped as he gulped on his next breath. 'They ain't got no numbers,' he replied sourly, 'names only – after Cornish coves, see?' He nodded towards a flight of carpeted stairs a few yards away. 'All upstairs.'

'And?'

He scowled. ''E's in Coverack – leastways, 'e was when 'e first checked in.'

'What do you mean by that?'

Snake-eyes shrugged. 'Only seen the feller once since 'e come. Stays in 'is room mostly – 'as 'is meals took up to him and left outside the door when 'e orders 'em. Real weirdo.'

But Benchley didn't wait to hear any more. Turning his back on him he headed for the stairs, thinking that, weirdo or not, maybe, just maybe, Vernon Wiles might have something new to tell him.

The musty damp smell hit him as soon as he got to the top of the stairs and he crinkled his nose in disgust as he stepped off the landing into a narrow corridor, surprised to see that there were no windows and the only light was provided by a couple of faintly glowing ceiling lights.

"Coverack" was the first room on the left and he almost tripped over a tray outside with plates and cutlery on it. He knocked sharply on the door, which stood ajar. There was no reply.

'Mr Wiles?' he called. 'It's the police.'

Still nothing. He frowned and knocked again. The door stirred slightly and he pushed against it with one hand until it swung slowly back to hit the wall with a soft thud. He winced, but there was no challenge from anyone. Curious, he stepped over the threshold and stood for a moment just inside, peering about him. Thick curtains had been pulled across the single window and only the feeble glow from the corridor lights trickled in behind him.

'Anyone here?' he said.

Automatically his hand felt for a light switch, found it and snapped it on. Then he simply stood there, feeling the bile rising in his throat as he stared at the double bed. The man lying crosswise on the rumpled, blood-stained duvet could not have answered him even if he had wanted to. Someone had put a bullet in his head, taking half the skull away on one side.

****

Lynn Giles knew all about festering bitterness She had suffered from it ever since the bomb outrage at The Philanderer's Club. But then it had all been about what had happened to her physically and how that single incident had ruined her life. This time it was different. This time her bitterness was motivated by suspicion and resentment. Suspicion because she sensed Alan Murray was not what he pretended to be, and resentment over the fact that he had deceived her so blatantly, just as she was falling for his charms.

Of course, she could be totally wrong about him. The spectacles could have been prescribed before the accident, which he said had claimed his sight as well as the lives of his family, but what about the optician's appointment, the field glasses, wristwatch and bedside clock – not to mention the ultra-clean house?

Other things occurred to her now too. When she had visited him at his home after their first meeting on the beach, how had he known it was her? All that nonsense about recognising the smell of her suntan oil and her lightness of step just didn't ring true. Then, the day she had seen him swimming off the little beach below his house, how had he managed to keep clear of the rocks in the cove and not only determine when to turn back, but to know in which direction the shoreline lay? Just as importantly, how had he managed to negotiate the narrow cliff path and steep steps to reach the beach, to start with? And how had he managed to find her house on his own, following the alleged incident with the jogger the night of Freddie Baxter's murder? None of it rang true and he'd certainly not been walking like a blind man when she'd seen him returning to the house, with Archie trotting ahead of him off the lead, after she had searched the damned place earlier.

Changing from her rain-soaked clothes into trousers and an over-blouse, she drained the glass of gin and tonic she had poured for herself and went through to the kitchen for tonic and lemon so she could prepare another drink, her mind as much in turmoil now as when she had fled Alan's house a couple of hours before. Why would someone claim to be blind and go to all the trouble of acting out that pretence, complete with guide dog and white stick, if it was all a load of rubbish? What would they have to gain, apart from public sympathy and the negligible benefit of eligibility for a disability allowance? And if it was all a con, it must have been a con which had taken some time and planning to set up, particularly where Archie was concerned. It was patently obvious from the way the Labrador acted that he had been trained as a guide dog and you couldn't just go to a pet shop and buy one of those off the shelf.

She was getting more and more confused by the minute. She had to find answers. Had to discover whether Alan was a fraud or whether her inherent paranoia was simply getting the better of her, as it had done in the past. There was only one way to resolve the issue too. She had to go back. Return to The Old Customs House and try to get into the locked cabinet in the main bedroom to see what secrets it held. If that failed, then it was a case of trying to get the truth out of Alan by surreptitious means. And the best place for learning truths was in bed. She smiled thinly, aware once again of a familiar itch despite her reservations about her mystery man.

Her mind made up, she crossed to the living room window and peered out into the rain. It was absolutely sheeting down now and out to sea she caught a multiple flash of lightning. The storm was gathering in strength and crossing the headland on foot in such conditions was obviously madness. It had to be the car, even if that meant taking a much longer way round. Quickly finishing her drink, she returned the dirty glass and bottle of gin to the sideboard. Then grabbing her anorak and ignition keys, she headed for the hall – only to stop in the act of opening the front door, a little voice in her head shouting a warning. "Now, just hold it, girl, think about what you're doing and where you are going. Think what could be behind all this."

She nodded to herself. Yeah, too right. She had no idea what she was getting into or who Alan Murray really was. He could be anyone. What if the whole blind man thing was not something she had just blundered into, but had actually been set up with her in mind? What if that first meeting with Alan on the beach had not been an accident, but part of a carefully organised plan – a plan conceived by the same people who had bombed The Philanderer's Club and who had now managed to trace her? The very idea that the handsome, sexy man she had slept with could be part of something like that seemed preposterous, but how could she be sure he wasn't?

Somehow, though, she needed to uncover the truth, regardless of the potential risks involved. It was in her nature to get to the bottom of things. It was a kind of compulsion. She had to know one way or the other and anyway, she was reassured by the fact that if Alan had meant her actual harm, he'd had plenty of opportunity to do the business in the last few days and hadn't, so it was unlikely that she would be more at risk now. Logic silencing the warning voice in her head, she opened the front door.

Rain lashed the car's windows as she started the engine of the big Mercedes and pulled out into the lane, heading for the main road. Way out to sea a brilliant white flash suddenly lit up an otherwise smudged grey horizon, heralding an ominous roll of thunder which seemed to go on and on. With a sharp stab of apprehension, she wondered whether this was actually some sort of bad omen.

CHAPTER 17

Detective Inspector O'Donnell was angrier than she had been for a long time and pulling up outside The Blue Ketch Inn, her eyes were blazing as she pushed past the uniformed policewoman guarding the front door from the shelter of the wooden porch and stormed into the bar, her anorak glistening and her hair plastered over her forehead from the downpour. Mick Benchley winced when he saw her, knowing full well that he couldn't have been more in the wrong place at the wrong time than he was at that precise moment.

'With respect, *sir*,' the DI challenged after sight of his police warrant card, 'what the devil are you doing here on my patch? Met taking over the Devon and Cornwall force area now too, are they?'

'My apologies,' he said. 'The fact is, I am the SIO in a London bombing investigation and—'

Her eyes narrowed. 'The Philanderer's Night Club?'

He raised his eyebrows, his surprise evident. 'And I came down here to see a key witness living on your manor—'

'Lynn Giles?' she finished for him. Living here under the assumed name, Mary Tresco?'

'You are on the ball.'

'I should be. Another of your witnesses – a certain Freddie Baxter – fell off a cliff near here a few nights ago.'

'I know – but are you sure he just fell?'

She smiled grimly. 'We thought so originally, but from information we've just received it seems more likely he was pushed, so it does.'

Benchley grimaced. 'In which case, it appears that you now have two murders on your hands.'

O'Donnell took a deep breath, forcing herself back in control. 'You'd better show me,' she said tightly and followed him up the stairs.

Another uniformed policeman stood outside the bedroom containing the corpse, but he stepped aside to allow them to peer through the doorway.

'SOCO are on their way, Ma'am,' the policeman said. 'An hour, tops.'

O'Donnell nodded, grimly surveying the room and the grisly cadaver on the bed. It looked even worse in a sudden flash of lightning which lit up the bedroom from end to end.

'Vernon Wiles,' she commented to no one in particular.

Benchley gave her a keen glance. 'It's apparently his room. But I've never met the man myself, so I couldn't say for certain. You know him?'

She nodded. 'I should do. He came down here with Baxter and I interviewed him about his friend's death.' She shuddered. 'Wee man seemed scared to death and it looks like he had good reason to be.'

Benchley pointed at a pillow lying to one side of the body. The blackened hole in the centre told its own story and some of its white feather innards were now stuck to the bloody head of the corpse like a gruesome tiara.

'Looks like his killer used the pillow to deaden the sound of the shot,' he said.

O'Donnell nodded. 'So, no silencer fitted then?'

'Unlikely if the pillow was necessary.'

'But surely someone would have heard something, even so?'

'Probably not. I bet a dive like this gets pretty lively at times and I happened to notice a poster over the bar when I walked in, advertising a nightly local band. This is an old building too, with thick walls and a heavy floor and, as I've already said, the pillow would have muffled the sound of the shot anyway – if he was actually murdered last night, that is.'

She frowned. 'What do you mean by that?'

He nodded towards the door. 'I had a look at the abandoned nosh outside on the tray. It's stew and badly congealed. Looks like it's been there forever. And Smiler behind the bar downstairs says the last time he remembers anything being taken up was lunchtime yesterday.'

'But didn't anyone here check why Wiles hadn't ordered anything else? And what about collecting the dishes and room cleaning?'

'This isn't The Ritz. I doubt whether they worry about anything until the guest leaves – if even then. I expect a lot of their guests don't eat at the pub anyway, but go out for meals. Can't say as I would blame them either, looking at that cow pat outside the door masquerading as stew.'

'Well, he was alive when I saw him the day before yesterday. So the bottom line is that he could have been shot any time after that?'

'Feasible, and the corpse looks less than fresh. You don't need to be a pathologist to see that the wound is quite a few hours old.'

She raised an eyebrow. 'And the motive, what would that be, Sherlock?' she said cheekily.

Benchley gave a faint smile. 'Elementary, my dear Watson. He was with Baxter the night he died. Maybe the killer thought there was a chance he had seen something and decided to make sure he kept schtum.'

She grunted and turned towards the uniformed constable. 'Anyone here see anything?'

The policeman shook his head. 'Not to my knowledge, Ma'am,' he said. 'That creepy barman was the only one about when we got here anyway.'

O'Donnell glanced quickly along the corridor. 'Anyone staying in the other rooms?'

Another shake of the head. 'Seems Wiles was the only one after Baxter died – apart from a young black woman who stayed just Tuesday night, then checked out.'

'Left well before I arrived,' Benchley commented. 'Smiler in the bar says she gave her name as Denise Cross, but her real name's Felicity Dubois and she was one of the late Freddie Baxter's models.'

'So it looks like she might have some explaining to do?'

'You can say that again.'

'But what would be her motive for murder?'

Benchley shrugged. 'We think Baxter had a hold over her – indecent pics – and it's feasible that she planted the bomb at The Philanderer's Club to get him off her back. When that failed, it's possible she followed him the day he came down here to see Lynn Giles and did the business on him then. We know she had a few days off before Baxter's death, so she had the opportunity. Maybe Wiles was in on Baxter's killing or saw Dubois carry it out, so she stiffed him to shut him up for good.'

'It all seems to fit. We have a witness who saw a woman push Baxter off the clifftop, though it was too dark for him to describe the assailant in detail.'

'Jigsaw pieces certainly seem to be falling into place.'

'Maybe, but I have to wonder why this Dubois woman would go to all the trouble of trying to disguise Baxter's death as an accident and then commit an obvious murder by shooting Wiles.'

Benchley grunted. 'Expediency, I would think? She needed to act fast to stop Wiles speaking out of turn. Could be he got nervous and phoned her, which would have forced her hand. From the evidence we have to date, our killer is not only persistent, but likes to clear up any loose ends afterwards. We've already found the body of the accomplice bomb-maker, shot in the head like Wiles here, which means the MO is virtually the same.'

'So all we have to do is find Dubois? What do we know about her?'

'Only that she's black and drives a maroon BMW 7 series.'

'Well, that's a start. Index number?'

Benchley pulled his notebook from his pocket and flicked it open at the relevant page to enable her to jot the number down on the back of an envelope, which she handed to the constable standing beside her. 'We'll get that circulated straight away,' she said as the constable reached for his personal radio. 'But she's probably already on her way back to the Smoke.'

Benchley seemed not have heard her, but had jerked his mobile out of his pocket and was stabbing the buttons with a fierce, almost desperate energy. The number he dialled rang and rang, then responded with a BT answerphone.

'Sod it!' he snapped. 'Still nothing.'

'Still nothing, what?'

He stared at her absently for a moment, obviously thinking. Then he seemed to surface from his thoughts with a jolt. 'Lynn Giles,' he answered finally. 'Called on her earlier and she was out. Seems she's not back even now. I don't like the sound of it.'

'You think Dubois will go after her?'

'Don't you?'

'Then we'd better check her place out,' O'Donnell replied. 'Like now.'

****

As Benchley and O'Donnell left The Blue Ketch Inn, Felicity Dubois turned into the lane leading down to The Beach House. Then a hundred yards or so from the bungalow, on the approach to a sharp bend, she pulled up and reversed back through an adjacent gateway to park just out of sight in the short, stubby grass behind a dry-stone wall, out of the buffeting wind. Switching off, she sat there smoking a cigarette, listening to the rain drumming on the roof and the occasional crack of thunder as she considered her next move.

By rights, she knew she should have headed straight back to London after what had happened at The Blue Ketch Inn. That would have been the most sensible thing to have done. In fairness it had been her first inclination too, and checking out of the inn in the previous day after visiting Lynn Giles she had high-tailed it towards the motorway, spending the next night at a motel on route to give her time to think things out. But her determination to finish her business with her former catwalk rival had finally won the day. After all, that was why she had driven all the way down to Cornwall in the first place, wasn't it? And that business would have been concluded but for the unexpected interruption by the swede kid delivering those bloody flowers.

She was totally indifferent to the grisly end of Vernon Wiles. The little shit had got what was coming to him and she wasn't going to allow that to divert her from her main purpose. Okay, so she was taking a big risk coming back to the area after what had happened. Although she had registered under a false name at The Blue Ketch Inn, being black made her easily identifiable if the police chose to extend their inquiries to the New Light agency, and in addition the snake-eyed barman might remember her saying that she was a friend of Lynn Giles. But so what? Why shouldn't she travel to Cornwall to see an old friend? And though technically naughty registering under a false name at the inn, as a well-known fashion model it was understandable that she would want to hide her identity in case of intrusive press interest.

As for Wiles himself, there was no way the swede plods would be able to connect him to her. He was Freddie Baxter's pal, after all, and nothing to do with New Light. Coupled with which, no one had seen her popping into his room that last afternoon anyway. So, once she had dealt with Lynn Giles, she could simply disappear back to London, with no one being any the wiser and everything well and truly sorted. She could hardly wait to see the ex-model's face in that final moment of truth, though. It would represent the ultimate satisfaction. The supreme triumph. And she was looking forward to savouring every last second of it.

Finishing her cigarette, she stubbed it out in the ashtray, grabbed a torch and reached for the handle of the door. Time to go. She accepted that she was about to get very wet, but had already decided that she was going to walk rather than drive the short distance to the bungalow to make her reappearance even more of a surprise. With the door half-open, however, she stopped short at the sound of a powerful engine starting up somewhere close by. Closing the door again and peering through the corner of the windscreen, she saw a flash of headlights and the rear lights of Lynn's Mercedes disappearing towards the main road.

'Now where the hell are *you* going?' she murmured to herself, and waiting a few seconds to give the Mercedes time to put some distance between them, she started the BMW and pulled out into the lane after her.

There was no sign of the big silver saloon when she got to the junction with the main road, but then she spotted it through the squalling rain. It had turned left towards Lizard Point and it was not hanging about either, despite the foul weather. Muttering an oath, she hit the accelerator hard and exited the lane with a screech of tyres – straight into the path of the police Traffic car as it rounded a sharp bend from the opposite direction with headlights blazing.

****

Lynn Giles pulled up some 20-30 yards from The Old Customs House, switching her headlights off, but leaving her engine running. Then she sat for a moment, studying the place from under hooded lids while she tapped out a tattoo on the steering wheel with both hands.

Well, now she was here what was she going to say to Alan? How was she going to justify dropping in on him like this? "Hi Alan, I'm feeling a bit fruity, so could you oblige?" She permitted herself a thin smile. Hardly. It was true that she had made impromptu visits to his place before, but each time she'd had a valid reason – the questioning by DI O'Donnell on the clifftop, for example, which had genuinely stressed her out. But this time nothing had happened for her to use as an excuse. Furthermore, much as she still fancied Alan, would she be able to give a convincing performance in bed, if it came to that, with all the newly arisen doubts about him still crowding her mind?

In the end, the decision was taken out of her hands as a figure suddenly appeared at the driver's window and tapped on the glass. Alan was wreathed in oilskins, from the sou'wester pulled down low over his face to the waterproofs tucked into his gumboots, and he gleamed black with the rain, which burst over him like the continuous fall of water erupting from the head of a fountain. For a second she jumped, hardly recognising him in his sinister-looking outfit, but then she saw Archie standing just behind him on a lead, looking forlorn and dejected.

'Can I help you?' Alan shouted. For a second she thought she had caught him out. So how did he know she was there? But then she realised her engine was still running. Damn it!

Pressing the button to lower the window, she felt the rain lash her face. 'It's me,' she said. 'Lynn.'

At first he seemed taken aback, but then he recovered and shook his head in apparent disbelief. 'What on earth are you doing out here in this weather?'

'What about you?' she shouted back.

He gave a hard laugh. 'Archie needed a walk,' he said. 'Got caught in this lot on the headland.'

He waved a hand towards the house. 'See you inside, if you feel like braving the rain.'

He didn't wait for a reply either, allowing Archie to lead him the few yards through the open gate to the front door. Grimacing, she eased the car forward to stop right beside the gate. Then switching off, she turned up the collar of her coat, and climbing out into the rain, kicked the door shut behind her and ran for the house.

Alan's boots and sou'wester were already lying on the floor and he was almost out of his waterproofs by the time she joined him in the hallway, slamming the front door against the rain-laden gusts as Archie stood and shook himself, sending water everywhere.

Alan took her coat and hung it up on a hook, then grinned. 'A nice stiff drink, I think,' he said, fumbling for a towel lying by the living room door, which he'd obviously dumped there before going out. 'You know where it is. Pour me a scotch, will you? I'll just see to Archie. He doesn't like storms, so I'll have to shut him in the kitchen with the blinds drawn to keep him quiet, I'm afraid.'

The house trembled under the onslaught of the wind and the dog whimpered and shrank away from him as he felt his way along the wall to the open doorway. Lynn could hear him coaxing the animal inside as she walked through into the living room, switched on the lights and flipped open the lid of the cocktail cabinet.

She was halfway through a gin and tonic by the time Alan joined her, wearing the ubiquitous dark glasses. She watched him carefully over the rim of her glass as he felt his way to the cabinet and fumbled for the glass of whisky she had poured for him. She frowned, wondering how he knew where she had left it – it could easily have been on the coffee table or a chair arm instead – unless he was either sighted or pretty damned good at assumptions.

'And to what do I owe this pleasure?' he said cheerfully, this time talking to the wrong wall.

She gave another frown, feeling confused. So was he genuinely blind or had he simply mastered the part he was playing?

'I ... I needed some company,' she said lamely, thinking that this was the question she had dreaded and which she was totally unprepared for. 'Just thought I'd call in to see you.'

He turned in the direction of her voice, then felt his way round the edge of the settee to where she was sitting and dropped down beside her. 'Glad you did,' he said, then added abruptly, 'Were you over earlier?'

She froze. That was one question she hadn't expected and it had completely thrown her. 'Ear ... earlier?' she prevaricated. 'I don't know what you mean?'

He laughed. 'Postman pulled my leg this morning after I had got back from walking Archie. Accused me of being a dark horse and having a bit on the side.'

'A bit on the side? I don't follow you?'

His smile was unconvincing. 'Said he thought he saw a young woman running away from the back of the house as he arrived.'

The lights dipped, then returned to full strength and she heard what sounded like a tile sliding off the roof. She took another sip of her drink, unable to face those thick black glasses even though the eyes they concealed were allegedly sightless. She could feel the tension mounting in the room. It was as though he already knew she had been in his house and was testing her response.

'Probably a mermaid,' she laughed back, knowing that her attempt at humour must have sounded equally false.

His smile broadened, but it still lacked any warmth. 'Then maybe I should try and net her next time?' he said softly. 'Any idea what I should use as bait?'

Before she could think of a suitably frivolous answer, his expression suddenly softened and he laughed again, this time with something akin to genuine humour. She took his cue and laughed with him, but the sound had a shaky note to it and carried more than just a hint of relief.

'Now,' he continued in a much brisker tone, 'you said you needed some company. For how long exactly?'

'How about the whole night?' she replied.

He nodded. 'I'll drink to that,' he said. 'What would you like to eat first?'

She took a deep breath. 'Perhaps we should just skip the food?' she said.

****

Lynn finished her shower and wrapped a big white towel around herself before returning to the bedroom to dress. The storm was gathering in even greater strength, with everything in the house seemingly shaking and rattling, and she shivered, feeling a sudden chill. Alan was no longer in the double bed and turning back out on to the landing, she heard the sound of clinking glasses coming from the direction of the living room downstairs.

'Shower's free, Alan,' she called down to him before returning to the bedroom to dry herself.

'Be up in a minute,' he shouted back. 'Just poured us a couple more drinks.'

Moments later she heard his heavy footsteps on the stairs, moving very slowly and apparently feeling for each step in turn. He appeared in the doorway as she was pulling on her clothes. He was barefoot, but wearing a short white robe and his glasses. She frowned. With the heavy curtains pulled in the bedroom and no lights lit during their love-making she had not been able to see his eyes, and now that the bedroom light had been switched on he had replaced his glasses and she was once more being denied the opportunity. The way he was holding his head, with his face slightly elevated and turned towards the far corner of the room, it appeared that he was not sure exactly where she was standing, but she was still not convinced. It could have been an act. But if it was, he was certainly damned good at it – a suspicion that had crossed her mind more than once before.

'Do you have to wear those things all the time?' she said sharply, unintentionally revealing her frustration.

He gave a slow smile. 'Why, do they bother you?'

She zipped up her trousers and grimaced. 'It ... it's just strange,' she replied.

He nodded, as if in understanding. 'I am very self-conscious about my eyes,' he said. 'When you lose your sight, their appearance sometimes changes and this can be very off-putting for sighted people.'

'It wouldn't bother me.'

'No,' he said drily, turning clumsily in the doorway, 'but it would bother me.' He felt his way across the landing towards the bathroom. 'I'll take my shower now,' he said. 'Won't be long. Drinks already waiting downstairs.'

She watched him go, biting her lip anxiously, and even when he had closed the bathroom door she still stood there, waiting and listening. She heard him using the toilet. Then there was the sudden gurgle of the shower. She swung back into the bedroom. She had very little time to do what she had come to do, but she was determined to do it anyway.

Picking up the pair of trousers he had left draped over the end of the bed, she felt in his pockets for his house keys and jerked them free of the lining in which they had become entangled. There were four or five keys on a brass ring and she immediately found the one she wanted. It was the only key that looked as if it might fit.

Wincing at a sudden thunder-clap, she crossed to the wardrobe. Then crouching down on all fours, she peered at the steel cabinet she had noticed on her earlier visit. If there was anything about Alan that needed to be hidden away, it would be in the cabinet, she was certain of it. After all, where else could it be? She was just able to make out the lock, but fumbled a little as she tried to insert the key into it. After the third attempt it went home easily. In the bathroom, the water still gurgled reassuringly and she heard Alan moving about in the shower cubicle.

She turned the key to the left, but it stuck and would go no further. Swearing under her breath, she turned it back and tried the other way. It still wouldn't budge in the lock. Damn it! She tried the left again and felt a thrill of excitement as it turned all the way. The door of the cabinet swung open. She listened again. But the shower was still gurgling.

Papers. The cabinet contained a sheaf of papers in a folder. Laying the folder on the floor in front of her, she began sifting through the contents. The photograph jumped out at her immediately and she held it up in the light. It was a picture of herself. She gaped as she scanned the typed report clipped to it. It was a complete résumé of her early life, right up to her teens and the death of her father in a fire in Maidenhead. There were also newspaper cuttings of the incident and photographs of his burned-out house. She felt an icy hand clutch at her heart and flicked over the pages. Pictures of her in several different fashion magazines as a model. One, a full-length nude in a French magazine, which had been taken very early in her career. There were also details of her National Insurance number, a copy of her birth certificate and other personal documents, including copies of some medical papers relating to a year she had spent in hospital after a nervous breakdown. What the hell was all this? Where had Alan got hold of the stuff and more importantly, why?

The shock of what she had discovered left her frozen to the spot for several seconds, like a victim of some 21st Century *Medusa*, unable to straighten up from her crouched position and reduced to staring into the gloomy depths of the cabinet in a bewildered, near vegetative state. How long she might have remained like that if she had been left to her own devices it is impossible to say, but as it was, she was denied the luxury of a gradual recovery, for it was at this point that her luck suddenly ran out.

It was the faint crack of a floorboard which first alerted her, cutting through the fug that clouded her brain and wrenching her back to reality. It was only when she lurched to her feet and stumbled round to face the bedroom door that she suddenly realised the shower in the bathroom had stopped running. Alan was standing there in his robe. He was no longer wearing his dark glasses and it was obvious from the way he was staring at her that he was no more blind than she was.

'I'm really sorry you had to find that,' he said quietly. 'It rather complicates things, you see.'

CHAPTER 18

Steam poured from under the crushed bonnet of the police Traffic car, spreading outwards in a wider vapour cloud as it mixed with the pouring rain, while the two uniformed officers hauled themselves groggily out of their vehicle. Felicity Dubois stared blankly at them through the driver's window of her BMW – like them, shocked, dazed and for a few moments unable to fully comprehend what had just happened. One thing soon became apparent: her car was going nowhere except perhaps to a breaker's yard. The police car had hit her with such force that it had slammed her back into the lane from which she had emerged and into a dry-stone wall, demolishing her front offside wing and burying the wheel under the twisted engine block.

Benchley and O'Donnell arrived on the scene in O'Donnell's CID car minutes after the Traffic officers had helped Dubois out of the her vehicle – stopping only just in time and pulling on to the grass verge behind them. As one of the officers ran back to the other side of the bend to put out warning beacons and bollards, the two detectives confronted Dubois, who was now sitting smoking a cigarette in the left-hand rear seat of the Traffic car, out of the wind and the rain.

'Felicity Dubois?' O'Donnell snapped, switching on the interior light and sliding into the seat beside her. 'This is a bit of a mess. In a hurry, were you?'

The model shrugged, without answering the question.

'You stayed at The Blue Ketch Inn two nights ago, didn't you?'

'So?'

'Why did you register in the name Denise Cross?'

'It's a free country.'

Benchley climbed into the front passenger seat and kneeling on it, turned round to face her between the two seats. 'Are you carrying?' he demanded, showing no interest in her shocked state or the nasty cut to her forehead.

Dubois treated him to a slow contemptuous smile. 'Carrying what, hon?' she replied. 'A shopping bag? A baby? Well, I'm not pregnant, so you must mean a shopping bag.' She looked around her and shook her head. 'But nope, no shopping bag either. Sorry.'

'You know what I mean,' he replied. 'A shooter. Are you armed?'

The model chuckled and held both her hands out in front of her, trailing smoke from her cigarette. 'Want to search me?' she offered. 'I'm game, if you are.'

'Do you think this is a joke?' O'Donnell snapped again.

Dubois shook her head. 'Hardly. Not after what those two cop dickheads did to my car.'

'You seem to have pulled out in front of them, not the other way about. So I'll ask you again, why the hurry?'

'I was visiting a friend, but saw her drive off as I arrived—'

'And went after her?'

'Nothing wrong with that, is there?'

'Not unless you write off a police car in the process. Was that friend Lynn Giles?'

'What if it was?'

O'Donnell went for shock tactics. 'So, after leaving a dead man back at The Blue Ketch, you casually drive over here as if nothing has happened?'

Dubois frowned. 'Dead man? What dead man?'

'Vernon Wiles.'

Dubois' eyes widened and she straightened up. 'Vernon?' she exclaimed, brazenly faking her surprise like an Equity pro. 'Vernon Wiles? You're saying he's dead?'

'Hardly surprising with half his skull blown away.'

Dubois continued with her pretence. 'You mean someone shot him?'

'Well, he didn't top himself and that's a fact.'

'Poor old Vernon. He was a nice little guy too.'

'You admit you knew him then?' Benchley queried.

''Course I knew him. He was Freddie Baxter's pal. But ... but I didn't kill him. Why would I? And anyway, I've never fired a gun in my life.'

'Maybe he saw you push Freddie Baxter off the cliff and you stiffed him to shut him up?'

'Freddie? You reckon I did him in too? Oh come on, hon, what do you think I am – a serial killer?'

O'Donnell gave a thin smile. 'That is exactly what I intend finding out, Miss Dubois. In the meantime, you are under arrest on suspicion of murder.'

****

Felicity Dubois took a long pull on her sixth cigarette and eyed Benchley and O'Donnell in turn through the smoke. 'Okay,' she said eventually, glancing briefly at the light on the tape machine which was winking at her from the corner of the police station interview room, 'when do you put on the thumbscrews?'

'Very funny,' O'Donnell replied, 'but there's nothing funny about the reason for your arrest.'

Dubois stubbed out her cigarette on the table-top in front of her. 'And you two won't be laughing when I sue you for wrongful arrest either,' she snapped back.

'You were offered a solicitor and you turned that down.'

Dubois shrugged. 'Don't need one. I haven't done anything wrong.'

'What about Vernon Wiles then? You're still saying you had nothing to do with his death?'

'I didn't even know he was dead until you told me.'

'Fine, but if we find your fingerprints in his room, how will you explain that?'

Dubois hesitated, her face creased into an ugly frown.

'Trying to remember what you touched in the room, are you?' Benchley said.

The model stared at him for a moment. 'I didn't kill him – or Freddie for that matter,' she muttered.

'But you were in his room?'

Dubois took a deep breath and abruptly capitulated. 'Okay. I admit I know what happened to him. When I checked in at The Blue Ketch a couple of days ago, I went to see him … to try and find out what he knew about Freddie's death, as I was pretty sure it wasn't an accident. But the little shit didn't answer the door. So I left it—'

'But you tried again?' Benchley encouraged.

Dubois nodded. 'The next day … yesterday … after I had called on Lynn. But again, he didn't answer the door and when I sneaked into his room, I found him with a hole in his head.'

'And you ran?'

'You bet I did. I didn't want to be framed for that, so I headed back to the Smoke, staying overnight in a motel on the way – and I have the receipt to prove it.'

'But what made you change your mind and turn around?'

'I wanted to see Lynn again.'

'Why? You two didn't get on. You were rivals.'

'So what? Maybe I was curious about how she was doing.'

'That's rubbish and you know it.'

Dubois selected another cigarette from a gold-coloured cigarette case. 'Think what you like,' she retorted, though her hand was trembling slightly as she lit up. 'But I'm not saying anything else. Except that I didn't kill Vernon or Freddie.'

Before either O'Donnell or Benchley could pursue the interview further, there was a sudden interruption. The knock on the door was rapid and urgent and O'Donnell got up quickly to answer it, verbally indicating for the benefit of the tape recorder that the interview was temporarily suspended and switching the machine off on the way.

The young uniformed constable was smiling confidently as he handed the DI the buff envelope. 'Found it when we turned over her car, ma'am,' he said. It was stuffed under the front passenger seat.'

O'Donnell nodded, and inserting her hand in the flap of the envelope, withdrew one of a number of black and white photographs. For a moment she stared at the first picture in astonishment. Then her expression changed to one of grim satisfaction. Thanking the officer and turning back into the room, she strolled over to the table and laid the photograph, followed slowly by several others, in front of Dubois, noting Benchley stiffen beside her as she did so.

The photographs had obviously been taken at a club of some sort and depicted a young Lynn Giles in a variety of indecent naked poses, cavorting on a stage or swinging on a long striped pole under powerful spotlights.

'Is this why you wanted to see Lynn Giles?' O'Donnell queried. 'Putting the squeeze on her about her early career as a pole-dancer, were you? After all, these pics wouldn't do her any good if they were to be made public, would they?'

Instead of being thrown by the photographs, Dubois drew nonchalantly on her cigarette and met her stare with arrogant amusement. 'How would

I know?' she replied. 'I found them in Freddie's office and was returning them to Lynn as a favour, so she could destroy them.'

'Why didn't you give them to her on your first visit?'

'She had company and I didn't want to embarrass her—'

'What a load of balls,' Benchley cut in, conscious of the fact that the tape recorder was no longer switched on.

Dubois shrugged again. 'Maybe,' she replied, 'but how are you going to prove otherwise? Lynn wouldn't want those pics used as evidence and you have nothing without her testimony anyway.' She leaned forward towards the Met man. 'But I'll tell you something else, Mr Detective. The pics sure as hell give me a reason for being down here – and that sort of throws your theory about me being a serial killer, doesn't it?'

****

'What now then?' O'Donnell said to Benchley in the CID office ten minutes later. 'We have nothing on Dubois, except a few naughty pictures of Lynn Giles, and she knows it.' She tapped the envelope containing the photographs, which was lying on the desk in front of her. 'We'd never get a blackmail conviction on the strength of what we have here.'

Benchley took a gulp of his coffee. 'I don't give a damn about the blackmail,' he said sourly. 'But the cunning little bitch is right when she says it lets her off the hook for murder. After all, why would Dubois want to kill Lynn Giles if she was out to blackmail her?'

'True, but if she's not our murderer, then someone else definitely is. The problem is who?'

The Met man nodded grimly. 'And more importantly, if Lynn Giles is to be their next target, how close are they to finding her?' He swore. 'Holy shit! She could be anywhere, which means we are buggered.'

O'Donnell snapped her fingers, her eyes gleaming. 'Maybe not,' she retorted, grabbing her coat from the back of the chair and heading for the door at a run. 'I think I know where she might have gone.'

'Now you're telling me?' Benchley shouted as he dumped his coffee in a wastepaper bin and raced after her. 'I just hope you're right and we're not already too late!'

****

Lynn Giles was scared – more scared than she had been for a long time – but she was also very angry. Dropping the folder on the floor, she snatched a pair of long-bladed scissors from the top of the bedside cabinet.

'What's this then – a miracle in the shower?' she shouted, holding the scissors out in front of her defensively and glaring at the man who had so cruelly deceived her. 'Not so blind now, are you, Mr Murray?'

Alan Murray smiled, but the smile lacked any genuine humour and his eyes – grey and penetrating – held an expression which was almost sad. 'Why don't you put the scissors down, Lynn?' he said.

'And why don't you tell me what the hell you are up to?' she retorted, her voice now trembling with suppressed emotion. 'Why you have got all this stuff on me?'

He shrugged. 'Background information,' he replied.

'Background information? Look, who the hell are you, and why all this blind man crap anyway?'

'I needed a convincing cover,' he said simply.

For a moment she just stared at him, her mouth hanging open in disbelief.

'Convincing cover?' she choked. 'What are you talking about? You slept with me, for frig's sake!'

He grimaced, his eyes focusing grimly on the scissors in her hand. 'Yes, and I'm sorry. I didn't mean it to go that far, but as it turned out, it was the only way.'

She shook her head several times, the scissors now shaking in her hand. 'The only way? The only way for what?'

He sighed. 'I had to get close to you. I knew you had been scarred by that bomb blast and realised you might wonder why a perfect stranger who was fully sighted would choose to hit on a young woman with your obvious disfigurements—'

She flinched at his brutal candour. 'You bastard,' she breathed. 'You total bastard!'

He lowered his gaze, but ploughed on. 'At the very least you would have expected me to question you about it, which could have compromised my position and put paid to any chance I had of forging a meaningful relationship with you. Look, do you mind if I sit down somewhere?'

'Stay there,' she grated. 'Where I can see you.'

He shrugged again and continued with his explanation, carefully leaning one shoulder against the wall. 'The blind man routine seemed to be the ideal solution, though I have to say, it took a lot of expert instruction to ensure that I could maintain a credible performance – plus an awful lot of money before I was able to persuade the appropriate people to loan me a fully-trained guide dog I could work with.'

She caught her breath. 'Archie.'

'Yes, Archie. We took to each other immediately, which is obviously very important in such situations.' He smiled faintly again. 'I must be a natural with animals.'

'Maybe Archie is as gullible as I've been,' she grated. 'He didn't realise what a prize shit you are either – though I must admit, I've had my suspicions about you all along. Especially when you managed to find your way to my place on your own, then fed me all that crap about being knocked over by a jogger—'

'Oh, that bit was true enough,' he cut in. 'Except that the character who knocked me over was not a jogger, but a rather unpleasant vagrant I caught watching your bungalow from the clifftop with a pair of binoculars. I chased after him, but lost him – and Archie – in the scrub.'

She showed little interest in his explanation. 'Whatever,' she almost spat. 'Now, I'll ask you again – exactly who the bloody hell are you?'

He pursed his lips, meeting her gaze again. 'Well, my name *is* Alan Murray, but I'm not a failed writer. Not a writer at all actually.'

'What then? Press?'

He gave a short laugh. 'Oh, nothing so exciting, I'm afraid. Just a run-of-the-mill investigator.'

'Investigator? Investigator for what?'

He sighed. 'I'm what you would call a freelance detective.'

'What, you mean like a … a private eye? A gumshoe?'

'More or less, yes. I work for major insurance companies.'

'Doing what exactly?'

'Looking into dodgy claims.'

'Dodgy claims? So why would you be interested in me?'

'Can't you see?'

'No, I damned well can't. How could I?'

He sighed heavily. 'Think about it, Lynn. Following the bombing of The Philanderer's Night Club, you made an injury claim against the New

Light Modelling Agency and received a very substantial pay-out from their insurers – the company I represent.'

'So what? Are you saying I wasn't entitled to that money?' She pointed to her scarred face. 'What's this – scotch mist? I was disfigured, hasn't that dawned on you yet?'

He nodded. 'Oh, your scars are real, that's beyond question, but it is how they were caused that the company I represent had doubts about. That's why I was sent down here to look into your claim.'

Lynn still didn't get it. 'Are you suggesting my injuries weren't caused by the bomb?'

His eyes glinted and touched by the shadows where the light from the table lamp failed to reach, his face seemed to have shrunk into a cold bleak mask. 'No, Lynn,' he said tightly, that's not the issue. It's the suspicion that you were in the act of planting the device yourself when it blew up prematurely, which would mean you got exactly what you deserved.'

¥¥¥¥

For a few seconds Lynn just stared at Murray, unintentionally lowering the scissors in her hand, hardly conscious of the rain crashing into the window behind her like millions of tiny marbles.

'Are you mad?' she breathed. 'Why on earth would I want to plant a bomb at The Philanderer's Club? That fashion show was to be my big chance. There were scouts from one of the top fashion houses there that day. Fat Freddie had already told me I was certain to get a contract with them.'

He nodded. 'But my earlier inquiries have revealed that he said much the same thing to your arch-rival, Felicity Dubois. Maybe she told you what he'd said – you know, catty one-upmanship. That would have got you really upset, wouldn't it? Upset enough possibly to decide to take out the competition altogether?'

'That's absolute crap and you know it.'

He sighed again. 'But it is feasible, isn't it? And then there is your previous history to add weight to things.'

'Previous history? What are you on about?'

He pursed his lips for a moment, as if trying to choose his words. 'This was the second major claim you benefitted from, wasn't it? You made one six years ago too when your father died in that house fire at Maidenhead.'

She looked totally bewildered now. 'My father? Yes, of course I claimed. But my solicitor dealt with it on my behalf. Dad … dad was a prominent member of a far right group and someone torched his home with him inside it. It was a dreadful business.'

'The police never caught the perpetrator, did they?'

'No. It was an isolated house and there were no witnesses and no forensic evidence left behind.'

'Convenient, wouldn't you say?'

She gaped at him. 'Are you suggesting I burned him?'

He shook his head. 'I suggest nothing, but you did have a good enough motive, didn't you? When you were a child, he took to abusing you after your mother died, didn't he? He was arrested and went to court. But he got off with it all in the absence of corroborative evidence and you ended up in psychiatric care after a nervous breakdown. My clients feel it was a bit of a coincidence that he died a month after you were released – and of course, there's this latest claim …'

She was shaking with emotion now, tears flooding down her cheeks. 'And … and you deliberately seduced me in an effort to extract a … a confession between the sheets?' she choked. 'You … you twisted, unfeeling bastard.'

He stepped forward quickly, then halted when the scissors in her hand jerked upright again as she stared at him through her tears, her face twisted into an expression of such bitter anguish that it made him visibly wince.

'I … I'm sorry, Lynn,' he said hesitantly, 'but I had a job to do and, as I said before, I hadn't meant things to go so far.'

She ran the back of her free hand over her eyes to try and sweep away the tears and gave an unnatural laugh. She was near to hysteria, he could see that. 'You had a job to do?' she ejaculated. 'So I was nothing more than … than a job, was I?'

He clenched his fists into tight balls by his side. 'That's not true,' he replied, his own voice breaking up with emotion. 'The fact is, I … I have fallen in love with you. I didn't mean to, but I just couldn't help it.'

'Fallen in love with me?' she echoed incredulously. 'Don't give me that load of balls, you hypocritical shit.'

There were tears in those grey eyes now. 'But it's true. I will always love you – no matter what you may have done.'

'What I may have done?' she almost screamed. 'I've done nothing. I am innocent – do you understand that? Innocent! I didn't plant that bomb. I had nothing to do with it and – and in case you were wondering, I didn't murder Freddie Baxter either.'

'No, you didn't,' an icy voice confirmed from the doorway. 'I did!'

As Lynn stared in disbelief over Murray's shoulder and he swung round to face the speaker, there was a loud *crack* and a tongue of flame seemed to leap towards his chest, sending him crashing to the floor in a heap.

'Hi there, Lynn,' Carol Amis sneered as she stepped into the room, an automatic pistol in one hand. 'Nice to see you again.

CHAPTER 19

There was silence in the small bedroom for several seconds, broken only by the fury of the storm. It was a long pregnant pause, during which Lynn Giles stayed perfectly still, her gaze fastened in shocked silence on Murray's prostrate body. Outside, the rain still lashed the windows, drumming on the roof tiles and pouring in cascades from the overfull gutters, and a crack of thunder produced a brilliant lightning flash, which sent the table lamp into a spasm of flickering.

Carol Amis tensed, obviously anticipating a sudden power-cut and conscious of the fact that if it happened, the room would be plunged into the deepening gloom, jeopardising the drop she had on Lynn. But after two or three seconds the lamp finally steadied into a single glaring eye and she smirked. 'Sorry about your boyfriend,' she said.

Lynn snapped out of her temporary paralysis and started towards Murray, only to be halted by Amis' sharp warning. 'Stay where you are. This is a .32 Tomcat semi-automatic, loaded with hollow point rounds. It's small but deadly, and as a former professional soldier and markswoman, I am a crack shot.'

Lynn wiped the rest of the tears from her eyes, gripping the scissors even more tightly in her hand. 'But he's hurt,' she choked, noting the pool of red spreading across the floor from under his out-flung arm. 'He's bleeding. I must help him.'

'Nothing you can do for him,' Amis retorted. 'He's dead. But drop the scissors.'

Lynn swayed drunkenly and gripped the edge of a small dressing table to stop her legs from buckling under her, the scissors falling from her nerveless fingers and clattering to the floor.

'That's better. Now we can have the little talk I always wanted.'

But Lynn was not listening. The shock of Amis' appearance and the ruthless shooting of Murray had achieved what no amount of regressive therapy had managed to achieve so far. As a violent stabbing pain in her head signalled the opening of a trapdoor in her brain, clarity was suddenly there in the form of a burning flashback, which served to answer all the questions that had been plaguing her for so many months.

'It was you I saw at The Philanderer's that day, wasn't it?' she accused in a strangled voice. 'I … I remember now. I went to the club a lot earlier than necessary to beat the traffic and caught sight of you leaving Felicity's changing room as I was coming out of the loo. But you had no reason to be there at all, had you? Freddie had left you at New Light's offices to hold the fort—'

'Ah, it's all come back to you now, has it?' Amis mocked. 'I feared it might eventually. That's why I knew I had to find you before it did. Problem was, Freddie was the only one who knew where you were hiding and he wasn't telling anyone. Bit of a bummer, wouldn't you agree?'

'So … so you followed him down here to Cornwall,' Lynn whispered, 'and after you had found me, you pushed him off the cliff?'

Amis seemed to relax a little and she smiled again. 'Very good, my dear. You win the prize. But I hadn't anticipated that the fat man's demise would cause so much heat, and as a result, I had to temporarily shelve the plans I had for you and Foxtrot-Oscar back to the Smoke until all the fuss died down.'

Lynn gave a bitter grimace. 'To think I suspected Cate Meadows and Felicity Dubois of being up to something when I ran into them down here,' she said, 'and all the time you were the one.'

Amis raised an eyebrow. 'What? Felice and the old Sidewinder are in Cornwall too now, are they? So almost the whole gang is here then? How nice. We could have had a party.'

'But I don't understand,' Lynn said, throwing a brief tortured glance at Murray as she forced herself to get a grip on her emotions in order to play for time while she desperately tried to work out what to do next. 'Why would you want to kill Freddie in the first place? You were his PA.'

Amis emitted a shrill unbalanced laugh. 'His PA, you say? Oh yes, I was his bloody PA all right but nothing more. Five long years I worked for that arsehole as his general dogsbody. Setting up his dodgy deals. Fiddling his accounts for him. Spying on his staff. Doing all his dirty work – and everything on the promise of a partnership in the business. Instead, he dumped me and started shagging that bitch, Felicity.' Her smouldering anger surfaced in a rush of emotion and the pistol trembled in her hand. 'And when I tackled him about it, do you know what he said? Do you know what that bastard said? He told me that if I didn't like it, I could always go and look for another job – after all I had done for him!'

Abruptly she recovered her composure, but her face had shrunk into a tight, vengeful mask. 'Well, I didn't like it, so I decided it was high time the fat man got what was coming to him – and his bit of tail too. I made contact with someone on the Dark Web who advertised "people solutions", met up with him at a derelict in London and paid him to make me a little package that went bang. He came up with a nice touch too: a box of chocolates with truffles on the first layer and oblivion on the next.'

She smirked. 'I knew Freddie would be sitting in the lounge at the club, as he always did during fashion events, and made sure when I planned the show with him that Felicity's changing room would be right next door, enabling me to plant my little device in her room and take out the pair of them in one hit.'

'Except that neither Freddie nor Felicity were in their appointed places when the bomb went off, were they?' Lynn breathed.

'No,' Amis replied with a sigh, 'and you got what was reserved for them, I'm afraid – though, rest assured, Felicity will get hers later. A little accident, I think. You can be thankful, however, that my dick-head of a bomb-maker economised on the quality and amount of charge he used, otherwise you wouldn't have survived the blast at all.'

'Sometimes I wish I hadn't,' Lynn retorted. 'Sometimes I think I would have been better off dead.'

Amis treated her to a cold smile. 'Don't worry,' my dear,' she said, 'your wish will soon be granted. Then it will all be over.'

'Nothing's over until the fat lady sings,' Lynn blurted again. 'You might kill me but there's still your bomb-maker and if the police trace him, there's every chance he will finger you.'

Amis chuckled. 'Ah, but I understand they already have traced him,' she sneered. 'The thing is, though, I put a bullet in his head after collecting my chocolate box, so talking is way beyond his capabilities now – as it is for that nasty little creep, Vernon Wiles.'

'You've murdered Vernon too?' Lynn gasped.

Amis simply shrugged in answer to her question. 'He wasn't worth anything anyway,' she said, 'but he had driven Freddie up on to the headland and was parked nearby, waiting for him, when I thumped the fat slob over the head with a tyre-lever I had taken along with me and pushed him off the cliffs. I thought it best to put him out of his misery, just in case he had seen something he shouldn't have seen. It's always best to tidy up properly after a hit, don't you think?'

'You're crazy – a proper head-case.'

Another cold smile, but Amis' eyes flashed dangerously. 'Maybe I am, my dear. The army certainly thought so, that's why they medically discharged me. Post- Traumatic Stress Disorder they called it. But then, when I really went off the rails and got a bit violent with people, I was sectioned and spent some time in a psychiatric unit until they apparently cured me. Same as you, dear – yes, I know all about your previous history and I overheard Mr Murray confirming it just now, which was most helpful.

'Thing is, you see, because of your past, no one will have any difficulty believing that you could have gone off the rails again and turned into a psychotic killer. A dangerous psychopath, in fact. Capable of planting a bomb at a fashion show to kill, not only your rival, but the boss who, you had discovered, was about to renege on his promise of a major modelling contract for you.

'Someone so full of vengeful hatred that you were prepared to pursue that boss to Cornwall when the first attempt failed, so you could finish the job. Someone who had good reason to waste, first the person who had made the bomb for you and then the man who had been with your boss on the clifftops the night he was murdered – to remove any possibility of him testifying against you in the future. And of course, someone who also had good reason to murder your own boyfriend after finding out that he was actually a private detective and was about to finger you for your indiscretions.'

Lynn swallowed hard, still trying to hold back her tears. 'Your madcap scheme will never work,' she said in a whisper. 'Someone will see through it.'

Amis' smile broadened. 'As the heroine always says towards the end of almost every gripping movie ever produced,' she mocked. 'The only difference here, though, is that this is a real situation, not a fictional one.'

'So how are you going to explain away my death – I assume you intend shooting me too?'

Amis' smile broadened. 'Suicide, my dear. You were so distraught after killing the man you had fallen for in such a big way that you put a bullet in your own head to end it all.'

Lynn backed away from her. 'But I have no intention of putting a bullet in my head.'

'No dear,' Amis accepted, stepping over Murray and advancing towards her, 'but I have – and how are you going to stop me? After all, you have nowhere to go and as long as I am within arm's length of you when I pull the trigger, who is to say your death was anything other than suicide? The powder burns alone will help police ballistics to their inevitable conclusion and I will leave my pistol in your hand as my parting present to you just to clinch things. So you see, my scheme is not as madcap as you think.'

At which point Lynn suddenly felt the wall at her back and realised that, unless there was a miracle, she was dead.

****

O'Donnell braked sharply as she turned into the lane leading down to Murray's house – and not just because of her speed either. The headlights of the CID car had caught the gleam of chrome to their left as they'd turned in off the main road. A vehicle of some sort seemed to have been driven into a gap in the undergrowth there. Benchley had seen it too. Pulling over, she switched off and jumped out of the CID car after him. The blue or black Mazda MX5 – it was difficult to tell which in the dark – had been reversed into the gap, obviously in an effort to conceal it from view, and foliage and branches were trapped under its rear bumper. The sports car was empty and locked up, but a quick check revealed that its radiator was still warm and the tyres smelled of road heat. This was one car that had been driven very hard and, at a guess, only minutes before.

'Seems Murray has another visitor, apart from Lynn Giles,' Benchley exclaimed, smoothing both hands down his face to wipe off the rain. 'No doubt an unwelcome one too.'

Before O'Donnell could reply, the Met man's mobile vibrated in his pocket. With an oath he dug the phone out and swiped the screen as he hurriedly clambered back into the car after O'Donnell, out of the rain.

'Guv'?' Moira Angel's breathless voice queried. 'Where are you?'

'Never mind that,' Benchley snapped back. 'But I can't talk now—'

'You must,' Angel persisted. 'It's urgent.'

Benchley scowled. 'Urgent?' He cast a quick sidelong glance at O'Donnell, who had turned towards him in her seat and was staring at him curiously, with one hand poised to turn the key in the ignition. 'What are you on about, woman?'

There was a burst of static. 'The checks you asked me to do?' came faintly.

'What about them?'

Angel's voice cut off, then returned and he only just managed to pick up on what she was saying through heavy crackling. 'Forget ... Dubois ... Not the one.'

'I already know that.'

Now Angel's voice was really breaking up. 'Checked staff offices ... New Light Modelling ...'

Lightning illuminated the inside of the car like a giant white flame and Angel's voice died again. Benchley swore. 'Moira? Can you hear me?'

More static, drowned by a roll of thunder, and then her voice coming through in fits and starts. '... Carol Amis ... ex-army ... Iraq, Afghanistan ... markswoman ... Discharged post-traumatic stress ... Psychotic history ...'

'What?' Benchley shouted back. 'You're saying Carol Amis is our killer?'

'Found couple .32 rounds ... back of desk drawer ... same calibre as weapon used... Islington job.'

More static and for a moment Benchley thought he had lost Angel altogether, but then her voice was back, this time without the static though very tiny. 'Guv, you still there? I think she's in Cornwall and she could be armed.'

Benchley glanced quickly through the rain streaming down his window at the sports car. 'What car does she own?' he shouted, conscious that he was losing her again.

Heavy static returned, but the tiny voice came through it again. 'Blue Mazda MX5—'

At which point the call was cut off completely, and as Benchley turned to relay the information to O'Donnell, it was apparent that she had picked up on what Angel had said from Benchley's own responses and was already on her police radio, requesting armed back-up. Seconds later, she had released the car's handbrake and they were coasting down the rest of the slope to Murray's house, ignition on, but engine off and lights extinguished.

****

The two detectives pulled up beside a silver Mercedes saloon which was parked close to the front gate of the property, also empty. 'Giles' car,' O'Donnell commented and stared up through the rain streaming down their windscreen to where lights flickered in the upper-floor windows of the house. 'Someone's definitely at home too.'

And as if to confirm the fact, the instant they climbed out of the car, the unmistakable *crack* of a gun-shot cut through the still mounting frenzy of the storm.

Instinctively, O'Donnell grabbed Benchley's arm as he started towards the front door of the house. 'Don't be a fool,' she said loudly, close to his ear. 'Wait for the ARV.'

He tore his arm free. 'You wait!' he retorted, wiping the rain out of his eyes. 'This is my mess and I'm going to sort it.'

Left with no alternative but to utter a few choice expletives at his disappearing figure, the DI grabbed a torch from the glove compartment and stumbled after him to the front porch of the house.

A quick check established that the front door was securely locked or bolted on the inside and as knocking was obviously out of the question under the circumstances, O'Donnell directed the beam of her torch down the side of the house. At first they could only make out a tangle of bushes writhing in the wind like spectral Dervishes, but then Nature came to their aid with a flash of sheet lightning which revealed a narrow path cutting through the bushes towards the back of the house.

The inevitable thunderclap came as they left the cover of the porch, using the torch to pick their way along the path. But almost immediately another lightning flash rendered the torch momentarily superfluous as an archway, set in a boundary wall and sporting what seemed to be climbing roses, stood out in stark relief to their right. Negotiating a short flight of stone steps leading up through it, they found themselves at the back of the house on a lamp-lit patio strewn with tables and chairs which had obviously been overturned by the wind. From somewhere inside the house a dog could be heard howling mournfully at the storm, but otherwise there was nothing save the sound of the wind and the rain.

Peering closely at a pair of patio doors, accessing what appeared to be a living room, O'Donnell tapped Benchley urgently on the arm. One of the doors seemed to be trembling in the light of the patio lamps, the catch apparently not fully engaged but the door itself held shut by the force of the wind off the sea. The Met man gave her a thumbs up sign in response, but it was no easy matter for him to prise the door open against the power of the wind and then to hold it there to prevent it slamming again after O'Donnell had slipped through after him.

Once inside, however, both detectives paused for a moment to listen. The howling of the dog was very close now and its frantic cries appeared to be issuing from a room on the other side of the open door to the hallway.

O'Donnell saw Benchley tense and grabbed his arm a second time, squeezing it hard in warning and pointing upwards. 'Wait for back-up,' she said again, her lips this time actually brushing his ear. 'We don't know what we're getting into.' But even as Benchley shook himself free, the decision was taken right out of their hands.

****

Lynn stared with a sort of horrible fascination at the pistol in Amis' hand. She was trapped and although her back was pressed so hard against the wall that she could feel the window-sill digging into her spine she was hardly conscious of the pain. All she was aware of was the fact that she was going to die and found herself wondering, in a peculiar detached sort of way, whether she would feel the .32 slug crash through her skull or whether it would be just an explosion of light and then total oblivion?

Amis was just feet away from her now, her face twisted into a sneer of anticipation. She was not hurrying, but advancing very slowly, as if to delay things for as long as possible to extract maximum enjoyment from her intended victim's trauma. She had already stepped over Murray's body and was raising her gun hand for the fatal shot she would deliver when she was up close and personal – the shot which would blast Lynn's brains through the window into the storm and leave the necessary powder marks around the wound to hoodwink the police into assuming her death was suicide.

'Any last requests?' she said softly, now just a couple of feet from Lynn who seemed frozen against the wall, like a rabbit mesmerised by the headlights of an oncoming vehicle.

'Go to hell!' Lynn whispered.

Amis' smile broadened. 'You first,' she replied, but just as her finger tightened on the trigger, the storm chose that precise moment to direct a powerful lightning strike at a distant electricity sub-station. At once the isolated clifftop house was plunged into total darkness.

****

In the small bedroom, two more gunshots. Bright muzzle flashes. The smell of cordite. Shadowy figures stumbling about in the darkness. Gasps. Expletives. Panicky cries. At the same time heavy feet thumping up the stairs towards the confusion. Then suddenly flashing blue light washing through the blackness as vehicles skidded to a halt and doors banged at the front of the house.

O'Donnell and Benchley, briefly stunned by the pandemonium above their heads, had reacted a little too late and had only just started up the stairs, using the pulsing light of the police strobes to see their way, when the fleeing figure hammering down from the upper floor slammed into them.

'What the hell—?' Benchley ejaculated, snatching at the gloom. His fingers closed briefly on the fold of a coat of some sort, but the figure tore itself free and in a moment was gone, swallowed up in the strobe-lit blackness of the hallway.

There was a brief pregnant pause, as if the house was holding its breath, and then the screaming started from somewhere at the top of the stairs – like a delayed reaction. At the same moment the front door burst open under the swing of a police ram, filling the hall with uniforms, while shouts and powerful flashlights were reflected in the windows from the sideway outside as other officers raced to the back of house.

Torn between responding to the screams and pursuing the fugitive, both Benchley and O'Donnell had hesitated. But then, with an oath, Benchley clambered up the remaining stairs as O'Donnell turned to face the officers pouring into the hallway below, shouting instructions at them regarding the fugitive.

The lights were restored by an unseen hand just as Benchley reached the landing, a uniformed woman police officer hard on his heels. He stopped short in the doorway of a lighted bedroom.

Lynn Giles was slumped on the floor just inside, with Alan Murray lying full-length in front of her. Her back was against the wall and Murray's head was resting in her lap, his face chalk-white and his eyes closed. He was wearing some kind of white robe which was gaping open from the waist up and soaked in blood – blood that streamed from a gaping wound in his chest. Lynn's own eyes were wide and staring. Her body shook fitfully as she stroked Murray's hair, sobbing her anguish and obviously in a state of severe traumatic shock.

'Get an ambulance – now!' Benchley snapped at the woman constable, adding, 'Hang in there, Lynn.' Then reluctantly turning on his heel, his mouth clamped shut in a hard line as the officer spoke rapidly into her personal radio, he thundered back down the stairs to where another drama was already unfolding on the patio.

Carol Amis had attempted to flee down the path at the side of the house. But she had been thwarted by the arrival of armed police officers who had suddenly emerged through the archway and she had fallen back to the low wall enclosing the lamp-lit patio. She was now facing the lead policeman, the pistol in her hand extended towards him as he covered her with what Benchley recognised as a deadly Heckler and Koch carbine.

'Armed police!' the officer shouted unnecessarily. 'Drop your weapon!'

Amis swung round in a panic as Benchley forced open the patio doors against the howling wind and joined O'Donnell just in front of them. The gun in Amis' hand swung in a jerky side-to-side motion between them and the officer with the H & K. Her leather coat glistened in the pouring rain and her free hand desperately tried to clear away the hair which was now plastered across her forehead, obstructing her line of vision.

'Don't shoot!' O'Donnell shouted at the armed policeman, noting that his colleague had come up beside him, similarly armed. In the circumstances, a Taser had obviously been considered an inappropriate alternative, which meant Carol Amis was just seconds away from being cut to pieces.

Another vivid flash of lightning illuminated the scene for a brief moment and the patio lights dipped, then strengthened as a clap of thunder directly overhead almost drowned Benchley's shout: 'Don't be a fool, Carol. Put down the gun. You can't win.'

But Amis was in no mood to listen. Demonstrating surprising agility, she swung herself up on to the wall, paused a moment, then dropped down the other side, leaving the armed police officers confused and unsure as to how to react.

Benchley was first across the patio after her and he was just in time to see her figure, now spot-lit by police flashlights, stumbling along the clifftop in the direction of the steps leading down to the beach. Where she thought she was going was not clear, but in her panic all sense seemed to have deserted her. The next instant, before Benchley's horrified gaze, she seemed to miss her footing and veer to her left, off the path. Then, silhouetted against the white-out of another powerful lightning flash, she threw up her arms like a grotesque puppet suddenly jerked away on its strings and was immediately swallowed up in the blackness, her terrified screams whipped away by the raging wind as she plunged over the edge of the cliff.

CHAPTER 20

The storm lost its destructive energy at around 2am and by dawn a soft pale light was reaching out across the ocean's easy swell to caress the rugged Cornish cliffs with exploratory fingers. But for a few felled trees, overturned refuse bins and missing tiles on the roofs of the coastal cottages, it was as if Nature's violent rampage had never happened and The Lizard seemed to be holding its breath in the hope of another fine day.

The helicopter from the police Air Operations Unit had been airborne for two hours – these days it worked with the Maritime and Coastguard's contracted Sikorsky helicopter out of Newquay after the closure of the Air-Sea Rescue base at Culdrose – as it swept low over the white caps, sticking to a collaborative search plan.

On the tiny beach at the foot of the cliffs, uniformed police officers, some armed with long poles, scrambled over the jumble of rocks exposed by the now retreating tide, carrying out a thorough search of the deep rock pools and crevices and the shallows of the creamy surf. But so far they had found only scuttling crabs, seaweed and the detritus washed ashore from the multitude of vessels using the busy shipping lanes off the coast.

More uniforms provided security cover around The Old Customs House, physically enforcing the exclusion zone which had been set up within the tapes drawn across the front door and rear patio doors. Inside the house itself, CSIs in their protective white overalls and face masks carried out a meticulous examination of the crime scene under the watchful eye of the crime scene manager, photographing and fingerprinting the bedroom where Murray had been shot. They had already carefully prised from the wall one of the two shells Amis had discharged at the moment of the power-cut, but the second had smashed through the window into the storm, never to be recovered.

On the patio Maureen O'Donnell's lone figure stood watching the helicopter's search operation through a pair of binoculars, her body trembling slightly in the dawn's chilly autumnal air which for the moment seemed to have replaced the brief Indian summer.

Mick Benchley mounted the patio steps behind her almost like an automaton. Exhaustion was written into his drawn, unshaven face, his eyes bloodshot and his body hunched into a borrowed Traffic policeman's anorak.

'Still no trace of her then?' he asked, pausing beside the DI.

She lowered her binoculars and turned towards him, eyeing him briefly before leaning back against the patio's low wall. She looked equally pale and drawn after a long, traumatic night without sleep.

'Nothing,' she said. 'Just a big fat zero so far.'

Benchley frowned. 'Just can't understand it,' he muttered. 'Hell, I saw her go over the edge and anyone who takes a dive off a cliff on to jagged rocks is hardly likely to get up and walk away afterwards, are they?'

O'Donnell shrugged. 'High tide, raging storm, heavy seas,' she summarised. 'She could have been swept out several miles, so she could.'

'Freddie Baxter wasn't swept out several miles,' he reminded her. 'He was lying where he had fallen.'

She nodded. 'Aye, but he landed on top of a heavy rock fall, well above normal sea level and in perfect weather – calm sea and so forth. We're talking about an entirely different set of circumstances here. Your woman may not have actually struck rock, but hit water instead.'

He sighed. 'Well, it's all over now anyway,' he said. 'And we got here just in time to prevent more fatalities. Even though Alan Murray did take a bullet, at least I'm told he'll survive.' He sighed. 'I must admit, it would have been more conclusive from a detection point of view to have had Amis' corpse on a slab to present to the coroner, rather than relying on the assumption that she is with the fishes. But we've got her bang to rights as our bomber and multiple killer nevertheless, so I suppose it's all pretty academic under the circumstances.'

O'Donnell nodded. 'And as there's nothing we can do here anymore, we might as well head back to the incident room for the final team debrief. You're welcome to join us, if you wish.'

He shrugged. 'Might as well before I head back to the Smoke to brief my own team.'

She treated him to a mischievous smirk. 'If you want to spend some of those inflated Met allowances we in the provinces can only dream about, you could always buy us both a nice breakfast afore you go.'

He returned her gaze with a wry smile and ran his eyes appreciatively over her shapely figure. 'And what do I get in return?' he queried, adopting a straight face.

Her smirk broadened. 'Well now,' she replied, 'if you're a really good boy, I might even offer to buy you a Cornish cream tea later.'

****

Just over 17 miles away, light and life greeted Lynn Giles dozing fitfully beside Alan Murray's hospital bed when she was awakened by his voice calling her name. Only just managing to keep her emotions in check after all that had happened at The Old Customs House, she had insisted on accompanying Murray to hospital in the ambulance, desperately praying that he wouldn't die. Despite the way he had treated her and the resentment and antagonism she had displayed towards him for his cruel deception just hours before, she knew deep down that she was hopelessly in love with this arrogant charlatan. Their affair had gone way beyond just carnal satisfaction. It had developed into something much deeper. Something she had never expected to happen and had never experienced in any previous relationship. Now she couldn't imagine life without him.

The surgeon who had removed the bullet from his chest several hours before had complimented him on his lucky escape. 'Another inch to the left and you would have been a goner,' he'd said cheerfully, showing him the twisted fragment of metal in its kidney-shaped basin. 'The lady with the gun obviously caught you on the turn, so the round missed your ticker, clipped your sternum and ended up in your shoulder.'

Given a sedative, trolleyed to a private room and placed under constant observation, the insurance investigator had slept for most of the afternoon. But now waking, he stared at Lynn through half-closed lids as she straightened and wiped the sleep from her own eyes. Squeezing his sound arm a little, she smiled. 'I ... I thought you were on the way out,' she said soberly, studying his pale, perspiring face.

He grunted. 'Too ornery for that,' he replied in a thick hesitant voice, obviously still partially under the influence of the sedative, which had been administered. 'Are you okay?'

She nodded. 'Shaken up, but otherwise unscathed,' she replied. 'Thanks to that power-cut, which threw the bitch's aim.'

He nodded slowly, then frowned. 'But what about Archie? He must have been terrified, what with the storm and everything.'

She squeezed his arm again. 'He's fine. Taken in by a police dog-handler just before I got in the ambulance with you. I saw him being fed a chocolate bar by the copper. He'll be his friend for life after that.'

He treated her to the ghost of a smile. 'Always liked his grub, did old Arch. He'll eat 'em out of house and home if he's not collected soon.'

'Will he have to go back to where you got him from, now that you no longer need him?' she queried.

He frowned. 'I sincerely hope not,' he said. 'I've got kind of used to the old feller now. Maybe they'll accept a hefty donation instead. We'll have to see.'

'Well, in the meantime you can leave him with me,' she said. 'I could do with some company at my place anyway.'

He grunted his thanks. 'So what happened to the mad woman with the gun?'

Lynn's mouth tightened. 'Went over the cliff, I'm told,' she replied. 'They haven't found her body yet. Poetic justice, though, in my opinion. It seems she was behind everything. The bombing of the club and three murders. All down to revenge after Freddie Baxter dumped her apparently, and she had planned for me to take the fall. A nice beauty.'

He tried to ease himself into a more comfortable position in the bed and winced at the pain. 'Seems I was wrong about everything then, doesn't it?' he blurted, after a pause. 'Especially you. I can only say how sorry I am.'

She manufactured a frown. 'What? Sorry I didn't turn out to be your multiple-murderess, you mean?'

'You know very well what I mean.' He hesitated, his good hand ruffling the bedsheet as he stared down at it. 'I meant what I said when I told you I had fallen in love with you,' he went on, his embarrassment apparent as he cleared his throat, unable to meet her gaze.

She raised an eyebrow. 'Despite all my scars?' she goaded, but with more than a trace of bitter cynicism in her tone.

He raised his head and treated her to a level stare. 'With or without the scars,' he said. 'It makes no difference to me. But I treated you very badly and I just don't know how I'm ever going to be able to make it up to you.'

She stood up and bent over him. 'Oh you'll make it up to me all right,' she said, leaning closer. 'Doc says you will be out of action for several weeks and when you leave hospital, I have to look after you until you get your strength back.' A glint of devilment was back in her eyes now as her lips brushed seductively against his. 'But after that, Mr Murray, you're going to make it up to me big time – and you'd better believe it.'

AFTER THE FACT

Darkness. Cold, dank and heavy. Pressing down on the young woman's broken body as she lay on her back, listening to the *plop, plop, plop* of water dripping on to her face from the blackness way above her head.

Carol Amis realised the police would be searching for her on the rocky beach below The Old Customs House. She had heard the muted clatter of the helicopters shortly after regaining consciousness. But they would be out of luck. She hadn't gone over the cliff edge at all, but had plunged into an old mine shaft hidden beneath a tangle of undergrowth just off the footpath she had tried to use as an escape route.

The shaft had been sunk into the ground maybe 100 years before by one of the many companies plundering the lonely promontory in the then relentless search for tin. But the steady erosion of the cliff face over the years had produced rock falls which had taken with them most of the remaining ruins of the mine's surface workings, leaving only the occasional broken wall and treacherous shaft to trap the unwary. She was its latest victim.

She must have fallen 40-50ft, landing heavily on the bed of broken rock, which choked the lower half of the shaft and the adits bored into the cliff face beneath her. Although it was a miracle she had survived the impact, it might have been better if she hadn't. She felt sure she had snapped part of her spine as there was no feeling below the waist anymore and one arm was trapped under her, useless and probably also broken. Blood streamed from a ripped shoulder. She could feel it running down her arm and over her hand. Mixing with the moisture which dripped incessantly on to her face and body. While she found she could still move the arm with difficulty, it turned out to be wasted effort. Her probing fingers encountered only a slimy wall streaming with water which chuckled with amusement as it trickled past her through holes in the rubble on its way into the buried depths.

Blind panic seized her. She was trapped. Entombed in stygian darkness. Unable to move and with almost no prospect of rescue. No one had seen her pitch into the shaft. The police search teams probably didn't even know it was there. Instead, they would assume she had smashed herself to pieces on the rocky beach and been swept out to sea in the storm.

God help her. Even after all she had done – the bombing, the ruthless taking of three lives – she couldn't be left to die like this.

Weakly at first, but then with renewed vigour as she marshalled what strength she had left, she shouted for help for the umpteenth time, her voice once more rebounding off the walls in the form of mocking echoes, which chased themselves around her with malevolent glee.

But there was still no response and as her shouts became wilder and more unhinged, the clatter of the search helicopters faded into silence, replaced solely by the sound of the trickling water and the muted screech of gulls wheeling above the empty clifftops, while the ghosts of the old Tommy knockers peered curiously down at her from their crevices in the shaft, waiting patiently for her soul to join them in their cold, dark world.

Also by the same author:

Crime Fiction:
Flashpoint
Burnout
Slice
Firetrap
Requiem
Strawfoot
Sandman
Deadly Secrets

Autobiography:
Reflections In Blue

Printed in Great Britain
by Amazon